Mothers in a Million

Celebrate Mother's Day with Harlequin® Romance!

Enjoy four very different aspects of motherhood and celebrate that very special bond between mother and child with four extra-special Harlequin® Romances this month!

Whether it's the pitter-patter of tiny feet for the first time, or finding love the second time around, these four Romances offer tears, laughter and emotion and are guaranteed to celebrate those mothers in a million!

For the ultimate indulgent treat, don't miss:

A FATHER FOR HER TRIPLETS by Susan Meier

THE MATCHMAKER'S HAPPY ENDING by Shirley Jump

SECOND CHANCE WITH THE REBEL by Cara Colter

FIRST COMES BABY… by Michelle Douglas

Dear Reader,

Mother's Day is bittersweet for me. The sweet part is that I have experienced the wondrous complexity, the bliss, the bond and the beauty of motherhood through my own daughter Cassidy. The bitter part is that my mom has been gone for seventeen years. She would have been seventy-four as I write this; June 2 was her birthday.

Whenever I see a middle-aged daughter with an elderly woman who is obviously her mother—having lunch together or out shopping or waiting in line for a movie—I feel that pang of envy and loss. I still pause sometimes, when I'm in a dilemma or enjoying a gorgeous sunset, and wonder, *What would Mom think of that?* In quiet moments of introspection I question if I returned her love as completely and unconditionally as she extended it.

In this book you will meet Mama Freda. My mom was not German. Or old. Or stocky. And yet somehow, in this character, my mom was with me once more, whispering that life is good, that everyone deserves a second chance and that ultimately love wins.

Enjoy your Mother's Day.

With love,

Cara

CARA
COLTER

Second Chance with the Rebel

&

Her Royal Wedding Wish

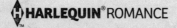

HARLEQUIN®ROMANCE

Recycling programs
for this product may
not exist in your area.

ISBN-13: 978-0-373-74242-4

SECOND CHANCE WITH THE REBEL

First North American Publication 2013

Copyright © 2013 by Cara Colter

HER ROYAL WEDDING WISH

Copyright © 2008 by Cara Colter

HARLEQUIN®
www.Harlequin.com

Printed in U.S.A.

CONTENTS

Cara Colter lives in British Columbia with her partner, Rob, and eleven horses. She has three grown children and a grandson. She is a recent recipient of an *RT Book Reviews* Career Achievement Award in the "Love and Laughter" category. Cara loves to hear from readers, and you can contact her or learn more about her through her website, www.cara-colter.com.

Books by Cara Colter

SNOWED IN AT THE RANCH
BATTLE FOR THE SOLDIER'S HEART
THE COP, THE PUPPY AND ME
TO DANCE WITH A PRINCE
RESCUED BY HIS CHRISTMAS ANGEL
WINNING A GROOM IN 10 DATES
RESCUED IN A WEDDING DRESS

Other titles by this author available in ebook format.

Second Chance with the Rebel

CHAPTER ONE

"HUDSON GROUP, HOW may I direct your call?"

"Macintyre Hudson, please."

Could silence be disapproving? Lucy Lindstrom asked herself. As in, you didn't just cold-call a multimillion-dollar company and ask to speak to their CEO?

"Mr. Hudson is not available right now. I'd be happy to take a message."

Lucy recognized the voice on the other end of the phone. It was that same uppity-accented receptionist who had taken her name and number thirteen times this week.

Mac was not going to talk to her unless he wanted to. And clearly, he did not want to. She had to fight with herself to stay on the line. It would have been so much easier just to hang up the phone. She reminded herself she had no choice. She had to change tack.

"It's an urgent family matter."

"He's not in his office. I'll have to see if he's in the building. And I'll have to tell him who is calling."

Lucy was certain she heard faint suspicion there, as if her voice was beginning to be recognized also, and was on the blocked-caller list.

"You could tell him it's Harriet Freda calling." She picked a fleck of lavender paint off her thumbnail.

"I'll take your number and have him call you back when I locate him."

"It's okay. I'll hold," Lucy said with as much firmness as she could muster.

As she waited, she looked down at the paper in her purple-paint-stained hand. It showed a neat list of names, all of them crossed off save for one.

The remaining name stood out as if it was written in neon tubing.

The boy who ruined my life.

Macintyre W. Hudson. A voice whispered from her past, *Everybody just calls me Mac.*

Just like that, seven years slipped away, and she could see him, Mac Hudson, the most handsome boy ever born, with those dark, laughing eyes, that crooked smile, the silky chocolate hair, too long, falling down over his brow.

Just like that, the shiver ran up and down her spine, and Lucy remembered exactly why that boy had ruined her life.

Only, now he wasn't a boy any longer, but a man.

And she was a woman.

"Macintyre Hudson did not ruin your life," Lucy told herself sternly. "At best he stole a few moments of it."

But what moments those were, a voice inside her insisted.

"Rubbish," Lucy said firmly, but her confidence, not in great supply these days anyway, dwindled. It felt as if she had failed at everything she'd set her hand to, and failed spectacularly.

She had never gone to university as her parents had hoped, but had become a clerk in a bookstore in the neighboring city of Glen Oak, instead.

She had worked up to running her own store, Books and Beans, with her fiancé, but she had eagerly divested herself of the coffee shop and storefront part of the business after their humiliatingly public breakup.

Now, licking her wounds, she was back in her hometown of Lindstrom Beach in her old family home on the shores of Sunshine Lake.

The deeding of the house was charity, plain and simple. Her widowed mother had given it to Lucy before remarrying and moving to California. She said it had been in the Lindstrom family for generations and it needed to stay there.

And even though that was logical, and the timing couldn't have been more perfect, Lucy had the ugly feeling that what her mother really thought was that Lucy wouldn't make it without her help.

"But I have a dream," she reminded herself firmly, shoring herself up with that before Mac came on the line.

Despite her failures, over the past year Lucy had developed a sense of purpose. And more important, she felt *needed* for the first time in a long time.

It bothered Lucy that she had to remind herself of that as she drummed her fingers and listened to the music on the other end of the phone.

The song, she realized when she caught herself humming along, was one about a rebel and had always been the song she had associated with Mac. It was about a boy who was willing to risk all but his heart.

That was Macintyre Hudson to a *T*, so who could imagine the former Lindstrom Beach renegade and unapologetic bad boy at the helm of a multimillion-dollar company that produced the amazingly popular Wild Side outdoor products?

Unexpectedly, the music stopped.

"Mama?"

Mac's voice was urgent and worried. It had deepened, Lucy was sure, since the days of their youth, but it had that same gravelly, sensuous edge to it that had always sent tingles up and down her spine.

Now, when she most needed to be confident, was not the time to think of the picture of him on his website, the one that had dashed her hopes that maybe he had gotten heavy or lost all his hair in the years that had passed.

But think of it she did. No boring head-and-shoulders shot in a nice Brooks Brothers suit for the CEO of Hudson Group.

No, the caption stated the founder of the Wild Side line was demonstrating the company's new kayak, Wild Ride. He was on a raging wedge of white water that funneled between rocks. Through flecks of foam, frozen by the camera, Macintyre Hudson had been captured in all his considerable masculine glory.

He'd been wearing a life jacket, a Wild Side product that showed off the amazing broadness of his shoulders, the powerful muscle of sun-bronzed arms gleaming with water. More handsome than ever, obviously in his element, he'd had a look in his devil-dark eyes, a cast to his mouth and a set to his jaw that was one of fierce concentration and formidable determination.

Maybe he didn't have any hair. He'd been wearing a helmet in the photo.

"Mama?" he said again. "What's wrong? Why didn't you call on my private line?"

Lucy had steeled herself for this. Rehearsed it. In her mind she had controlled every facet of this conversation.

But she had not planned for the image that materialized out of her memory file, that superimposed itself above the image of him in the kayak.

A younger Mac Hudson pausing as he lifted himself out of the lake onto the dock, his body sun-browned and perfect, water sluicing off the rippling smooth lines of his muscles, looking up at her, with laughter tilting the edges of his ultra-sexy eyes.

Do you love me, Lucy Lin?

Never *I love you* from him.

The memory hardened her resolve not to be in any way vulnerable to him. He was an extraordinarily handsome man, and he used his good looks in dastardly ways, as very handsome men were well-known to do.

On the other hand, her fiancé, James Kennedy, had been homely and bookish and had still behaved in a completely dastardly manner.

All of which explained why romance played no part in her brand-new dreams for herself.

Fortified with that, Lucy ordered herself not to stammer. "No, I'm sorry, it isn't Mama Freda."

There was a long silence. In the background she could hear a lot of noise as if a raucous party was going on.

When Mac spoke, she took it as a positive sign. At least he hadn't hung up.

"Well, well," he said. "Little Lucy Lindstrom. I hope this is good. I'm standing here soaking wet."

"At work?" she said, surprised into curiosity.

"I was in the hot tub with my assistant, Celeste." His tone was dry. "What can I do for you?"

Don't pursue it, she begged herself, but she couldn't help it.

"You don't have a hot tub at work!"

"You're right, I don't. And no Celeste, either. What we have is a test tank for kayaks where we can simulate a white-water chute."

Lucy had peeked at their website on and off over the years.

The business had started appropriately enough, with Mac's line of outdoor gear. He was behind the name brand that outdoor enthusiasts coveted: Wild Side. First it had been his canoes. It had expanded quickly into kayaks and then accessories, and now, famously, into clothing.

All the reckless abandon of his youth channeled into huge success, and he was still having fun. Who tested kayaks at work?

But Mac had always been about having fun. Some things just didn't change.

Though he didn't sound very good-humored right now. "I'm wet, and the kayak didn't test out very well, so this had better be good."

"This is important," she said.

"What I was doing was important, too." He sighed, the sigh edged with irritation. "Some things just don't change, do they? The pampered doctor's daughter, the head of student council, the captain of the cheerleading squad, used to having her own way."

That girl, dressed in her designer jeans, with hundred-dollar highlights glowing in her hair, looked at her from her past, a little sadly.

Mac's assessment was so unfair! For the past few years she had been anything but pampered. And now she was trying to turn the Books part of Books and Beans into an internet business while renting canoes off her dock.

She was painting her own house and living on macaroni and cheese. She hadn't bought a new outfit for over a year, socking away every extra nickel in the hope that she could make her dream a reality.

And that didn't even cover all the things she was running next door to Mama Freda's to do!

She would have protested except for the inescapable if annoying truth: she *had* told a small lie to get her own way.

"It was imperative that I speak to you," she said firmly.

"Hmmm. Imperative. That has a rather regal sound to it. A princess giving a royal command."

He was insisting on remembering who she had been before he'd ruined her life: a confident, popular honor student who had never known trouble and never done a single thing wrong. Or daring. Or adventurous.

The young Lucy Lindstrom's idea of a good time, pre-Mac, had been getting the perfect gown for prom, and spending lazy summer afternoons on the deck with her friends, painting each other's toenails pink. Her idea of a great evening had been sitting around a roaring bonfire, especially if a sing-along started.

Pre-Mac, the most exciting thing that had ever happened to her was getting the acceptance letter from the university of her choice.

"Pampered, yes," Mac went on. "Deceitful, no. You are the last person I would have ever thought would lower yourself to deceit."

But that's where he was dead wrong. He had brought out the deceitful side in her before.

The day she had said goodbye to him.

Hurt and angry that he had not asked her to go with him, to hide her sense of inconsolable loss, she had tossed her head and said, "I could never fall for a boy like you."

When the truth was she already had. She had been so crazy in love with Mac that it had felt as though the fire that burned within her would melt her and everything around her until there was nothing left of her world but a small, dark smudge.

"I needed to talk to you," she said, stripping any memory of that summer and those long, heated days from her voice.

"Yes. You said. Imperative."

Apparently he had honed sarcasm to an art.

"I'm sorry I insinuated I was Mama Freda."

"Insinuated," he said silkily. "So much more palatable than lying."

"I had to get by the guard dog who answers your phone!"

"No, you didn't. I got your messages."

"Except the one about needing to speak to you personally?"

"Nothing to talk about." His voice was chilly. "I've got all the information you gave. A Mother's Day Gala in celebration of Mama Freda's lifetime of good work. A combination of her eightieth birthday and Mother's Day. Fund-raiser for all her good causes. She knows about the gala and the fund-raiser but has no idea it's honoring her. Under no circumstances is she to find out."

Lucy wondered if she should be pleased that he had obviously paid very close attention to the content of those messages.

Actually, the fund-raiser was for Lucy's good cause, but Mama Freda was at the very heart of her dream.

At the worst point of her life, she had gone to Mama Freda, and those strong arms had folded around her.

"When your pain feels too great to bear, *liebling,* then you must stop thinking of yourself and think of another."

Mama had carried the dream with Lucy, encouraging her, keeping the fire going when it had flickered to a tiny ember and nearly gone out.

Now, wasn't it the loveliest of ironies that

Mama was one of the ones who would benefit from her own advice?

"Second Sunday of May," he said, his tone bored, dismissive, "black-tie dinner at the Lindstrom Beach Yacht Club."

She heard disdain in his voice and guessed the reason. "Oh, so that's the sticking point. I've already had a hundred people confirm, and I'm expecting a few more to trickle in over the next week. It's the only place big enough to handle that kind of a crowd."

"I remember when I wasn't good enough to get a job busing tables there."

"Get real. You never applied for a job busing tables at the yacht club."

Even in his youth, Mac, in his secondhand jeans, one of a string of foster children who had found refuge at Mama's, had carried himself like a king, bristling with pride and an ingrained sense of himself. He took offense at the slightest provocation.

And then hid it behind that charming smile.

"After graduation you had a job with the town, digging ditches for the new sewer system."

"Not the most noble work, but honest," he said. "And real."

So, who are you to be telling me to get real? He didn't say it, but he could have.

Noble or not, she could remember the ridged edges of the sleek muscles, how she had loved to touch him, feel his wiry strength underneath her fingertips.

He mistook her silence for judgment. "It runs in my family. My dad was a ditchdigger, too. They had a nickname for him. Digger Dan."

She felt the shock of that. She had known Mac since he had come to live in the house next door. He was fourteen, a year older than she was. When their paths crossed, he had tormented and teased her, interpreting the fact she was always tongue-tied in his presence as an example of her family's snobbery, rather than seeing it for what it was.

Intrigue. Awe. Temptation. She had never met anyone like Mac. Not before or since. Ruggedly independent. Bold. Unfettered by convention. Fearless. She remembered seeing him glide by her house, only fourteen, solo in a canoe heavily laden with camping gear.

She would see his campfire burning bright against the night on the other side of the lake. It was called the wild side of the lake because it was undeveloped crown land, thickly forested.

Sometimes Mac would spend the whole weekend over there. Alone.

She couldn't even imagine that. Being alone over there with the bears.

The week she had won the spelling bee he had been kicked out of school for swearing.

She got a little Ford compact for her sixteenth birthday, while he bought an old convertible and stripped the engine in the driveway, then stood down her father when he complained. While she was painting her toenails, he was painstakingly building his own cedar-strip canoe in Mama's yard.

But never once, even in that summer when she had loved him, right after her own graduation from high school, had Mac revealed a single detail about his life before he had arrived in foster care in Lindstrom Beach.

Was it the fact that he had so obviously risen above those roots that made him reveal that his father had been nicknamed Digger Dan? Or had he changed?

She squashed that thing inside her that felt ridiculously and horribly like hope by saying, proudly, "I don't really care if you come to the gala or not."

She told herself she was becoming hardened to rejection. All the people who really mattered to Mama—except him—had said they would come. But her own mother had said she would be in Africa on safari at that time and many people from Lucy's "old" life, her high-school days, had not answered yet. Those who had, had answered no.

There was silence from Mac, and Lucy allowed herself pleasure that she had caught him off guard.

"And I am sorry about messing up *your* Mother's Day."

"What do you mean, *my* Mother's Day?" His voice was guarded.

That had always been the problem with Mac. The insurmountable flaw. He wouldn't let anyone touch the part of him that *felt*.

"I chose Mother's Day because it was symbolic. Even though Mama Freda has never been a biological mother, she has been a mother to so many. She epitomizes what motherhood is."

That was not the full truth. The full truth was that Lucy found Mother's Day to be unbearably painful. And she was following Mama Freda's own recipe for dealing with pain.

"I don't care what day you chose!"

"Yes, you do."

"It's all coming back now," he said sardonically. "Having a conversation with you is like crossing a minefield."

"You feel as if Mother's Day belongs to you and Mama Freda. And I've stolen it."

"That's an interesting theory," he said, a chill in his voice warning her to stop, but she wasn't going to. Lucy was getting to him and part of her liked it, because it had always been hard to get to Mac Hudson. It might seem as if you were, but then that devil-may-care grin materialized, saying *Gotcha, because I don't really care.*

"Every Mother's Day," she reminded him quietly, "you outdo yourself. A stretch limo picks her up. She flies somewhere to meet you. Last year Engelbert Humperdinck in concert in New York. She wore the corsage until it turned brown. She talked about it for days after. Where you took her. What you ate. Don't tell me it's not your day. And that you're not annoyed that I chose it."

"Whatever."

"Oh! I recognize that tone of voice! Even after all this time! Mr. Don't-Even-Think-You-Know-Me."

"You don't. I'll put a check in the mail for whatever cause she has taken up. I think you'll find it very generous."

"I'm sure Mama will be pleased by the check. She probably will hardly even notice your absence, since all the others are coming. Every single one. Mama Freda has fostered twenty-three kids over the years. Ross Chillington is clearing his filming schedule. Michael Boylston works in Thailand and he's coming. Reed Patterson is leaving football training camp in Florida to be here."

"All those wayward boys saved by Mama Freda." His voice was silky and unimpressed.

"She's made a difference in the world!"

"Lucy—"

She hated it that her name on his lips made her feel more frazzled, hated it that she could remember leaning toward him, quivering with wanting.

"I'm not interested in being part of Lindstrom Beach's version of a TV reality show. What are you planning after your black-tie dinner? No, wait. Let me guess. Each of Mama's foster children will stand up and give a testimonial about being redeemed by her love."

Ouch. That was a little too close to what she did have planned. Did he have to make it sound cheap and smarmy instead of uplifting and inspirational?

"Mac—"

"Nobody calls me Mac anymore," he said, a little harshly.

"What do they call you?" She couldn't imagine him being called anything else.

"Mr. Hudson," he said coolly.

She doubted that very much since, she could still hear a raucous partylike atmosphere unfolding behind him.

It occurred to her she would like to hang up on him. And she was going to, very shortly.

"Okay, then, Mr. Hudson," she snapped, "I've already told you I don't care if you don't come. I know it's way too much to ask of you to take a break from your important and busy schedule to honor the woman who took you in and pulled you back from the brink of disaster. Way too much."

Silence.

"Still, I know how deeply you care about her. I know it's you who has been paying some of her bills."

He sucked in his breath, annoyed that she knew that.

She pushed on. "Aside from your Mother's Day tradition, I know you took her to Paris for her seventy-fifth birthday."

"Lucy, I'm dripping water on the floor and shivering, so if you could hurry this along."

She really had thought she could get through her life without seeing him again. It had been a blessing that he came back to Lindstrom Beach rarely, and when he had, she had been away.

Because how could she look at him without remembering? But then hadn't she discovered you could remember, regardless?

Once, a long, long time ago, she had tried, with a desperation so keen she could almost taste its bitterness on her tongue, to pry his secrets from him. Lying on the sand in the dark, the lake's night-blackened waters lapping quietly, the embers of their fire burning down, she had asked him to tell her how he had ended up in foster care at Mama Freda's.

"I killed a man," he whispered, and then

into her shocked silence, he had laughed that laugh that was so charming and distracting and sensual, that laugh that hid everything he really was, and added, "With my bare hands."

And then he had tried to divert her with his kisses that burned hotter than the fire.

But he had been unable to give her the gift she needed most: his trust in her.

And that was the real reason she had told him she could never love a boy like him. Because, even in her youth, she had recognized that he held back something essential of himself from her, when she had held back nothing.

If he had chosen to think she was a snob looking down her nose at the likes of him, after all the time they had spent together that summer, then that was his problem.

Still, just thinking of those forbidden kisses of so many years ago sent an unwanted shiver down her spine. The truth was nobody wanted Mac to come back here less than she did.

"I didn't phone about Mama's party. I guess I thought I would tell you this when you came. But since you're not going to—"

"Tell me what?"

She had to keep on track, or she would be swamped by these memories.

"Mac—" she remembered, too late, he didn't want to be called that and plunged on "—something's wrong."

"What do you mean?"

"You knew Mama Freda lost her driver's license, didn't you?"

"No."

"She had a little accident in the winter. Nothing serious. She slid through a stop sign and took out Mary-Beth McQueen's fence and rose bed."

"Ha. I doubt if that was an accident. She aimed."

For a moment, something was shared between them. The rivalry between Mama and Mary-Beth when it came to roses was legendary. But the moment was a flicker, nothing more.

All business again, he said, "But you said it wasn't serious?"

"Nonetheless, she had to see a doctor and be retested. They revoked her license."

"I'll set her up an account at Ferdinand's Taxi."

"I don't mind driving her. I like it actually.

My concern was that before the retesting I don't think she'd been to a doctor in twenty years."

"Thirty," he said. "She had her 'elixir.'"

Lucy was sure she heard him shudder. It was funny to think of him being petrified of a little homemade potion. The Mac of her memory had been devil-may-care and terrifyingly fearless. From the picture on his website, that much had not changed.

"I guess the elixir isn't working for her anymore," Lucy said carefully. "I drive her now. She's had three doctors' appointments in the last month."

"What's wrong?"

"According to her, nothing."

Silence. She understood the silence. He was wondering why Mama Freda hadn't told him about the driver's license, the doctor's appointments. He was guessing, correctly, that she would not want him to worry.

"It probably *is* nothing," he said, but his voice was uneasy.

"I told myself that, too. I don't want to believe she's eighty, either."

"There's something you aren't telling me."

Scary, that after all these years, and over

the phone, he could do that. Read her. So, why hadn't he seen through her the only time it really mattered?

I could never fall for a boy like you.

Lucy hesitated, looked out the open doors to gather her composure. "I saw a funeral-planning kit on her kitchen table. When she noticed it was out, she shoved it in a drawer. I think she was hoping I hadn't seen it."

What she didn't tell him was that before Mama had shoved the kit away she had been looking out her window, her expression un-characteristically pensive.

"Will my boy ever come home?" she had whispered.

All those children, and only one was truly her boy.

Lucy listened as Mac drew in a startled breath, and then he swore. Was it a terrible thing to love it when someone swore? But it made him the *old* Mac. And it meant she had penetrated his guard.

"That's part of what motivated me to plan the celebration to honor her. I want her to know—" She choked. "I want her to know how much she has meant to people before it's too late. I don't want to wait for a funeral to bring to light all the good things she's done and been."

The silence was long. And then he sighed.

"I'll be there as soon as I can."

"No! Wait—"

But Mac was gone, leaving the deep buzz of the dial tone in Lucy's ear.

CHAPTER TWO

"WELL, THAT WENT well," Lucy muttered as she set down the phone.

Still, there was no denying a certain relief. She had been carrying the burden of worrying about Mama Freda's health alone, and now she shared it.

But with Mac? He'd always represented the loss of control, a visit to the wild side, and now it seemed nothing had changed.

If he had just come to the gala, Lucy could have maintained her sense of control. She had been watching Mama Freda like a hawk since the day she'd heard, *Will my boy ever come home?*

Aside from a nap in the afternoon, Mama seemed as energetic and alert as always. If Mama had received bad news on the health front, Lucy's observations of her had convinced her that the prognosis was an illness of the slow-moving variety.

Not the variety that required Mac to drop everything and come now!

The Mother's Day celebration was still two weeks away. Two weeks would have given Lucy time.

"Time to what?" she asked herself sternly.

Brace herself. Prepare. Be ready for him. But she already knew the uncomfortable truth about Macintyre Hudson. There was no preparing for him. There was no getting ready. He was a force unto himself, and that force was like a tornado hitting.

Lucy looked around her world. A year back home, and she had a sense of things finally falling into place. She was taking the initial steps toward her dream.

On the dining-room table that she had not eaten at since her return, there were donated items that she was collecting for the silent auction at the Mother's Day Gala.

There were the mountains of paperwork it had taken to register as a charity. Also, there was a photocopy of the application she had just submitted for rezoning, so that she could have Caleb's House here, and share this beautiful, ridiculously large house on the lake with young women who needed its sanctuary.

One of her three cats snoozed in a beam of sunlight that painted the wooden floor in front of the old river-rock fireplace golden. A vase of tulips brought in from the yard, their heavy heads drooping gracefully on their slender stems, brightened the barn-plank coffee table. A book was open on its spine on the arm of her favorite chair.

There was not a hint of catastrophe in this well-ordered scene, but it hadn't just happened. You had to work on this kind of a life.

In fact, it seemed the scene reflected that she had finally gotten through picking up the pieces from the last time.

And somehow, *last time* did not mean her ended engagement to James Kennedy.

No, when she thought of her world being blown apart, oddly it was not the front-page picture of her fiancé, James, running down the street in Glen Oak without a stitch on that was forefront in her mind. No, forefront was a boy leaving, seven years ago.

The next morning, out on her deck, nestled into a cushioned lounge chair, Lucy looked out over the lake and took a sip of her coffee. Despite the fact the sun was still burning off the early-morning chill, she was cozy in her pajamas under a wool plaid blanket.

The scent of her coffee mingled with the lovely, sugary smell of birch wood burning. The smoke curled out of Mama Freda's chimney and hung in a wispy swirl in the air above the water in front of Mama's cabin.

Birdsong mixed with the far-off drone of a plane.

What exactly did *I'll be there as soon as I can* mean?

"Relax," she ordered herself.

In a world like his, he wouldn't be able just to drop everything and come. It would be days before she had to face Macintyre Hudson. Maybe even a week. His website said his company had done 34 million dollars in business last year.

You didn't just walk away from that and hope it would run itself.

So she could focus on her life. She turned her attention from the lake, and looked at the swatch of sample paint she had put up on the side of the house.

She loved the pale lavender for the main

color. She thought the subtle shade was playful and inviting, a color that she hoped would welcome and soothe the young girls and women who would someday come here when she had succeeded in transforming all this into Caleb's House.

Today she was going to commit to the color and order the paint. Well, maybe later today. She was aware of a little tingle of fear when she thought of actually buying the paint. It was a big house. It was natural to want not to make a mistake.

My mother would hate the color.

So maybe instead of buying paint today, she would fill a few book orders, and work on funding proposals for Caleb's House in anticipation of the rezoning. Several items had arrived for the silent auction that she could unpack. She would not give the arrival of Mac one more thought. Not one.

The drone of the plane pushed back into her awareness, too loud to ignore. She looked up and could see it, red and white, almost directly overhead, so close she could read the call numbers under the wings. It was obviously coming in for a landing on the lake.

Lucy watched it set down smoothly, turn-

ing the water, where it shot out from the
pontoons, to silvery sprays of mercury. The
sound of the engine cut from a roar to a purr
as the plane glided over the glassy mirror-
calm surface of the water.

Sunshine Lake, located in the rugged interior of British Columbia, had always been a
haunt of the rich, and sometimes the famous.
Lucy's father had taken delight in the fact that
once, when he was a teenager, the queen had
stayed here on one of her visits to Canada.
For a while the premier of the province had
had a summer house down the lake. Pierre
LaPontz, the famous goalie for the Montreal
Canadiens, had summered here with friends.
Seeing the plane was not unusual.

It became unusual when it wheeled around
and taxied back, directly toward her.

Even though she could not see the pilot for
the glare of the morning sun on the wind-
shield of the plane, Lucy knew, suddenly and
without a shade of a doubt, that it was him.

Macintyre Hudson had landed. He had arrived in her world.

The conclusion was part logic and part instinct. And with it came another conclusion.
That nothing, from here on in, would go as she

expected it. The days when choosing a paint color was the scariest thing in her world were over.

Lucy had thought he might show up in a rare sports car. Or maybe on an expensive motorcycle. She had even considered the possibility that he might show up, chauffeured, in the white limo that had picked up Mama Freda last Mother's Day.

Take that, Dr. Lindstrom.

She watched the plane slide along the lake to the old dock in front of Mama Freda's. The engines cut and the plane drifted.

And then, for the first time in seven years, she saw him.

Macintyre Hudson slid out the door onto the pontoon, expertly threw a rope over one of the big anchor posts on the dock and pulled the plane in.

The fact he could pilot a plane made it more than evident he had come into himself. He was wearing mirrored aviator sunglasses, a leather jacket and knife-creased khakis. But it was the way he carried himself, a certain sureness of movement on the bobbing water, that radiated confidence and strength.

Something in her chest felt tight. Her heart was beating too fast.

"Not bald," she murmured as the sun caught on the luscious dark chocolate of his hair. It was a guilty pleasure, watching him from a distance, with him unaware of being watched. He had a powerful efficiency of motion as he dealt with mooring the plane.

He was broader than he had been, despite all the digging of ditches. All the slenderness of his youth was gone, replaced with a kind of mouthwatering solidness, the build of a mature man at the peak of his power.

He looked up suddenly and cast a look around, frowning slightly as if he was aware he was being watched.

Crack.

The sound was so loud in the still crispness of the morning that Lucy started, slopped coffee on her pajamas. Thunder?

No. In horror Lucy watched as the ancient post of Mama Freda's dock, as thick as a telephone pole, snapped cleanly, as if it was a toothpick. As she looked on helplessly, Mac saw it coming and moved quickly.

He managed to save his head, but the falling

post caught him across his shoulder and hurled him into the water. The post fell in after him.

A deathly silence settled over the lake.

Lucy was already up out of her chair when Mac's head reemerged from the water. His startled, furious curse shattered the quiet that had reasserted itself on the peaceful lakeside morning.

Lucy found his shout reassuring. At least he hadn't been knocked out by the post, or been overcome by the freezing temperatures of the water.

Blanket clutched to her, Lucy ran on bare feet across the lawns, then through the ancient ponderosa pines that surrounded Mama's house. She picked her way swiftly across the rotted decking of the dock.

Mac was hefting himself onto the pontoon of the plane. It was not drifting, thankfully, but bobbing cooperatively just a few feet from the dock.

"Mac!" Lucy dropped the blanket. "Throw me the rope!"

He scrambled to standing, found the rope and turned to look at her. Even though he had to be absolutely freezing, there was a long pause as they stood looking at one another.

The sunglasses were gone. Those dark,

melted-chocolate eyes showed no surprise, just lingered on her, faintly appraising, as if he was taking inventory.

His gaze stayed on her long enough for her to think, *He hates my hair.* And *Oh, for God's sake, am I in my Winnie-the-Pooh pajamas?*

"Throw the damn rope!" she ordered him.

Then the thick coil of rope was flying toward her. The throw was going to be slightly short. But if she leaned just a bit, and reached with all her might, she knew she could—

"No!" he cried. "Leave it."

But it was too late. Lucy had leaned out too far. She tried to correct, taking a hasty step backward, but her momentum was already too far forward. Her arms windmilled crazily in an attempt to keep her balance.

She felt her feet leave the dock, the rush of air on her skin, and then she plunged into the lake. And sank, the weight of the soaked flannel pajamas pulling her down. Nothing could have prepared her for the cold as the gray water closed over her head. It seized her; her whole body went taut with shock. The sensation was of burning, not freezing. Her limbs were paralyzed instantly.

In what seemed to be slow motion, her body

finally bobbed back to the surface. She was in shock, too numb even to cry out. Somehow she floundered, her limbs heavy and nearly useless, to the dock. It was too early in the year for a ladder to be out, but since Mama no longer fostered kids she didn't put out a ladder—or maintain the dock—anyway.

Lucy managed to get her hands on the dock's planks, and tried to pull herself up. But there was a terrifying lack of strength in her arms. Her limbs felt as if they were made of Jell-O, all a-jiggle and not quite set.

"Hang on!"

Even her lips were numb. The effort it took to speak was tremendous.

"No! Don't." She forced the words out. They sounded weak. Her mind, in slow motion, rationalized there was no point in them both being in the water. His limbs would react to the cold water just as hers were doing. And he was farther out. In seconds, Mac would be helpless, floundering out beyond the dock.

She heard a mighty splash as Mac jumped back into the water. She tried to hang on, but she couldn't feel her fingers. She slipped back in, felt the water ooze over her head.

Lucy had been around water her entire life.

She had a Bronze Cross. She could have been a lifeguard at the Main Street Beach if her father had not thought it was a demeaning job. She had never been afraid of water.

Now, as she slipped below the surface, she didn't feel terrified, but oddly resigned. They were both going to die, a tragically romantic ending to their story—after all these years of separation, dying trying to save one another.

And then hands, strong, sure, were around her waist, lifting her. Her head broke water and she sputtered. She was unceremoniously shoved out of the water onto the rough boards of the dock.

Lucy dangled there, her elbows underneath her chest, her legs hanging, without the strength even to lift her head. His hand went to her bottom, and he gave her one more shove—really about as unromantic as it could get—and she lay on the dock, gasping, sobbing, coughing.

Mac's still in the water.

She squirmed around to look, but he didn't need her. His hands found the dock and he pulled himself to safety.

They lay side by side, gasping. Slowly she became aware that his nose was inches from her nose.

She could see drops of water beaded on the sooty clumps of his sinfully thick lashes. His eyes were glorious: a brown so dark it melted into black. The line of his nose was perfect, and faint stubble, twinkling with water droplets, highlighted the sweep of his cheekbones, the jut of his jaw.

Her eyes moved to the sensuous curve of his lips, and she felt sleepy and drugged, the desire to touch them with her own pushing past her every defense.

"Why, little Lucy Lindstrom," he growled. "We have to stop meeting like this."

All those years ago it had been her capsized canoe that had brought them—just about the most unlikely of loves, the good girl and the bad boy—together.

A week after graduation, having won all kinds of awards and been voted Most Likely to Succeed by her class, she realized the excitement was suddenly over. All her plans were made; it was her last summer of "freedom," as everybody kept kiddingly saying.

Lucy had taken the canoe out alone, something she never did. But the truth was, in that gap of activity something yawned within her, empty. She had a sense of her own life getting away from her, as if she was falling in with other people's plans for her without really ever asking herself what *she* wanted.

A storm had blown up, and she had not seen the log hiding under the surface of the water until it was too late.

Mac had been over on the wild side, camping, and he had seen her get into trouble. He'd already been in his canoe fighting the rough water to get to her before she hit the log.

He had picked her out of the water, somehow not capsizing his own canoe in the process, and taken her to his campsite to a fire, to wait until the lake calmed down to return her to her world.

But somehow she had never quite returned to her world. Lucy had been ripe for what he offered, an escape from a life that had all been laid out for her in a predictable pattern that there, on the side of the lake with her rescuer, had seemed like a form of death.

In all her life, it seemed everyone—her parents, her friends—only saw in her what they wanted her to be. And that was something that filled a need in them.

And then Mac had come along. And effortlessly he had seen through all that to what was real. Or so it had seemed.

And the truth was, soaking wet, gasping for air on a rotting dock, lying beside Mac, Lucy felt now exactly as she had felt then.

As if her whole world shivered to life.

As if black and white became color.

It had to be near-death experiences that did that: sharpened awareness to a razor's edge. Because she was so aware of Mac. She could feel the warmth of the breath coming from his mouth in puffs. There was an aura of power around him that was palpable, and in her weakened state, reassuring.

With a groan, he put his hands on either side of his chest and lifted himself to kneeling, and then quickly to standing.

He held out his hand to her, and she reached for it and he pulled her, his strength as easy as it was electrifying, to her feet.

Mac scooped the blanket from the dock where she had dropped it, shook it out, looped it around her shoulders and then his own, and then his arms went around her waist and he pulled her against the freezing length of him.

"Don't take this personally," he said. "It's a matter of survival, plain and simple."

"Thank you for clarifying," she said, with all the dignity her chattering teeth would allow. "You needn't have worried. I had no intention of ravishing you. You are about as sexy as a frozen salmon at the moment."

"Still getting in the last shot, aren't you?"

"When I can."

Cruelly, at that moment she realized a sliver of warmth radiated from him, and she pulled herself even closer to the rock-hard length of his body.

Their bodies, glued together by freezing, wet clothing, shook beneath the blanket. She pressed her cheek hard against his chest, and he loosed a hand and touched her soaking hair.

"You hate it," she said, her voice quaking.

"It wasn't my best entrance," he agreed.

"I meant my hair."

"I know you did," he said softly. "Hello, Lucy."

"Hello, Macintyre."

Standing here against Mac, so close she could feel the pebbles of cold rising on his chilled skin, she could also feel his innate strength. Warmth was returning to his body and seeping into hers.

The physical sensation of closeness, of sharing spreading heat, was making her vulnerable to other feelings, the very ones she had hoped to steel herself against.

It was not just weak. The weakness could be assigned to the numbing cold that had seeped into every part of her. Even her tongue felt heavy and numb.

It was not just that she never wanted to move again. That could be assigned to the fact that her limbs felt slow and clumsy and paralyzed.

No, it was something worse than being weak.

Something worse than being paralyzed.

In Macintyre Hudson's arms, soaked, her Winnie-the-Pooh pajamas providing as much protection against him as a wet paper towel, Lucy Lindstrom felt the worst weakness of all, the longing she had kept hidden from herself.

Not to be so alone.

Her trembling deepened, and a soblike sound escaped her.

"Are you okay?" he asked.

"Not really," she said as she admitted the

full truth to herself. It was not the cold making her weak. It was him.

Lucy felt a terrible wave of self-loathing. Was life just one endless loop, playing the same things over and over again?

She was cursed at love. She needed to accept that about herself, and devote her considerable energy and talent to causes that would help others, and, as a bonus, couldn't hurt her.

She pulled away from him, though it took all her strength, physical and mental. The blanket held her fast, so that mere inches separated them, but at least their bodies were no longer glued together.

History, she told herself sternly, was *not* repeating itself.

It was good he was here. She could face him, puncture any remaining illusions and get on with her wonderful life of doing good for others.

"Are you hurt?" he asked, putting her away from him, scanning her face.

She already missed the small warmth that had begun to radiate from him. Again, she had to pit what remained of her physical and mental strength to resist the desire to collapse against him.

"I'm fine," she said tersely.

"You don't look fine."

"Well, I'm not hurt. Mortified."

His expression was one of pure exasperation. "Who nearly drowns and is mortified by it?"

Whew. There was no sense him knowing she was mortified because of her reaction to him. By her sudden onslaught of uncertainty.

They had both been in perilous danger, and she was worried about the impression her hair made? Worried that she looked like a drowned rat? Worried about what pajamas she had on?

It was starting all over again!

This crippling need. He had seen her once, when it seemed no one else could. Hadn't she longed for that ever since?

Had she pursued getting that message to him so incessantly because of Mama Freda? Or had it been for herself? To feel the way she had felt when his arms closed around her?

Trembling, trying to fight the part of her that wanted nothing more than to scoot back into his warmth, she reminded herself that feeling this way had nearly destroyed her. It had had far-reaching repercussions that had torn her family and her life asunder.

"This is all your fault," she said. Thankfully, he took her literally.

"I'm not responsible for your bad catch."

"It was a terrible throw!"

"Yes, it was. All the more reason you shouldn't have reached for the rope. I could have thrown it again."

"You shouldn't have jumped back in the water after me. You could have been overcome by the cold. I'm surprised you weren't. And then we both would have been in big trouble."

"You have up to ten minutes in water that cold before you succumb. Plus, I don't seem to feel cold water like other people. I white-water kayak. I think it has desensitized me. But under no circumstances would I have stood on the pontoon of my plane and watched anyone drown."

Gee. He wasn't sensitive, and his rescue of her wasn't even personal. He would have done it for anyone.

"I wasn't going to drown," Lucy lied haughtily, since only moments ago she had been resigned to that very thing. He'd just said she had ten whole minutes. "I've lived on this lake my entire life."

"Oh!" He smacked himself on the forehead with his fist. "How could I forget that? Not only have you lived on the lake your entire life, but so did three generations of your family before you. Lindstroms don't drown. They die like they lived. Nice respectable deaths in the same beds that they were born in, in the same town they never took more than two steps away from."

"I lived in Glen Oak for six years," she said.

"Oh, Glen Oak. An hour away. Some consider Lindstrom Beach to be Glen Oak's summer suburb."

Lucy was aware of being furious with herself for the utter weakness of reacting to him. It felt much safer to transfer that fury to him.

He had walked away. Not just from this town. He had walked away from having to give anything of himself. How could he never have considered all the possibilities? They had played with fire all that summer.

She had gotten burned. And he had walked away.

And he had never even said he loved her. Not even once.

CHAPTER THREE

"YOU KNOW WHAT, Macintyre Hudson? You were a jerk back then, and you're still a jerk."

"May I remind you that you begged me to come back here?"

"I did not beg. I appealed to your conscience. And I personally did not care if you came back."

"You were a snotty, stuck-up brat and you still are. Here's a novel concept," Mac said, his voice threaded with annoyance, "why don't you try thanking me for my heroic rescue? For the second time in your life, by the way."

Because of what happened the first time, you idiot.

"If I needed a hero," she said with soft fury, "you are the last person I would pick."

That hit home. He actually flinched. And she was happy he flinched. *Snotty, stuck-up brat?*

Then a cool veil dropped over the angry sparks flickering in his eyes, and his mouth turned upward, that mocking smile that was his trademark, that said *You can't hurt me—don't even try.* He folded his arms over the deep strength of his broad chest, and not because he was cold, either.

"You know what? If I was looking for a damsel in distress, you wouldn't exactly be my first pick, either. You're still every bit the snooty doctor's daughter."

She felt all of it then. The abandonment. The fear she had shouldered alone in the months after he left. Her parents, who had always doted on her, looking at her with hurt and embarrassment, as if she could not have let them down more completely. The friends she had known since kindergarten not phoning anymore, looking the other way when they saw her.

She felt all of it.

And it felt as if every single bit of it was his fault.

"Just to set the record straight, maybe it's you who should be thanking me," she told him. "I came down here to rescue you. You were the one in the water."

"I didn't need your help...."

So, absolutely nothing had changed. She was, in his eyes, still the town rich girl, the doctor's snooty daughter, out of touch with what he considered to be real.

And he was still the one who didn't *need*.

"Or your botched rescue attempt."

The fury in her felt white-hot, as if it could obliterate what remained of the chill on her. Lucy wished she had felt *that* when she had seen him get knocked off the dock by the post. She wished, instead of running to him, worried about him, she had marched into her house and firmly shut the door on him.

She hadn't done that. But maybe it was never too late to correct a mistake. She could do the right thing this time.

She stepped in close, shivered dramatically, letting him believe she was weak and not strong, that she needed his body heat back. Mac was wary, but not wary enough. He let her slip back in, close to him.

Lucy put both her hands on his chest, blinked up at him with her very best will-you-be-my-hero? look and then shoved him as hard as she could.

With a startled yelp, which Lucy found extremely satisfying, Macintyre Hudson lost his footing and stumbled off the dock, back into the water. She turned and walked away, annoyed that she was reassured by his vigorous cursing that he was just fine.

She glanced back. More than fine! Instead of getting out of the water, Mac shrugged out of his leather jacket and threw it onto the dock. Then, making the most of his ten minutes, he swam back to his plane.

Within moments he had the entire situation under control, which no doubt pleased him no end. He fastened the plane to the dock's other pillar, which held, then reached inside and tossed a single overnight bag onto the dock.

She certainly didn't want him to catch her watching. Why was she watching? It was just more evidence of the weakness he made her feel. What she needed to be doing was to be heading for a hot shower at top speed.

Lucy had crossed back into her yard when she heard Mama's shout.

"Ach! What is going on?"

She turned to see Mama Freda trundling toward her dock, hand over her brow, trying to see into the sun. Then Mama stopped, and a light came on in that ancient, wise face that seemed to steal the chill right out of Lucy.

"Schatz?"

Mac was standing on the dock, and had removed his soaking shirt and was wringing it out. That was an unfortunate sight for a girl trying to steel herself against him. His body was absolutely perfect, sleek and strong, water sluicing down the deepness of his chest to the defined ripples of his abs.

He dropped the soaked shirt beside his jacket and sprinted over the dock and across the lawn. He stopped at Mama Freda and grinned down at her, and this time his grin was so genuine it could have lit up the whole lake. Mama reached up and touched his cheek.

Then he picked up the rather large bulk of Mama Freda as if she were featherlight, and swung her around until she was squealing like a young girl.

"You're getting me all wet," she protested loudly, smacking the broadness of his shoulders with delight. *"Ach.* Put me down, galoothead."

Finally he did, and she patted her hair into

place, regarding him with such affection that Lucy felt something burn behind her eyes.

"Why are you all wet? You'll catch your death!"

"Your dock broke when I tried to tie to it."

"You should have told me you were coming," Mama said reproachfully.

"I wanted to surprise you."

"Surprise, schmize."

Lucy smiled, despite herself. One of Mama's goals in life seemed to be to create a rhyme, beginning with *sch,* for every word in the English language.

"You see what happens? You end up in the lake. If you'd just told me, I would have warned you to tie up to Lucy's dock."

"I don't think Lucy wants me tying up at her dock."

Only Lucy would pick up his dry double meaning on that. She could actually feel a bit of a blush moving heat into her frozen cheeks.

"Don't be silly. Lucy wouldn't mind."

He could have thrown her under the bus, because Mama would not have approved of anyone being pushed into the water at this time of year, no matter how pressing the circumstances.

But he didn't. Her gratitude that he hadn't thrown her under the bus was short-lived as Mac left the topic of Lucy Lindstrom behind with annoying ease.

"Mama, I'm freezing. I hope you have *apfelstrudel* fresh from the oven."

"You have to tell me you're coming to get strudel fresh from the oven. That's not what you need, anyway. Mama knows what you need."

Lucy could hear the smile in his voice, and was aware again of Mama working her magic, both of them smiling just moments after all that fury.

"What do I need, Mama?"

"You need elixir."

He pretended terror, then dashed back to the dock and picked up his soaked clothing and the bag, tossed it over his naked shoulder. He returned and wrapped his arm around Mama's waist and let her lead him to the house.

Lucy turned back to her own house, her eyes still smarting from what had passed between those two. The love and devotion shimmered around them as bright as the strengthening morning sun.

That was why she had gone to such lengths

to get Macintyre Hudson to come back here. And if another motive had lain hidden beneath that one, it had been exposed to her in those moments when his arms had wrapped around her and his heat had seeped into her.

Now that it was exposed, she could put it in a place where she could guard against it as if her life depended on it.

Which, Lucy told herself through the chattering of her teeth, it did.

Out of the corner of his eye, Mac saw Lucy pause and watch his reunion with Mama.

"Is that Lucy?" Mama said, catching the direction of his gaze.

"Yeah, as annoying as ever."

"She's a good girl," Mama said stubbornly.

"Everything she ever aspired to be, then."

Only, she wasn't a girl anymore, but a woman. The *good* part he had no doubt about. That was what was expected of the doctor's daughter, after all.

Even given the circumstances he had noted the changes. Her hair was still blond, but it no longer fell, unrestrained by hair clips or elastic bands, to the slight swell of her breast.

Plastered to her head, it hadn't looked like

much, but he was willing to bet that when it was dry it was ultrasophisticated, and would show off the hugeness of those dazzling green eyes, the pixie-perfection of her dainty features. Still, Mac was aware of fighting the part of him that missed how it used to be.

She had lost the faintly scrawny build of a long-distance runner, and filled out, a fact he could not help but notice when she had pressed the lusciousness of her freezing body into his.

She seemed uptight, though, and the level of her anger at him gave him pause.

Unbidden, he wondered if she ever slipped into the lake and skinny-dipped under the full moon. Would she still think it was the most daring thing a person could do, and that she was risking arrest and public humiliation?

What made her laugh now? In high school it seemed as if she had been at the center of every circle, popular and carefree. That laugh, from deep within her, was so joyous and unchained the birds stopped singing to listen.

Mac snorted in annoyance with himself, reminding himself curtly that he had broken that particular spell a long time ago. Though if that was completely true, why the reluctance to return Lucy's calls? Why the aversion to coming back?

If that was completely true, why had he told Lucy Lindstrom, of all people, that his father had been a ditchdigger?

That had been bothering him since the words had come out of his mouth. Maybe that confession had even contributed to the fiasco on the dock.

"What's she doing?" Mama asked, worried. "Is she wet, too? She looks wet."

"We both ended up in the lake."

"But how?"

"A comedy of errors. Don't worry about it, Mama."

But Mama was determined to worry. "She should have come here. I would look after her. She could catch her death."

Mama Freda, still looking after everyone. Except maybe herself. She was looking toward Lucy's house as if she was thinking of going to get her.

He noticed the grass blended seamlessly together, almost as if the lawns of the two houses were one. That was new. Dr. Lindstrom had gone to great lengths to accentuate the boundaries of his yard, to lower any risk of association with the place next door.

Despite now sharing a lawn with its shabby neighbor, the Lindstrom place still looked like something off a magazine spread.

A bank of French doors had been added to the back of the house. Beyond the redwood of the multilayered deck, a lawn, tender with new grass, ended at a sea of yellow and red tulips. The flowers cascaded down a gentle slope to the fine white sand of the private beach.

On the L-shaped section of the bleached gray wood of the dock a dozen canoes were upside down.

What was with all the canoes? He was pretty sure that Mama had said Lucy was by herself since she had come home a year ago.

A bird called, and Mac could smell the rich scent of sun heating the fallen needles of the ponderosa pine.

As he gazed out over the lake, he was surprised by how much he had missed this place. Not the town, which was exceptionally cliquey; you were either "in" or you were "out" in Lindstrom Beach.

Lucy's family had always been "in." Of

course, "in" was determined by the location of your house on the lake, the size of the lot, the house itself, what kind of boat you had and who your connections were. "In" was determined by your occupation, your membership in the church and the yacht club, and by your income, never mentioned outright, always insinuated.

He, on the other hand, had been "out," a kid of questionable background, in foster care, in Mama's house, the only remaining of the original cabins that had been built around the lake in the forties. Her house, little more than a fishing shack, had been the bane of the entire neighborhood.

And so the sharing of the lawn was new and unexpected.

"Do you and Lucy go in together to hire someone to look after the grounds?" he asked.

"No, Lucy does it."

That startled him. Lucy mowed the expansive lawns? He couldn't really imagine her pushing a lawn mower. He remembered her and her friends sitting on the deck in their bikinis while the "help" sweated under the hot sun keeping the grounds of her house immaculate. But he didn't want Lucy to crowd back into his thoughts.

"You look well, Mama," he said, an invitation for her to confide in him. He should have known it wouldn't be that easy.

"I look well. You look terrible." She gave his freezing, naked torso a hard pinch. "No meat on your bones. Eating in restaurants. I can tell by your coloring."

He thought his coloring might be off because he had just had a pretty good dunking in some freezing water, but he knew from long experience that there was no telling Mama.

They approached the back of her house. The porch door was choked with overgrown lilacs, drooping with heavy buds. Mac pushed aside some branches and opened the screen door. It squeaked outrageously. He could see the floorboards of her screened porch were as rotten as her dock.

He frowned at the attempt at a repair. Had she hired some haphazard handyman?

"Who did this?" he said, toeing the new board.

"Lucy," she said, eyeing the disastrous repair with pride. "Lucy helps me with lots of things around here."

His frown deepened. Somehow that was

a Lucy he could never have imagined, nails between teeth, pounding in boards.

Though Mama had said nothing, he had suspected for some time the house was becoming too much for her, and this confirmed it.

"You should come to Toronto with me," he said. It was his opening move. In his bag he had brochures of Toronto's most upscale retirement home.

"Toronto, schmonto. No, you should move back here. That big city is no place for a boy like you."

"I'm not a boy anymore, Mama."

"You will always be my boy."

He regarded her warmly, searching her face for any sign of illness. She was unchanging. She had seemed old when he had first met her, and she really had never seemed to get any older. There was a sameness about her in a changing world that had been a touchstone.

Why hadn't she told him she had lost her license?

She was going to be eighty years old three days before Mother's Day. He held open the inside door for her, and they stepped through into her kitchen.

It, too, was showing signs of benign neglect: paint chipping from the cabinets, a door not closing properly, the old linoleum tiles beginning to curl. There was a towel tied tightly around a faucet, and he went and looked.

An attempted repair of a leak.

"Lucy's work?" he guessed.

"Yes."

Again, the Lucy he didn't know. "You just have to tell me these things," he said. "I would have paid for the plumber."

"You pay for enough already."

He turned to look at Mama, and without warning he was fourteen years old again, standing in this kitchen for the first time.

Harriet Freda's had been his fifth foster home in as many months, and despite the fact this one had a prime lakeshore location, from the outside the house seemed even smaller and dumpier and darker than all the other foster homes had been.

Maybe, he had thought, already cynical, they just sent you to worse and worse places.

The house would have seemed beyond humble in any setting, but surrounded by the magnificent lake houses, it was painfully shacklike and out of place on the shores of Sunshine Lake.

That morning, standing in a kitchen that cheerfully belied the outside of the house, Mac had been fourteen and terrified. That had been his first lesson since the death of his father: never let the terror show.

She had been introduced to him as Mama Freda, and she looked stocky and ancient. Her hair was a bluish-white color and frizzy with a bad perm. She had more wrinkles than a Shar-Pei. Mac thought she was way too old to be looking after other people's kids.

Still, she looked harmless enough, standing at her kitchen table in a frumpy dress that showed off her chunky build, thick arms and legs, ankles swollen above sensible shoes. She had been wearing a much-bleached apron, once white, aged to tea-dipped, and covered with faded blotches of berry and chocolate.

The niceties were over, the social worker was gone and he was standing there with a paper bag containing two T-shirts, one pair of jeans and a change of underwear. Mrs. Freda cast him a look, and there was an unmistakable friendly twinkle in deep-set blue eyes.

Well, there was no sense her thinking they were going to be on friendly terms.

"I killed a man," he said, and then added, "With my bare hands." He thought the *with my bare hands* part was a nice touch. It was actually a line from a song, but it warned people to stay back from him, that he was dangerous and tough.

And if Macintyre Hudson had wanted one thing at age fourteen, it was for people to stay back from him. He had been like a wounded animal, unwilling to trust again.

Mama Freda glanced up from what she was doing, stretching out an enormous piece of dough, thin and elastic, over the edges of her large, round kitchen table. She regarded him, and he noticed the twinkle was gone from her eyes, replaced with an immense sorrow.

"This is a terrible thing," she said, sinking into a chair. "To kill a man. I know. I had to do it once."

He stared at her, his mouth open. And when she beckoned to the chair beside hers, he abandoned his meager bag of belongings and went to it, as if drawn to her side by a magnet.

"It was near the end of the war," she said, looking at her hands. "I was thirteen. A soldier, he was—" she glanced at Mac, trying to decide how much to say "—hurting my sister. He had his back to me. I picked up a cast-iron pan and I crept up behind him and I hit him as hard as I could over his head. There was a terrible noise. Terrible. He fell off my sister. I think he was already dead, but I knew if he ever got up we were all doomed, and so I hit him again and again and again."

Mac had never heard silence like he heard in Mama Freda's kitchen right then. The clock ticking sounded explosive.

"So I know what this thing is," she said finally, "to kill a man. I know how you carry it within you. How you think of his face, and wonder who he was before the great evil overcame him. I wonder what his mother felt when he never came home, and if his sisters grieve him to this day, the way I grieve the brother who went to war and never came home."

Her hand crept out from under her apron and she laid it, palm up, on the table. An invitation. And Mac surprised himself by not being able to refuse that invitation. He put his hand on the table, too. Her hand closed around his, surprisingly strong for such an old lady.

"Look at me," she said.

And he did.

She did not say a word. She didn't have to. He looked deep into her eyes, and for the first time in a long, long time, he felt he was not alone.

That someone else knew what it was to suffer.

Later they ate the *apfelstrudel* she had finished rolling out on her kitchen table, and it felt as if his taste buds had come awake, as if he could taste for the first time in a long, long time, too, as if he had never tasted food quite so wondrous.

He started, in that moment, with warm strudel melting in his mouth, to do what he had sworn he would never do again. But he was careful never to call it that, and never to utter the words that would solidify it and make it real. For him, the admission of love was the holding of a samurai's sword that you would eventually plunge into your own heart.

But he had never altered the story he had told her that day, not even when she had said to him once, "I know, *schatz,* there is nothing in you that could kill another person. Or anything. Not even a baby robin that fell from its nest. I have watched you carry bugs outside rather than swat them."

But he had never doubted that she really had killed that soldier, and she, too, carried bugs outside rather than swatting them.

Mama, with her enormous capacity to care for all things, had saved him.

And he owed it to her to be there for her if she needed him. It was evident from the state of her house that he hadn't been there in the ways she needed. And that Lucy, the one he had called the spoiled brat, had been. He felt the faintest shiver of something.

Guilt?

"Go shower," Mama said, and he drew himself back to the present with a shake of his head. "Nice and hot."

She was already reaching up high into her cabinet and Mac shuddered when the ancient brown bottle of elixir came down, and he hightailed it for the tiny bathroom at the top of the stairs.

When he came down, in dry clothes, she had a tumbler of the clear liquid poured.

"Drink. It will ward off the cold."

"I'm not cold."

"The cold you will get if you don't drink

it!" She had that look on her face, her arms folded over her ample bosom.

There was no sense explaining to Mama you didn't get colds from being cold, that you got them from coming in contact with one of hundreds of viruses, none of which were very likely to be living in the freezing-cold water of Sunshine Lake.

He took the tumbler, plugged his nose and put it back. It burned to his belly and he felt his toes curl.

He set the glass down, and wiped his watering eyes. "For heaven's sakes, its schnapps!"

"Obstler," she said happily. "Not peppermint sugar like they drink here. Ugh. Mine is made with apples. Herbs."

She was right, though—if there was any sneaky virus in him, no matter what the source, it would be gone now.

"Homemade, from my great-grandmother's recipe. Now, take some to Lucy. I have it ready." She passed him an unlabeled brown bottle of her secret elixir.

"I'm not taking it to Lucy." After that encounter on the dock, the less he had to do with Lucy the better.

He'd wanted to believe, after all this time,

that Lucy, the girl who had not thought he was good enough, would have no power over him. He had seen the world. He'd succeeded. He'd expected Lucy and this town to be nothing more than a speck of dust from the past.

What he hadn't expected was the rush of feeling when he had seen her. Even dripping wet, near frozen, seeing Lucy on the dock calling to him, he had felt a pull so strong it felt as if his heart was coming from his chest. He'd been vulnerable, caught off guard, but still, there had always been something about her.

She still had that face, impish, unconventionally beautiful, that inspired warmth and trust, that took a man's guard right down, and left him in a place where he could be shoved into a lake by someone who weighed sixty pounds less than he did.

An old hurt surfaced, its edges knife-sharp. *I could never fall for a boy like you.*

That was the problem with coming back to a place you had left behind, Mac thought. Old hurts didn't die. They waited. And those words, coming from Lucy, the one he had trusted with his ever-so-bruised heart…

"She needs the elixir! She'll catch her death."

Since he didn't want to tell Mama why he didn't want to see Lucy—because he had fully expected to be indifferent and had been anything but—now might be a good time to explain viruses. But his explanation, he knew, would fall on deaf ears.

"She's a doctor's daughter. I'm sure she knows what she needs."

Mama looked stubborn.

"Mama, it's probably illegal to make this stuff, let alone dispense it."

She regarded him, her eyes narrow, and then without warning, "Are you speaking to your mother yet, *schatz?*"

He glared at her stonily.

"Nearly Mother's Day. Just two weeks away. She must be lonely for you."

The only thing his mother had ever been lonely for was her bank account. But he wasn't being drawn into this argument. And he could clearly see Mama had grabbed on to it now, like a dog worrying meat off a bone.

"How many years?" she asked softly, stubbornly.

He refused to answer out loud, but inside, he did the math.

"It's time," she said.

On this, and only this, he had refused her from the first day he had come here. There would be no reconciliation with his mother.

"Just a card, to start," she said, as if they had not played out this scene a hundred times before. "I think I have the perfect one right here."

It was one of Mama's things. She always had a cupboard devoted to greeting cards. She had one suitable for every occasion.

Except son and mother estranged for fourteen years.

Without a word he picked up the bottle of homemade schnapps and went out the squeaking door. When he glanced back over his shoulder, Mama had her back to him, rummaging through the card cupboard, singing with soft satisfaction.

He noticed how hunched she was.

Frail, somehow, despite her bulk.

He noticed how badly the house needed repair, and felt guilty, again, that he had somehow let it get this bad.

Mac was not unaware that he had been back in Lindstrom Beach all of half an hour and all these uncomfortable feelings were rising to the surface. He didn't like feelings.

Lucy had been here when he had not. Well, he'd take over from her now.

It occurred to him that this trip was probably not going to be the quick turnaround he had hoped for. Still, a few days of intense work, and he'd be out of here, leaving all these uneasy feelings behind him.

"Make sure she drinks some," Mama shouted as the screen creaked behind him. "Make sure. Don't come back here unless she does."

And much as he didn't want Lucy to be right about anything, and much as he didn't like the unexpected feelings, he realized, reluctantly, she had been right to insist he come back here.

Mama needed him.

And yes, the time to honor his foster mother was definitely now. But he would leave the gala to Lucy, and honor his foster mother by making sure her house was livable before he left again.

CHAPTER FOUR

MAC CROSSED THE familiar ground between the two houses. He noted, again, that Lucy's property was everything Mama's was not. Even with the lawns melting together, the properties were very different: Mama's ringed in huge trees—that were probably hard to mow around—the Lindstrom place well-maintained, oozing the perfect taste of old money.

From the tidbits of information dropped by Mama, Mac knew Lucy had taken over the house from her mother a year or so ago. Hadn't there been something about a broken engagement?

How did she find time to do the work that it used to take an entire team of gardeners to do?

Unless she doesn't have a life.

Which, also from tidbits dropped by Mama,

Lucy didn't. She ran some kind of online book business. A life, yes, but not the life he had expected the most popular girl in high school would have ended up with.

I don't care, Mac told himself, but if he really didn't, would he even have to say that to himself?

He debated going to the front of the house, keeping everything nice and formal, but in the end, he stayed in the back and went across the deck. He stopped and surveyed the house. The stately white paint was faded and peeling; a large patch of a sample paint color had been put up.

It was a pale shade of lavender. Several boards underneath it had samples of what he assumed would be trim color, ranging from light lilac to deep purple.

The paint color made him think he didn't know Lucy at all.

Which, of course, he didn't. She was no more the same girl she had been when he'd left than he was the same man. He became aware of the sound of water running inside the house, assumed Lucy was showering and was grateful for the reprieve from another encounter with her.

He wasn't a little kid anymore. And neither was Lucy. He respected Mama, but he couldn't take her every wish as a command. *Make sure she drinks it.* Lucy could find the bottle and make up her own mind whether to drink it.

He would take his chances. If he didn't return for a while, Mama might not question how he had completed his assignment. And, hopefully, she would be off the topic of his mother by then, as well.

Mac set Mama's offering at Lucy's back door, and then strolled down to her dock to look over the canoes. They weren't particularly good quality—different ages and makes and colors. Then he saw a sign, fairly new, nailed to a wharf post like the one that had broken at Mama's.

Lucy's Lakeside Rentals. It outlined the rates and rules for renting canoes.

Lucy was renting canoes? He *really* didn't know her anymore. In fact, it almost seemed as if their roles were reversed. He had arrived, he knew every success he had ever hoped for, and she was mowing lawns and scraping together pennies by renting canoes.

He thought he should feel at least a moment's satisfaction over that. A little gloating from the kind of guy Lucy could never fall for might be in order. But instead, Mac felt oddly troubled. And hated it that he felt that way.

He looked at the house. He could still hear water running. He eased a canoe up with his toe. The paddles were stored underneath it.

Then Mac maneuvered the canoe off the dock and into the water, got into it and began to paddle toward the other side of the lake.

Even more than Mama's embrace, the silent canoe skimming across the water filled him with what he dreaded most of all—a sense of having missed this place, a sense that even as he had tried to leave it all behind him, this was home.

An hour later, eyeing Lucy's house for signs of life and relieved to find none, Mac put the canoe back on the dock. He felt like a thief as he crept up to her back door. The elixir was gone. He could report to Mama with a clear conscience. Still, the feeling of being a thief was not relieved by sticking twenty bucks under a rock to cover the rental of the canoe.

"Hey," Lucy cried, "Wait!"

He turned and looked at her, put his hands

into his pockets. He looked annoyed and impatient.

"What are you doing?" Lucy called.

"I took one of your canoes out. There's rental money under the rock." This was said sharply, as if it was obvious, and she was keeping him from something important.

"I never said you could rent my canoe."

"I have to pass a character test?"

Below the sarcasm, incredibly, Lucy thought she detected the faintest thread of hurt. After all these years, could it still be between them?

I could never fall for a boy like you.

No, he was successful and worldly, and it was written in every line of his stance that he didn't give a hoot what she thought of him.

"I didn't say that. You can't just take a canoe."

"I didn't just take it. I paid you for it."

"You need to tell me where you're going. What if you didn't come back?"

"I've been paddling these waters since I was fourteen. I've kayaked some of the most dangerous waters in the world. I think I can be trusted with your canoe."

Trust. There it was again. The missing ingredient between them.

"It's not the canoe I'm worried about. I need to give you a life jacket."

"You're worried about me, Lucy Lin?" Now, aggravatingly, he was pulling out the charm to try to disarm her.

"No!"

"So what's the problem?"

"You should have asked."

"Maybe I should have. But we both know I'm not the kind of guy who does things by the book."

Again she thought she heard faint challenge, a hurt behind the mocking tone.

She sighed. "I don't want your money, Mac. If you want to take a canoe, take one. But let someone know where you're going. At least Mama, if you don't want to talk to me."

She was unsettled to realize now she was the one who felt hurt. Not that she had a right to be. Of course he wouldn't want to talk to her. She'd pushed him into the lake. Though she had a feeling his aversion to her went deeper than that recent incident.

"I don't need your charity," he said, "I'd rather pay you."

"Well, I don't need your charity, either."

"You know what? I'll just have my own equipment sent up."

"You do that."

She watched him walk away, his head high, and felt regret. They needed to talk about Mama, if nothing else. But he hadn't returned her calls, and he didn't want to talk to her now, either.

Lucy picked up his twenty-dollar bill, stuck it in an envelope, scrawled his name across it. Not bothering to dress, she crossed the lawns between the two houses in her housecoat, but didn't knock on the door.

She followed his lead. She put the envelope under a rock and walked away. When she got home, she inspected the canoes, saw which one he had been using, and shoved a life jacket underneath it.

"What's this?" Mama said, handing him the envelope.

Mac looked in it and sighed with irritation. Trust Lucy. She was always going to have the last word.

Except this time she wasn't, damn her. He folded the envelope, tucked it in his pocket and went out the back door. The last person he would ever accept charity from was Lucy. He owed her for the canoe, fair and square, and the days of her—or anyone in this town—feeling superior to him were over.

He lifted his hand to knock on her back door to return the money to her. Raised voices drifted out the open French doors and he moved away from the paint and peered into Lucy's house.

"You're wrecking the neighborhood!" someone said shrilly.

"It's just a sample." That voice was Lucy's, low and conciliatory.

"Purple? You're going to paint your house purple? Are you kidding me? It's an absolute monstrosity. When Billy and I saw it from the boat the other day, I nearly fell overboard."

Lucy had a perfect opportunity to say, *too bad you didn't,* but instead she defended her choice.

"I thought it was funky."

"Funky? On Lakeshore Drive?"

No answer to that.

Mac tried the door, and it was unlocked. He pulled it open and slid in. After a moment, his eyes adjusted to being inside and he saw Lucy at her front door, still wrapped in a housecoat, her hands folded defensively over her chest, looking up at a taller woman, the other woman's slenderness of the painful variety.

Now, there was a face from the past. Claudia Mitchell-Franks. Dressed in a trouser suit he was going to guess was linen, her makeup and hair done as if she was going to a party. Her thin face was pinched with rage.

Lucy was everything Claudia was not. Fresh-scrubbed from the shower, her short hair was towel-ruffled and did not look any more sophisticated than it had fresh out of the drink. She was nearly lost inside a white housecoat, the kind that hung on the back of the bathroom door in really good hotels.

Her feet were bare, and absurdly that struck him as far sexier than her visitor's stiletto sandals.

"And don't even think you're renting canoes this year! Last summer it increased traffic in this area to an unreasonable level, and you don't have any parking. The street above your place was clogged. And I had riffraff paddling by my beach."

"There's no law against renting canoes," Lucy said, but without much force.

This was the same Lucy who had just pushed him into the water? Why wasn't she telling old Claudia to take a hike?

"I had one couple stop and set up a picnic on my front lawn!" Claudia snapped.

"Horrors," Lucy said dryly. He found himself rooting for her. *Come on, Lucy, you can do better than that.*

"I am not spending another summer explaining to people it's a private beach," Claudia said.

Shrilly, too, he was willing to bet.

"It isn't," Lucy said calmly. "You only own to the high-water mark, which in your case is about three feet from your gazebo. Those people have a perfect right to picnic there if they want to."

Mac felt a little unwilling pride in her. That was information he'd given her all those years ago when he'd thumbed his nose at all those people trying to claim they owned the beaches.

"I hope you don't tell *them* that," Claudia said.

"I have it printed on the brochure I give out

at rental time," she said, but then backtracked. "Of course I don't. But can't we share the lake with others?"

The perfectly coiffed Claudia looked as if she was going to have apoplexy at the idea of sharing the lake. Mac was pretty sure Claudia was one of the girls who used to sit on that deck painting her toenails while the "riffraff" slaved in the yard.

"Well, you won't be giving out any brochures this year, no, you won't! You'll need a permit to run your little business. And you're not getting one. And you know what else? You can forget the yacht club for your fundraiser."

"I've already paid my deposit," Lucy said, clearly rattled.

"I'll see that it's returned to you."

"But I have a hundred confirmed guests coming. The gala is only two weeks away!" There was a pleading note in her voice.

"This is what you'll be up against if you even try rezoning. This is a residential neighborhood. It always has been and it always will be."

"That's what this is really about, isn't it?"

"We finally no longer have to put up with

the endless parade of young thugs next door to this house, and you do this?"

He'd heard enough. He stepped across the floor.

"Lucy, everything okay here?"

Lucy turned and looked at him. He could see her eyes were shiny, and he hoped he was the only person in the room who knew that meant she was close to tears.

He thought she might be angry that he had barged into her house, but instead he saw relief on her delicate features as he approached her. Despite the brave front, he could tell that for some reason she felt as if she was in over her head. Maybe because this attack was coming from someone who used to be her friend?

"You remember Claudia," she said.

He would have much rather Lucy told Claudia to get the hell out of her house instead of politely making introductions.

Claudia was staring at him meanly. Oh, boy, did he ever remember that look! The first time he'd taken Lucy out publicly, for an ice cream cone on Main Street, they had run into her, and she'd had that same look on her skinny, malicious face.

"I know you," she said tapping a hard, bloodred-lacquered fingernail against a lip that matched.

He waited for her to recognize him, for the mean look to deepen.

Instead, when recognition dawned in her eyes, her whole countenance changed. She smiled and rushed at him, blinked and put her claw on his arm, dug her talon in, just a little bit.

"Why, Macintyre Hudson." She beamed up at him. "Aren't you the small-town boy who has done well for himself?"

He told himself he should find this moment exceedingly satisfactory, especially since it had happened in front of Lucy. Instead, he felt a sensation of discomfort—which Lucy quickly dispelled.

Because behind Claudia, Lucy crossed her arms over her chest and frowned. Then she caught his eye and pantomimed gagging.

He didn't want to be charmed by Lucy, but he couldn't help but smile. Claudia actually thought it was for her. He didn't let the impression last. He slid out from under her fingertips.

"I seem to remember being one of the

young thugs from next door. *And* the riffraff who had the nerve to paddle by your dock. I might even have had the audacity to eat my lunch on your beach now and again."

She hee-hawed with enthusiasm. "Oh, Mac, such a sense of humor! I've always *adored* you. My kids—I have two boys now—won't wear anything but Wild Side. If it doesn't have that little orangey kayak symbol on it, they won't put it on."

He tried not to show how appalled he was that his brand was the choice of the elite little monkeys who lived around the lake.

"What brings you home?" Claudia purred.

Over Claudia's bony shoulder, he saw Lucy now had her hands around her own neck, the internationally recognized symbol for choking. He tried to control the twitching of his lips.

"Lucy's having a party to honor my mother. I wouldn't have missed it for the world."

Considering that it had given him grave satisfaction to snub Lucy by giving the event a miss, this news came as a shock to him.

"Oh. That. I wasn't expecting *you* would come for *that*. There's been a teensy problem with location. Anyway, it's not as if she's your *real* mother."

Unaware how insensitive that remark was, Claudia forged ahead, her red lips stretched over teeth he found very large.

"I'm afraid the committee has voted to revoke our rental to Lucy. And we don't meet again until next month, and that's too late. But you know, the elementary-school gym is probably available. I'd be happy to check for you."

"No thanks."

"Don't be mad at *me*. It's really Lucy's fault. Norman Avalon is president of the yacht club this year. Do you remember him?"

An unpleasant memory of a boy throwing a partially filled Slurpee cup on him while he was shoveling three tons of mud out of a ditch came to mind.

"They live right over there. If Lucy paints the place purple, his wife, Ellen—you remember Ellen, she used to be a Polson—will have to look at it all day. She's ticked. Royally. And that was before the rezoning application. Macintyre, it is just sooo nice seeing you."

He didn't respond, tried not to look at Lucy, who had her eyes crossed and her tongue hanging out, her hands still around her own throat.

"Congrats on your company's success. I know Billy would love to see you if you have time. We generally have pre-dinner cocktails at the club on Friday."

Behind Claudia, Lucy dropped silently to her knees, and was swaying back and forth, holding her throat.

"The club?" As if there was only one in town, which there was.

"You know, the yacht club."

"Oh, the one Lucy isn't renting anymore. To honor *my* mother."

"Oh." With effort, since her expression lines had been removed with Botox, Claudia formed her face into contrite lines and lowered her voice sympathetically. "If you wanted to drop by on Friday and talk to Billy about it, he might be able to use his influence for *you*."

Lucy keeled over behind her, her mouth moving in soundless gasping, like a beached fish.

"Billy who?"

"Billy. Billy Johnson. Do you remember him?"

"Uh-huh," he said, noncommittal. He seemed to remember smashing his fist into the face of the lovely Billy after he had made a guess about his heritage.

Claudia held up a hand with an enormous set of rings on it. "That's me now, Mrs. Johnson. Don't forget—cocktails. We dress, by the way."

"As opposed to what?"

"Oh, Mac, you card, you. Toodle-loo, folks."

She turned and saw Lucy lying on the ground, feigning death.

She stepped delicately over her inert body, and hissed, "Oh, for God's sake, Lucy, grow up. This man's the head of a multimillion-dollar company."

And she was gone, leaving a cloying cloud of perfume in her wake.

For a moment Lucy actually looked as if she'd allowed Claudia's closing barb to land. Her eyes looked shiny again. But then, to his great relief, she giggled.

"Oh, for God's sake, Lucy," he said sternly, "grow up."

She giggled more loudly. He felt his defenses falling like a fortress made out of children's building blocks. He gave in to the temptation to play a little.

"Hey, I'm the head of a multimillion-dollar company. A little respect."

And then she started to laugh, and he gave in to the temptation a little more, and he did, too. It felt amazingly good to laugh with Lucy.

"You are good," he sputtered at her. "I got it loud and clear. Charades. Three words. *She's killing me.*"

He went over, took her hand and pulled her to her feet. She collapsed against him, laughing, and for the second time that day he felt the sweetness of her curves in his arms.

"Mac," she cooed, between gasps of laughter. "I've always *adored* you."

"The last time you looked at me like that, I got pushed in the lake."

She howled.

"What was that whole horrid episode with Claudia about?" he finally said, putting her away from him, wiping his eyes.

The humor died in her eyes. "Apparently if you even think of painting your house purple, you're off the approved list for renting the yacht club."

He had a sense that wasn't the whole story between the two women, but he played along.

"Boo-hoo," he said, and they were both laughing again.

"I haven't laughed like that for a long time."

She hadn't? Why? Suddenly, protecting himself did not seem quite as important as it had twenty minutes ago when he had come across her lawn to give her her money back.

"It's really no laughing matter," Lucy said, sobering abruptly. "Now I've gone and ticked her off—"

"Royally," he inserted, but she didn't laugh again.

"And I've got a caterer coming from Glen Oak, but they have to have a kitchen that's been food-safe certified. The school won't do."

"Don't worry. We'll fix it."

"We?" she said, raising an eyebrow at him, but if he wasn't mistaken she was trying valiantly not to look relieved.

"I told Claudia I came back for the party."

"But you didn't."

"When I saw Mama's place falling down, I realized I might be here a little longer than I first anticipated."

"Her place *is* in pretty bad repair," Lucy said. "I was shocked by it when I first came home. I've done my best."

"Thanks for that. I appreciate it. But don't quit your day job."

"She would love it if you were here for a while. Being at the gala would be a bonus. For her, I mean."

Mama *would* love it. But staying longer than he'd anticipated was suddenly for something more than getting Mama's house back in order. When he'd seen that barracuda taking a run at Lucy, he'd felt protective.

He didn't want to feel protective of Lucy. He wanted to hand her her money and go. He wanted to savor the fact she was on the outs with her snobbish friends.

But he was astonished to find that not only was he not gloating over Lucy's fall from grace, he felt as if he couldn't be one more bad thing in her day. Mama Freda would be proud: despite his natural inclination to be a cad, he seemed to be leaning toward being a better man.

Lucy seemed to realize she was in her housecoat and inappropriately close to him.

She backed off, and looked suddenly uncomfortable.

"Claudia is right. I'm embarrassed. What made me behave like that? You, I suppose. You've always brought out the worst in me."

"Look, let's get some things straight. Claudia is *never* right, and I *never* brought out the worst in you."

"You didn't? Lying to my parents? Sneaking out? You talked me into smoking a cigar once. I drank my first beer with you. I—" Her face clouded, and for a moment he thought she was going to mention the most forbidden thing of all, but she said, "I became the kind of girl no one wanted sitting in the front pew of the church."

"That would say a whole lot more about the church than the kind of girl you were. I remember you laughing. Coming alive like Sleeping Beauty kissed by a prince. Not that I'm claiming to be any kind of prince—"

"That's good."

"I remember you being like a prisoner who had been set free, like someone who had been bound up by all these rules and regulations learning to live by your own guidelines. And learning to be spontaneous. I think it was the very best of you."

"There's a scary thought," she said, running a hand through her short, rumpled hair, not looking at him.

"I think the seeds of the woman who would paint her house purple were planted right then."

"You like the color?" she asked hopefully. "You saw my sample when you came in, didn't you?"

He hated it that she asked, as if she needed someone's approval to do what she wanted. "It only matters if you like the color."

"I wish that were true," she said ruefully.

"I remember when you used to be friends with Mrs. Billy-Goat Johnson," he said.

"I know. But I think the statute of limitations has run out on that one, so I won't accept responsibility for it anymore." She tried to sound careless, but didn't quite pull it off.

Suddenly it didn't seem funny. Lucy had changed. Deeply. And that change had not been accepted by the people around her. He suspected it went a whole lot deeper than her painting her house purple.

Well, so what? People did change. He had

changed, too. Though probably not as deeply. He tended to think he was much the same as he had always been, a self-centered adrenaline junkie, driven by some deep need to prove himself that no amount of success ever quite took away. In other words, when Lucy had called him a jerk she hadn't been too far off the mark.

The only difference was that now he was a jerk with money.

She had helped Mama when he had not, and for that, if nothing else, he was indebted to her.

But now Lucy seemed somehow embattled, as if she desperately needed someone on her side.

Not me, he told himself sternly. He wasn't staying here. He owed Lucy nothing. He was getting a few of the more urgent things Mama needed done cleared up. Okay, it wouldn't hurt to stay a few more days for Lucy's party. That would make Mama happy. It wasn't about protecting Lucy from that barracuda. Or maybe it was. A little bit. But tangling his life with hers?

It occurred to him that he may have lied to himself about his reasons for never coming back to Lindstrom Beach. He had told himself it was because it was the town that had scorned him. The traditional place full of Brady Bunch families, where he'd been the kid with no real family and a dark, secret history.

He'd played on that and developed a protective persona: adrenaline junkie, renegade, James Dean of the high-school set. It had brought a surprising fan base from some of the kids, though not their parents.

Not the snooty doctor's daughter, either. Not at first.

But now, standing here looking at Lucy, it occurred to him none of that was the reason he had avoided returning to this place.

Had he always known, at some level, that coming home again would require him to be a better man?

But would that mean looking out for the girl who had rejected him?

"May I use your phone?" he asked. "My cell got wrecked in the lake."

Her expression asked if he had to, she suddenly seemed eager to divest herself of him. But she looked around and handed him a cordless. Now that he had decided to be a better man, he was going to follow through before he changed his mind.

He could look at it as putting Claudia in her place as much as helping Lucy.

"Casey?" he said to his assistant. "Yeah, away for a few days…My hometown…You didn't know I had a hometown?…Hatched under a rock? Thanks, buddy." He waggled his eyebrows at Lucy, but she was pretending not to listen.

"Look, I need twenty thousand dollars of clothing products, sizes kid to teen, delivered to the food bank, boy's and girl's club and social services office of Lindstrom Beach, British Columbia. Make sure some of it gets to every agency that helps kids within a fifty-mile radius of that town…Yeah, giveaways.

"Of course you've never heard of Lindstrom Beach. When that's done—if you can have the whole area blanketed by tomorrow—take out a couple of ads on the local TV and radio stations thanking the Lindstrom Beach Yacht Club for donating their facilities for the Mother's Day Gala.

"Thanks, buddy. Don't know when I'll be back and don't bother with the cell. I made the mistake of not bringing the Wild Side waterproof case. Oh, throw some of those in with the other donations. I'll pick up another cell phone in the next few days."

Lucy was no longer pretending not to listen. She was staring at him as he found the button and turned off her phone. He handed it back to her. If he was not mistaken, she was struggling not to look impressed.

"Just admit it," he said. "That was great. Two birds with one stone."

"Everybody does not call you Mr. Hudson," she said, pleased. "Two birds?"

"Yeah. Claudia's stuck-up kids just became a whole lot less exclusive, and unless I miss my guess, you are *in* at the yacht club."

"You hate the yacht club," she reminded him.

"I've always had a strange hankering for anything anybody tells me I can't have."

Her arms folded more tightly over her chest and her eyes looked shiny again.

"I didn't mean you," he said softly.

"Let's not kid ourselves. That was part of the attraction. Romeo and Juliet. Bad boy and good girl."

"I don't think that was part of the attraction for me," he said, slowly. "It was more what

I said before. It was watching you come into yourself, caterpillar to butterfly."

"Actually," she said, and she shoved her little nose in the air, reminding him of who she had been before he'd taught her you didn't go to hell for saying *damn*, "I don't want to have this discussion. In fact, if you don't mind, I need to get dressed."

"I have to give this to you first. Special delivery," he said, holding out the money to her. "What was that about rezoning?"

She ignored the envelope. "I think it had to do with the canoes. I think you're supposed to rezone to run a business."

But she suddenly wasn't looking at him. He was startled. Because, scanning her face, he was sure she was being deliberately evasive. What did renting canoes have to do with finally getting rid of the young thugs next door? Though it was Claudia they were dealing with. That was a leap in logic she could probably be trusted to make.

"I can put a lawyer on it if you want."

"I don't need you to fix things. I already told you I'm not in the market for a hero."

"Take your money."

"No. Are you in my house without an invitation?" she asked, annoyed.

"Boy, I saved you from drowning *and* from Claudia, and your gratitude, in both instances, seems to be almost criminally short-lived."

"Oh, well," she said.

"Anyone could come in your house without an invitation. You should consider locking the back door at least."

"Don't you dare tell me what to do! This is not the big city. And don't show up here after all these years and think you are going to play big brother. I don't need one."

But it was evident from what he had just seen that she needed something, someone in her court. Still, he was no more eager to play big brother to her than she was to cast him in that role.

But again, if that was what being a better man required of him, he'd suck it up. No looking at her lips, though. Or at the place her housecoat was gapping open slightly, revealing the swell of a deliciously naked breast.

"Lindstrom Beach may not be the big city," he said, reaching out and gently pulling her housecoat closed. "But it's not the fairy tale you want to believe in, either."

She glanced down, slapped his hand away, and held her housecoat together tightly with her fist. "As a matter of fact, I gave up on fairy tales a long time ago."

"You did?" he said skeptically.

"I did," she said firmly.

He looked at her more closely, and there was that subtle anger in her again suddenly. He missed the girl who had lain on the floor, clutching her throat. He also felt the little ripple of unease intensify—the one that had started when he saw her clumsy repair job in Mama's porch. It was true. There was something very, very different about her.

In high school she had been confident, popular, perky, smart, pretty. She'd been born with a silver spoon in her mouth and had the whole world at her feet. Her crowd, including Claudia, expected it that way.

But Claudia had always had a certain hard smoothness to her, like a rock too polished. In Lucy, he remembered a certain dewy-eyed innocence, a girl who really did believe in Prince Charming, and for some of the happiest moments of his life, had mistakenly believed it was him.

But Lucy Lindstrom no longer had the look of a woman waiting for her prince.

In fact, from behind the barrier of her newly closed housecoat, she looked stubborn and offended. So, she did not want a hero. Or a prince. Good for her. And he was not looking for a damsel in distress. Or a princess.

So they were safe.

Except, he didn't really feel safe. He felt some danger he couldn't identify, so heavy in the air he might be able to taste it, the same way a deer could taste a threat on the wind.

"What happened to your fiancé?" he asked.

"What fiancé?"

"Mama told me you were going to get married."

"I changed my mind."

"She told me that, too."

"But she didn't give you the details?"

"No. Why would she know the details?"

"You're not from around these parts, are you, son?" She did a fairly good impression of a well-known TV doctor.

"I don't know what you mean."

"My engagement breakup was front-page news after my fiancé was chased naked down a quiet residential street in Glen Oak by a gun-wielding man who just happened to be the cuckolded husband of a woman who was my friend and the barista in our bookstore coffee shop."

It seemed Lucy Lindstrom's fall from grace had been complete. Mac ordered himself to feel satisfied. But that wasn't what he felt at all. He couldn't even pretend.

"Aw, Lucy." Her eyes had that shiny look again. He wanted to reach for her and hold her, but he knew if he did she would never forgive him.

"Don't feel sorry for me, please." She held up her hand. "Everything is on film these days. Someone caught the whole thing on their phone camera. It was a local sensation for a few days."

"Aw, Lucy," he said again, his distress for her genuine.

"Aren't you going to ask me if I never guessed something was going on? Everyone else asks that."

"No, I'm going to ask you if you want me to track him down and kill him."

"With your bare hands?" she asked, and though her voice was silky her eyes were shining again.

"Is he the one who made you quit believing in fairy tales?"

"No, Mac," she said quietly. "That happened way before him."

Her eyes lingered for just a moment on his lips, and then she licked hers, and looked away.

Mac turned from the sudden intensity, and made himself focus on the house—anything but her lips and the terrible possibility it was him who had made her stop believing in fairy tales.

"This isn't how I remember it."

Once, he had made the mistake of going to the front door when she was late meeting him at the dock for a canoe trip.

He'd stepped inside and it had reminded him of an old castle: dim and grim, the front room so crowded with priceless antiques that it felt hard to breathe. He found out he'd been invited inside to get a piece of her father's mind, and that's when he'd discovered that Lucy had been seeing him on the sly.

I forbid you to see my daughter.

After all these years Mac wasn't sure, but the word *riffraff* might have come into play. Of course, being *forbidden* to see Lucy had only made him come up with increasingly creative ways to spend time with her.

And it had intensified the pleasure of sneaking into this very room, when her parents were asleep upstairs, and kissing her until they had both been breathless with longing.

That first meeting with her father had been nothing in comparison to the last one.

There's been a rash of break-ins around the lake. My house is about to be broken into. The police are going to find the stolen goods next door, in your bedroom. You'll be arrested and it will be the final straw for that rotten place. I've always wanted to buy it. Someday, Lucy and the man she marries will live there.

Mac had known for a long time that he had to go. That there was no future for him in Lindstrom Beach and never would be.

He'd told her about her father's threat and said he couldn't stand it in this town for one more second. And that's when she had said it.

I could never fall for a boy like you.

Had her father convinced her he was a thief? That he was behind the break-ins that had happened that summer?

Or had she just come to her senses and realized it wasn't going to work? That a guy like him was never going to be able to give a girl like her the things she had become accustomed to?

It seemed to him that there was a lot of space between them that was too treacherous to cross. They'd caused each other pain, he was sure, but he was sure he had caused her more than she had caused him.

Maybe he had been the one who wrecked fairy tales for her.

But he'd already been a world away from fairy tales by the time he met her.

Safer to focus on the here and the now.

"There used to be a wall here," he said. *And a couch here.* He decided that focusing on the here and now meant not mentioning the couch. Not even thinking about it would have been good, too, but it was too late for that.

"My mom actually opened the walls ups after my dad died."

Which meant they were not, technically, even in the same room they had once made out in. The ghosts of their younger selves, breathless with need, were not here.

Mac somehow doubted her mother had

achieved the almost tangible quality of sanctuary that the room had. Her mother, as he recalled her, had been much like Claudia. This room would have had the benefit of an interior designer, the magazine-shoot-perfect layout. It would have been designed with an eye for entertaining. And impressing.

But Lucy had created a space that was casual and inviting. It was a place where a person could read a book or stay in their housecoat all day. But there was something about it that he couldn't quite put his finger on.

Mac went through to the dining-room table to set down the envelope of money. There were papers stacked neatly on it. It was not the space of someone who entertained or had large dinner parties. He put his finger on it: her space had a feeling of surprising solitude clinging to it.

Lucy? Who had been at the heart of a crowd, directing all the action, without even knowing she was? Imposing her standards on others as unconsciously as breathing?

Lucy? Who had been the most popular girl in her graduating class, not standing up for herself with the likes of Claudia Mitchell-Franks?

Lucy? Who had always been "in," now suddenly having to beg for use of the yacht club in the town named for her grandfather?

Lucy? Who had been as conservative as her parents before her, now tentatively painting her house purple and enraging the community by running a commercial venture from her dock?

"What happened to you?" he asked softly.

And he saw more than secrets in her eyes—enormous, green, dazzling. But if he didn't allow himself to be dazzled, he was sure he saw something he really didn't want to see. He saw fear.

CHAPTER FIVE

FOR ONE MOMENT Lucy was almost overcome by a desire to tell him. Everything. That after he had left that summer, her whole world as she had known it had changed irrevocably and forever.

But she was not giving in to impulses—she already regretted the charade behind Claudia's back—and especially not where Mac was concerned.

"Nothing happened to me. I grew up. That's all."

She didn't want him to look too closely at the table. The charitable foundation registration was sitting there. So was the rezoning application that would allow her to turn this house into a group home for unwed mothers.

She was not getting into that. Not with him. Not now and not ever.

Still clutching her housecoat closed, she

went over and inserted herself between him and her secrets.

"Is there something on that table you don't want me to see?"

She was close enough that she could smell him, the scent of the pure lake water not quite eradicated by a faint soapy scent.

"No."

"Unlike Claudia," he said, "you are developing a little worry furrow right here."

He touched between her brows.

And she wanted, weakly, to lean into his thumb and share her burdens. She had secrets. She was worrying. It was none of his business. He was a man she had known back when he was a boy. To think she knew anything about him now, on the basis of that, would be pure folly.

Unless she remembered she couldn't trust him.

"Seven years," he said, peering over her shoulder. "What could possibly be on your table after seven years that you wouldn't want me to see?" He waggled his eyebrows at her in that fiendish way that he had. "The possibility of a lingerie catalog is making me look harder."

Enough. She snatched the money from where he had set it on the table, and looked at it with exaggerated interest. "I don't want this."

Mac shrugged. "Donate it to your favorite charity."

"All right," she said stiffly. There was an irony in that that he never had to know about. In fact, he did not need to know one more thing about her. She was all done laughing for the day. It felt like a total weakness that he coaxed that silly part from her. And the story of her broken engagement.

She didn't like how that had changed him, some wariness easing in him as he looked at her.

"Now, I have to go get dressed, so if you'll excuse me…"

"What *is* your favorite charity?"

She shook her head, felt put out that he was trying to make conversation with her instead of obediently heading for the door.

"Why? Do you want the receipt?"

He turned, and relieved, Lucy thought that she had insulted him and he was going. Instead, he went into her living room and sat down in one of her overstuffed chairs. If she was not mistaken, the only reason he was still here was that he was devilishly enjoying her discomfort.

At least he'd moved away from the rezoning documents.

He appeared totally relaxed, deeply enjoying the view out her window.

She cocked her head at him, unforthcoming. Who could outwait whom?

He picked up the book that was open on the arm, but she raced over and snatched it away—not quickly enough.

"Interesting reading material for a girl who has given up on fairy tales. *To Dance with a Prince?*"

She bit back an urge to defend her choice of reading material, but he had already moved on.

"I like what you've done to the place," he said. "Kind of ski-lodge chic instead of Victorian manor house. I doubt that was your mom. I bet the exterior paint color wasn't her choice, either. It's surprisingly Bohemian for this neck of the woods."

"The paint is barely dry and the neighbors have lost no time in letting me know they don't appreciate me indulging my secret wild side."

And then it was there, the danger. It sizzled in the air between them. Her secret wild side was interwoven with their history. Those heated summer nights of discovery, bodies melting together. That hunger they'd had, an almost desperate sense of not being able to get enough of each other.

She found his eyes on her lips and the memory was scalding.

She was shocked by what she wanted. To be wild. To taste him just one more time. To throw caution to the wind.

"I would have pictured you in a very different life, Lucy."

"Really?"

"Traditional. A big house. A busy husband. A vanload of kids, girls who need to get to ballet lessons, boys who need to be persuaded not to keep their frogs in the kitchen sink."

She was silent.

"I thought you would be living a life very similar to that of your parents, that you'd be hanging with all those kids you grew up with. Friday drinks with friends at the yacht club, water-skiing on weekends in the summer, trips to the ski hill in the winter."

She arched an eyebrow at him. "I'm surprised you pictured me at all."

It was his turn to be silent. The view out the window seemed to hold his complete attention. And then he said, quietly, "A man never forgets his first love."

Something trembled inside her. "I didn't know I was your first love."

"How could you not know? Those crazy weeks, Lucy. I'd wake up thinking of you. I'd go to sleep thinking of you. We spent every moment we could together. It felt as if I couldn't breathe unless you were there to give me air."

How well she remembered the intensity of those few weeks.

"You never said you loved me," she whispered.

He looked at her and smiled. She distrusted that smile. It could still turn her insides to jelly. That devil-may-care smile made him the most handsome man alive, but it said that nothing mattered to him. It was the wall he put up.

"I never say I love anyone," he said. "Not even Mama."

"You've never told Mama you love her?"

"I don't think so."

"Well, that just stinks."

"Anyway, those days are a long way behind us, Lucy."

Yes, they were and it would do nothing but harm to dredge them up. Even now, she could feel her heart beating way too quickly at his admission that he had spent night and day doing nothing but thinking of her. At the time, he certainly hadn't let on that's what was going on for him!

"So, what does the grown-up Lucy do for fun?"

The question took her aback. "Fun?" she asked uncomfortably.

"You were the girl at the center of the fun, as hokey and wholesome as I found it at the time. The water fight on the front lawn of the high school. The fund-raising car wash where they shut down Main Street and brought out the fire truck. The three-day bike excursion to Bartlett. The canoe trip across the lake, camping on the Point.

"I remember standing over at Mama's one night when you had a group of kids here at your fire pit. You know what I couldn't believe? You had them all singing! All these kids who considered themselves cooler than cool, singing *Row Row Row Your Boat*."

"I thought those days were a long way behind us," she muttered. "Besides, you never participated in any of those things!"

"No, I didn't."

"Why?"

"I felt I didn't fit in."

It was an admission of something real about him, and for the second time Lucy was startled. He had never once said anything like that when they were together. He had revealed more about himself in the last ten minutes than he had the whole time they were together.

"That never showed," she said. "You always seemed so supremely confident. Everybody thought you were so cool. Unafraid, somehow. Bold. If you wore a pair of jeans with a rip in the knee, half the school had ripped their jeans by the next week."

"It wasn't that I didn't have the right stuff—the clothes, the great bike, though I didn't—it wasn't that. It was that your crowd was all so damn *normal*. Two parents. Nice houses. A dog. Allowances. Born into expectations of how they would behave and what they would become. I felt excluded from that. Like I could never belong, only be a visitor."

"I hope I never made you feel like that."

"No, Lucy, you never did. In fact, for those few weeks—" He stopped.

"For those few weeks what?" she breathed.

But he rolled his shoulders, like a fighter shrugging off a blow. "Nothing."

And the veil was down over his eyes, and that was what she remembered most about him. Get close, but not too close.

"You kind of bucked all those expectations of you, didn't you, Lucy?"

Oh, yeah. Because she had had one life before Mac and a completely different one after.

"My life may not be what my father and mother expected, but I have a really good life. I love what I do."

"Mama keeps me posted."

She felt mortified, and he saw it and laughed.

"Don't worry, nothing juicy, just tidbits of news. I heard about your online bookstore, and according to Mama, you do very well at it, too."

"Ah, well," Lucy said, wryly self-deprecating, "You know Mama. When she loves you, you can do no wrong."

"When did you two become so close? When I lived here there was always a kind of barrier, imposed by the doctor, between your family and her. You and Mama were polite to each other, and good neighbors, but you weren't mowing her lawn or repairing her house."

Again, Lucy had to fight with a voice inside her that said, *Wouldn't it be nice to tell him?*

But she reminded herself, firmly, that that summer when she had loved him, she had given and given and given until she had not a secret left. And he had not divulged anything about himself. Laughing at her efforts to find out.

I killed a man. With my bare hands.

"I don't remember the exact details," she lied. But oh, she remembered them so clearly. Flying across that lawn in the dark, the emotional pain in her so great, she was unaware she had stepped on a sharp rock and her foot was bleeding.

The door opening and Mama standing there. Liebling! *What is it?*

"So, to get back to my original question, what do you do for fun?"

"My work's fun," she said firmly.

"I hope you're joking."

She felt mutinous. "What do you do for fun?"

"My work *is* fun. I developed a company that's all about fun. I think the roots of Wild Side started right here."

"So, your work is what you do for fun, too."

"Touché," he said. "But I do love the white-water kayaking. It is so physical and requires such intense concentration. It makes me feel more alive than just about anything I've ever done."

But a sudden memory flashed through his eyes and it was as if she could see it, too: lying in the sand beside him, the moonlight bathing them, never having ever felt quite so alive as that before.

Or since.

"I guess that's what I'm asking, Lucy. What makes you feel like that?"

"Like what?' she stammered.

"The way I feel when I am in a kayak. Alive. Totally engaged. Intensely in the moment. What makes you feel like that?"

If she said nothing, he would think she was a total loser. And in fact there was something that made her feel exactly like that.

"I have something," she said reluctantly. And she did. "It makes me feel alive, but I'm pretty sure you wouldn't call it fun."

"Try me."

"Not today." To tell him would just make her feel way too vulnerable.

"Drink the schnapps and I'll ask again."

She marched into her kitchen, got down a shot glass, filled it from Mama's bottle and went back out. She slammed the liquid back. She blinked hard.

"Okay," he said. "What do you do for fun, Lucy Lin?"

"You already figured it out," she said, "I work. Now, shoo. Because I have a lot of that to do today."

Shoo. She wished she had worded that differently. He looked way too closely at her. He was too close to striking a nerve.

He turned to go. "I'll be back."

"I was afraid you would say that," she muttered as she watched him go. Even though she ordered herself not to, even though she knew she shouldn't, Lucy went and watched him cross the yards back to Mama's house.

He was whistling and the melody drifted in her open door, mingled with the scent of the trees, and tingled along her spine.

Rebel. It was a warning if she had ever heard one, and yet Lucy was aware that she felt alive in ways she had not for a long, long time.

Mac went back across the lawns, pensive. Something was so different about Lucy. What had changed in her?

He got the sense that maybe she had become an outcast from the Lindstrom Beach crowd, which was the most surprising thing of all.

As surprising as her mowing lawns and trying to fix floorboards and renting canoes.

Her new aloneness in this community, was it her choice or theirs?

What mattered, really, was that Lucy was shouldering all that responsibility for Mama and he had let her. She seemed alone, and she seemed just a little too grim about life.

Somewhere in her was a woman who

wanted to paint her house purple, and probably wasn't going to.

Without an intervention. He was going to be the man Mama expected him to be.

Before he left here, he was going to help Lucy have some fun.

Lucy actually felt light-headed.

It was the schnapps, she told herself, not Mac Hudson crash-landing in her world. She went back upstairs and looked at herself critically in her bedroom's full-length mirror. First soaking wet, now in her housecoat! These were not the impressions she had intended!

She had intended to look sophisticated and coolly professional. Even if she did have a job where she could work in her pajamas if she wanted to.

Lucy found herself dressing for the potential of another meeting with him, and then made herself get to work. First, she turned on her computer and reviewed orders that had come in overnight. There were also a dozen more RSVPs for the Mother's Day Gala, three of them from girls she had gone to high school with, saying "will NOT be able to attend."

She felt something sag within her, and told herself it was not disappointment. It was pragmatic: the people refusing to come were the ones who could make the best donations to her cause.

But, of course, her cause was at odds with their vision for life around the lake.

Lucy forced herself to think of something else. She went into a spare room that had become the book room, retrieved the book orders and began to package them.

Later, she would review her rezoning proposal for Caleb's House, the documents lying out on her dining room table where she hadn't wanted Mac to see them.

As the day warmed, Lucy moved out onto her deck to work, as she often did. She told herself it was a beautiful day, but was annoyed at herself for sneaking peeks at Mama's house.

She could hear enormous activity—saws and hammers—but she didn't see Mac.

She wanted to go see what he was doing over there, but pride made her stay at home.

When she had finally succeeded in putting

him out of her mind, the radio was on and she heard the ad about the donation of the Wild Side clothing in thanks for the donation of the yacht club for the Mother's Day Gala.

Within an hour she had been phoned by several representatives of the yacht club—notably not Claudia—falling all over themselves to make sure she knew she was most welcome to the space for the Mother's Day Gala, and that the regular charge had been waived.

Now, as evening fell, Lucy was once again cozy in her pajamas, trying to concentrate on a movie. She found herself resentful that he was next door. She and Mama often watched a movie or a television show together in the evenings.

She hated it that she felt lonely. She hated it that she was suddenly looking at her life differently.

When had she allowed herself to become so boring? Her phone rang.

"Hello, Lucy."

"Mac," she said. "I've been meaning to call and thank you. The yacht club has confirmed."

He snickered. So did she.

"You didn't tell me Mama's car isn't even insured."

"Why would she insure a car she can't drive?"

"I took it to town three times for building materials before she remembered to tell me, ever so casually, that the insurance had lapsed. I could have been arrested!"

From loneliness to this: laughter bubbling up inside her.

"Anyway, Mama would like to see a movie tonight. Can you drive me to town so I can get one for her?"

"You're welcome to borrow my car anytime you need one."

"I'll keep that in mind, thanks, but Mama says I'm not allowed to pick a movie without you there. She says I'll bring home something awful. A man movie, she called it. You know. Lots of action. Blood. Swearing."

"Yuck."

"Just what Mama said. On the other hand, if we send you to get a movie without me, it'll probably be a two-hanky special, heavy on the violin music."

"Why don't you and Mama go get the movie?"

"She's making *apfelstrudel*." He sighed happily. "She says it's at the delicate stage. It'll be ready by the time we bring the movie back. She says you have to come have some."

It was one of Mama's orders. Unlike an invitation, you could not say no. As if anyone could say no to Mama's strudel, anyway. Still, it was not as if Lucy was agreeing to spend time with him. Or plotting to spend time with him. It was just happening.

"She hasn't stopped cooking since you got there, has she?"

"No, because I also made a grocery run before I found out I was driving illegally. She made schnitzel for supper," he said happily. "You know something? Mama's schnitzel would be worth risking arrest for. She's already started a new grocery list. Would you mind if we picked up a few things while we're in for the movie?"

Lucy did mind. She minded terribly that she had been feeling sorry for herself and lonely, and that now she wasn't. That life suddenly seemed to tingle with possibility.

From going for a movie and to the grocery store.

Her life *had* become too boring.

Of course, she wasn't kidding herself. The tingle of possibility had nothing to do with the movie or groceries.

Sternly, Lucy reminded herself she was not a teenager anymore. Back then, being around Mac had seemed like pure magic. But she'd been innocent. As he had pointed out earlier, she had believed in fairy tales. She'd been a hopeless romantic and a dreamer and an optimist.

It would be good to see how Mac fared with her adult self! It would be good to do a few ordinary things with him. Certainly that would knock him down off the pedestal she had put him on when she was nothing more than a kid. It would be good to see how her adult self fared around Mac.

It was like a test of all her new intentions, and Lucy planned on passing it!

"Meet me in the driveway," she said. "In ten minutes."

Did she take extra care in choosing what to wear? Of course she did. It was only human that while she wanted to break her fascination with Mac, it would be entirely satisfying to see his with her increase.

She wanted to be the one in the power position for a change.

If she looked at her life that was the whole problem. She had always given away too much power to others. Fallen all over herself trying to win approval.

If she had a fatal flaw, it was that she had mistaken approval for love.

"You know," Mac said, a few minutes later, "they say that people's choice of cars says a lot about them."

Lucy looked at her car, a six-year-old compact in an almost indistinguishable color of gray.

She frowned. The car was almost a perfect reflection of the life she seemed to be newly reassessing. "It's reliable," she said defensively.

"I can cross driving off the list of things you do for fun."

"What do you drive?"

"What do you think?" he said.

"I'm guessing something sporty that guzzles up more than your fair share of the world's resources!"

"You'd be guessing right, then. I have two

vehicles. One a sports car and the other an SUV great for hauling equipment around."

"Both bright red?" she asked, not approvingly.

"Of course. One's a convertible. You'd like it."

"Flashy," she said.

"I don't enjoy being flashy," he said without an ounce of sincerity. "I just want to find my vehicle in the parking lot. It's crowded in the big city."

They got in the car. She did not offer to let him drive. It wasn't that her car would be a disappointment after what he was accustomed to. It was that she was not letting him take charge. It was a small thing, but she hoped that it said something about her, too.

"I'm glad you came with me," he said after her disapproving silence about his flashy car lengthened between them.

Something in her softened. What was the point of being annoyed at him? He wanted to be with her. She ordered her heart to stop. She glanced at him, and he was frowning at the list.

"I didn't want to have to ask a clerk where to find this." He held the list under her nose.

"Hey! I'm trying to drive."

It was a good reminder that the point of being annoyed with him was to protect herself.

"It's after seven. There's no traffic on this road." Still he withdrew the list. "C-u-m-i-n."

"Cumin?"

"I wouldn't have pronounced it like that. What is it, anyway?

"A spice."

He rapped himself on the forehead. "See? I thought it had something to do with feminine hygiene."

"Mac. You're incorrigible! What an awful thing to say!"

"Why are you smiling then?"

"My teeth are gritted. Do not mistake that for a smile! I do not find off-color remarks funny."

"Now you sound like you've been at finishing school with Miss Claudia. Don't take life so seriously, Lucy. It's over in a blink."

That was twice as annoying because she had said almost the very same thing to herself earlier. Lucy simmered in silence.

CHAPTER SIX

"SAME OLD PLACE," Mac said, as they entered the town on Lakeshore Drive, wound around the edge of the lake, through a fringe of stately Victorian houses, and then passed under the wooden arch that pronounced it Main Street.

Lucy's house was two miles—and a world—away from downtown Lindstrom Beach. Main Street had businesses on one side, quaint shops that sold antiques and ice cream and rented bicycles and mopeds. Bright planters, overflowing with petunias, hung from old-fashioned light standards.

On the other side of the street mature cottonwoods formed a boundary to the park. Picnic tables underneath them provided a shaded sitting area in the acres of white-sand beach that went to the water's edge.

"Charming," she insisted.

"Sleepy," he said. "No. Make that exhausted."

The shops would be open evenings in the peak of the summer season, but now they were closed, their bright awnings rolled up, outdoor tables and chairs put away against the buildings. There were two teenagers sitting at one of the picnic tables. She was pretty sure they were both wearing Wild Side shirts.

They left downtown and the main road bisected a residential area. Lucy Lindstrom loved her little town, founded by her grandfather. This part of it had wide tree-shaded boulevards, a mix of year-round houses and enchanting summer cottages.

Under the canopy of huge trees, in the dying light, kids had set up nets and were playing street hockey. They heard the cry of "car!" as the kids raced to get their nets out of the way.

"I bet you don't see that in the big city."

"See?" he said. "You still believe in the fairy tale."

"I don't really think it's so much a fairy tale," she said, a trifle defensively. "This town, my house, the lake, they give me a sense of sanctuary. Of safety. Of the things that don't change."

In a few weeks, as spring melted into summer, the lake would come alive. Main Street Beach, which Lucy could see from her dock, would be spotted with bright umbrellas, generations enjoying it together.

There would be plump babies in sun hats filling buckets with sand, mothers slathering sunscreen on their offspring and passing out sandy potato chips and drinks, grandmothers and grandfathers snoozing in the shade or lazily turning the pages of books.

Along Lakeshore Drive, boards would come off the windows of the summer houses. Power boats, canoes and the occasional plane would be tied up to the docks. The floats would be launched and quickly taken over by rowdy teenagers pushing and shoving and shouting. There would be the smell of barbecues and, later, sparks from bonfires would drift into a star-filled sky.

"I'm unchanging. As incorrigible as ever."

"Can you ever be serious?"

"I don't see the point."

"I love this town," she said, stubbornly staying on the topic of the town, instead of the topic of *him*. "How could anyone not love it?"

Now, added to that abundance of charm

that was Lindstrom Beach, Lucy had her dream, and it was woven into the peace and beauty and values of her town. The dream belonged here, even if Claudia Johnson didn't think so!

And so did she. Even if Claudia Johnson disapproved of her.

"How could anyone not like it here?" She could have kicked herself as soon as it slipped out. It sounded suspiciously like she cared that he didn't like it here.

"How much you like Lindstrom Beach depends on your pedigree." Suddenly he sounded very serious, indeed.

She glanced at him. His mouth had a firm line to it, and he took a pair of sunglasses out of his pocket and put them on. She was pretty sure those sunglasses had been in the lake yesterday.

"It does not."

"Spoken by the one with the pedigree. You have no idea what it was like to be a kid from the wrong side of the tracks in Lindstrom Beach."

This time the chill in the voice was hers. "That may be true, but it certainly wasn't for lack of trying."

Suddenly, the pain felt fresh between them, like fragile skin that had been burned only an hour or two before. He had been right. There was no point being so serious.

If she could, she would have left things as they were, lived contentedly in the lie that she was all over that, the summer she had spent loving Mac nothing more than the foolish crush of a woman barely more than a girl. She'd only been seventeen, after all.

He had teased her about it then. The perfect doctor's daughter having her walk on the wild side. When she had first heard the name of his company, she had wondered if he was taunting her for what she had missed. But he had never asked her to go on that journey with him. And besides, that brief walk on the wild side had been a mistake.

The repercussions had torn her oh-so-stable family apart. And then, there was the little place on a knoll behind the house, deeply shaded by hundred-year-old pines, that she went to, that reminded her what a mistake it had been.

Leave it, a voice inside her ordered. But she was not at all sure that she could.

"Macintyre Hudson," Lucy said, her voice

deliberately reprimanding, "you lived next door to me, not on the wrong side of the tracks."

But underneath the reprimand, was she still hoping she could draw something out of him? That she could do today what she had not been able to do all those years ago?

Find out who he really was, what was just beneath the surface of the incorrigible facade he put on for the world?

He snorted. "The wrong side of the tracks is not a physical division. Your father hated Mama's old cottage, hardly more than a fishing shack, being right next door to his mansion. He hated it more that she brought children of questionable background there. His failures in life: he failed to have Mama's place shut down, and he failed to bully her in to moving."

Mac didn't know that, in the end, her father had considered *her* one of his failures, too.

"But it looks like Claudia Johnson née Mitchell-Franks has taken over where he left off," he said drily. And then he grinned, as if he didn't care about any of it. "I think we should attend her little shindig on Friday night at the yacht club."

The grin back, she knew her efforts to get below the surface had been thwarted. Again. She should have known better than to try.

"I wouldn't go there on Friday night if my life depended on it," she said.

"Really? Why?"

"First of all, I wasn't invited."

"You need an invitation?"

A little shock rippled through her. All those years ago, was it possible that he had never thought to invite her to go with him when he left Lindstrom Beach? That he had just thought if she wanted to go, she would have taken the initiative?

Lucy did not want to be thinking about ancient history. She was not allowing herself to dwell on what might have been.

But still, she said, "Yes, I need an invitation."

"Your grandfather built the damned place."

"I never renewed my membership when I came back."

"You're going to allow Claudia to snub you? I'd go just to tick her off. It could be fun."

But Lucy felt something dive in the bottom of her stomach at the thought of going somewhere where she wasn't wanted, all that old crowd looking at her as if she was the one who had most surprised them all, and not in a good way.

Fun. His diversionary tactic when anything got too serious, when anything threatened the fortress that was him.

"Well, showing up where I'm not wanted is not exactly my idea of a good time."

"I have a lot to teach you," he said, then, "And here we are at the grocery store. Which is open at—" he glanced at his watch "—half past seven. Good grief." He widened his eyes at her in pretended horror and whispered, "Lucy! Are they open Sunday?"

"Since I've moved back, yes."

"I'll bet there was a petition trying to make it close at five, claiming it would be a detriment to the town to have late-night and Sunday shopping. Ruin the other businesses, shut down the churches, corrupt the children."

She sighed. "Of course there was a petition."

The tense moment between them evaporated as he got out of the car and waited for her. "Come on, Lucy Lin, let's go find the cumin. And just for fun, we have to buy one thing that neither of us has ever heard of before."

"Would you quit saying the word *fun* over and over as if you don't think I know what it is? Besides, this is Lindstrom Beach, I don't think you'll find anything in this whole store that you've never heard of before."

"You're already wrong, because I'd never heard of cumin. Would you like to make a bet?"

Don't let him suck you into his world of irreverence, she ordered herself sternly.

"If I find something neither of us has ever heard of, you have to eat it, whatever it is," he challenged her.

"And if you don't?"

"You can pick something I have to eat."

It was utterly childish, of course. But, reluctantly she thought, it did seem like it might be fun. "Oh, goody. Pickled eggs for you."

"You remember that? That I hate those?"

Unfortunately, she remembered everything.

And suddenly it was there between them again, a history. An afternoon of canoeing, a picnic on an undeveloped beach on the far shore. Her laying out the picnic lunch she had packed with a kind of shy pride: basket, blanket, plates, cold chicken, drinks. And then the jar of eggs. Quail eggs, snitched from her mother's always well-stocked party pantry.

She had made him try one. He had made a big deal out of how awful it was. In fact, he had done a pantomime of gagging that surpassed the one she had done of Claudia yesterday. But, at that moment that he had started gagging on the egg, they had probably been going deeper, talking about something that mattered.

"I'm not worried about having to eat pickled eggs," he said. "I'm far too competitive to worry. I'll find something you've never heard of before. Unlike you, who are somewhat vertically challenged, I am tall enough to see what they tuck away on the top shelves."

As he grabbed a grocery cart, Lucy desperately wanted to snatch the list from him and just do it the way she had always done it. Inserting playfulness into everyday chores seemed like the type of thing that could make one look at one's life afterwards and find it very mundane.

And with Mac? There was going to be an

afterward, because he was restless and he would never be content in a place like this.

"Here's something now," he said, at the very first aisle. "Sasquatch Bread. I mean, really?"

"It's from a local bakery. It's Mama's favorite."

"We'll get some, then. How about this?" He picked up a container. *"Chapelure de blé?"*

"What?"

"I knew it. Here less than thirty seconds, and I've already won."

She looked at what he was holding. "You're reading the French side. It's bread crumbs."

"Trust the French to make bread crumbs sound romantic. We'll take some of these, too. You never know when you might need romantic bread crumbs."

She was not sure she wanted to be discussing romance with Mac, not even lightly, but the truth was he was hard to resist. Even complete strangers could see how irresistible he was. She did not miss the sidelong glance of a mother with a baby in her buggy or the cheeky smile of leggy woman in short shorts.

But it seemed as if his world was only about her. He didn't even seem to notice those

other women, his focus so intent she could be
giddy with it.

If she didn't know better than to steel herself.

But even with steeling herself against his
considerable charm, just like that the most
ordinary of things, shopping for groceries,
was fun! He scoured the store for oddities,
blowing dust from obscure items on the top
shelves.

He thought he had her at quinoa, but when
she said she made a really good salad with it,
that went in the cart, too.

The strangest thing was that she was in a
grocery store that she had been in thousands
of times. And it felt as if she was discovering
a brand-new world.

"Got it," he finally said. He held out a large
jar to her. "You have never heard of this!"

"Rolliepops," she read. "Pickled herring
wrapped around a savory filling. Ugh!"

"Gotcha!"

He bought the largest size he could find,
and they found the rest of the things on the
list, plus items he deemed essential for movie
night: popcorn, red licorice and chocolate-
covered raisins.

"You are really going to enjoy snacking on your Rolliepops during the movie," he told her as they strolled out of the store with their laden cart.

"I'd rather eat the bread crumbs."

"Then you shouldn't have admitted you knew what they were. Retribution for the quail eggs all those years ago," he said happily as he stowed all the things he had bought— most of them not on the list and completely impractical—in the trunk of her car.

The video store was also fun as they wrangled over movies. This was the part of being with him that she had forgotten: it was easy.

It had always astonished both of them what good friends they became and how quickly. They had thought they would be opposites. Instead, they made each other laugh. They thought their worlds would be miles apart, instead they were comfortable in the new world they created.

And now it was as if seven years didn't separate them at all. She felt as if she had seen him just yesterday.

Finally, after much haggling, they settled on a romantic comedy.

By the time they got back, it never even

occurred to Lucy not to join him at Mama's house for the movie and fresh strudel. They parked the car back in her driveway and walked over with the groceries.

The strudel was excellent, the movie abysmal, Mama got up halfway through it and went to bed.

Suddenly, they were alone. Too late, Lucy remembered what else had come so easily and naturally to them.

When they were alone, an awareness of each other tingled in the air between them.

Back then, they had explored it. She with guilt, he with hunger, both of them with a sense of incredible discovery. The memory of that made her ache with wanting.

He was so close. She could smell the familiar, intoxicating scent of him. If she reached out, she could touch his arm.

"I have to go," she said, jumping up abruptly.

"Something urgent to do? Feed your fish? Put up a new swatch of color?"

"Something like that," she said.

"Don't forget, you owe me. You still have to eat a Rolliepop."

She grimaced. "I think I'd have nightmares. Herring wrapped around something 'savory'? Not my idea of a bedtime snack, but you know what? A bet is a bet."

"Yes, it is, but even though we had a deal, I'll let you off the hook. For tonight. I'll enjoy having something to hold over you."

He insisted on walking her back across the darkened lawns. A loon called on the lake and they both stopped to listen to its haunting cry.

"I don't like it that Mama was tired tonight," she said as they stood there. "She always insists on watching every movie to the end, even if it's awful. She told me once she always gives it a chance to redeem itself."

"People. Movies. She's all about second chances, our Mama. I'm concerned she's wearing herself out cooking for me. I told her to stop, but she won't."

"What rhymes with stop?" Lucy asked.

"Schnop," he said, and they shared a quiet laugh, but grew serious again as they continued walking across the backyard.

"I'm worried that it's not cooking that's wearing her out."

"Me, too."

It felt entirely too good to have someone to share these worries with.

"Has she said anything? About her health?" Lucy asked.

"No. I've been probing, too, but she says she's fine. While repairing the bathroom, I looked through the medicine cabinet. There was a prescription bottle, but she doesn't have internet, so I couldn't check what it's for."

"I can."

"I know, but it makes me feel guilty. Like I'm spying on her. It's kind of an affront to her dignity. So, I'm just going to hang out and fix the house, and keep my eyes and ears open and see if she tells me."

He stopped on her back porch.

"Good night, Lucy."

"Mac." It seemed to her suddenly she was a long way from her goal of proving to herself that he had no power over her anymore.

In fact, it felt like everything it had always felt like with him: as if the ordinary became extraordinary, as if she'd been sleeping and was coming awake, feeling the utter glory of life shimmering through her very pores.

The moonlight and the call of the loons wrapped her in their spell.

On an impulse she stepped in close to him. She needed to know.

On an impulse she stood up on her tiptoes. She needed to know if that was the same.

She wasn't sure why she had to do this. Maybe because she felt he believed she was way too predictable, from her car to her loyalty to her little town to what he presumed was the lack of fun in her life.

She had kissed other men since then. She had something to compare him to now. She had not back then. She would not be as easy to dazzle as that girl, a virgin whose only experiences with kisses had been spin-the-bottle at parties.

Or maybe she just had something to prove to herself when she took his lips.

That she could have the power. That she didn't need to wait for other people to instigate.

But whatever her intention was, it was lost the second their lips connected. He groaned and pulled her close to him, surrendered to her and claimed her at the very same time.

Oh, no. It was the same.

It was the same way as it had always been. She had never felt it before him, and never after, either. Certainly not with the man she had nearly married.

Oh, God, had she picked James precisely because he didn't make her feel like this? No wonder he had gone elsewhere for his passion!

When Mac's lips met hers, it was as if the world melted, as if the stars began to swirl in that dark sky, faster and faster until they melted right into it and everything became one. The stars, the sky, the loons, the lake, her, Mac.

All one incredible, swirling energy that was life itself.

How was it possible that she had convinced herself she could live without this?

She could feel the danger of being sucked right into the vortex of all that energy. She could feel the danger of wanting to be sucked into it.

Instead, she forced herself to yank away.

"Damn it all to hell," she said.

"Whoa. Not the normal reaction when a woman kisses me."

Was that often? Of course it was! Look at the man!

"You stud muffin, you," she said to hide how rattled she was.

"I have the feeling if we were on the dock,

I'd be getting shoved in again. Why are you so angry with me, Lucy Lin?"

"I'm not!" she said.

And she wasn't. That was the whole problem. She wasn't angry with him at all. She loved it that he was making her laugh, and making ordinary things seem fun, and carrying the burden of Mama with her.

She loved the taste of his lips and the way his arms closed around her. It felt like a homecoming for one who had wandered too long in foreign lands.

She loved the way women looked at him in the grocery store, confirming what she always knew: Mac Hudson was about the most handsome man ever born.

And she hated herself for loving all those things.

She was angry with herself because she hadn't proved what she wanted at all. In fact, the exact opposite was true!

She had proved her life was empty and passionless, despite all her good causes!

She went in her house and closed the door, and forced herself not to look back to see him crossing the lawn in the moonlight.

"Stay on your own side of the fence!" she ordered herself grimly.

When Mac got back in, Mama was up, watching the end of the movie.

"I thought you were tired," he said.

"*Ach,* at my age, being tired doesn't mean you get to sleep. I thought the movie might redeem itself."

"Has it?"

"No. Why is this funny, people treating each other so badly?"

"I don't know, Mama." He sat down beside her, and she turned off the movie.

"What's wrong, *schatz?*"

"Mama, have I ever told you that I love you?"

"Of course," she said, with no hesitation. "Just not with words. You take time from your busy work and come to help me. What is that, if not love?"

"Too bad all women aren't as wise as you."

"When you look like me, you develop wisdom."

"I think you're beautiful," he said.

"See? What is that, if not love?"

"I'm worried about you, Mama. Living

here by yourself. The house getting to be too much for you. I'm worried you're sick and not telling anyone."

"This is a good thing, my boy. To worry about someone else, hmm? It means you are not thinking of yourself all the time."

It was hard to be offended when it was true. He lived a hedonistic lifestyle. Self-indulgent. His business had allowed him to travel the world. Collect every toy. Seek increasing levels of adventure to fill himself, for a while. His lack of commitment made him responsible to no one but himself.

When he started feeling vaguely empty, he raced to the next rush, hoping it would be the thing that would fill him.

"When you feel pain, you have to do something for another."

"I can build you a new house."

"Would that make *you* feel better?"

"Wouldn't you like it?"

"I consider having more than what I need a form of stealing."

Hmm. Hadn't Lucy said something almost the same? About his vehicles. Taking more than his share of the world's resources?

"Everybody filling up their lives full, full,

full with stuff," Mama said. "What is it they don't want to feel?"

"Lonely, I guess," he surprised himself by saying. "Less than."

"Do something for someone else."

"I am. I'm doing something for you."

"You should do something nice for Lucy."

Wasn't that what he'd already decided? But now, that kiss changed everything. He felt as if he was floundering.

"She seems angry at me."

"So, that stops you? You can only offer kindness if there is something in it for you? Why is she angry at you?"

"I don't know. I mean, you know we had a little thing that summer before I left. I knew she couldn't come with me. She loved it here. The little bit of time that she was with me put her at odds with her friends and family. Her dad threatened to have me arrested he was so put out by the whole thing. We were both stupidly young. How could that have worked?"

Mama was silent, and then she said, "You left her to the only life she'd ever known. Maybe that was love, also, hmm, *schatz?*"

He was suddenly nearly blinded with a memory of how it had felt being with Lucy.

Waking up with a smile on his face, needing to be with her. Practically on fire with the sensation of being alive.

He shook it off and sighed. "I'm not sure I'm capable of such nobility," he said. "She wanted more of me than I could give her."

"Ah."

"Maybe," he said hopefully, "it's not me that she's angry with. Her recent fiancé took a pretty good run at her self-esteem by the sounds of it. And something is going on with her old crowd. I hate it that Claudia Stupid-Johnson feels better than her."

"No," Mama said softly. "What you hate is that Lucy lets her."

He felt like he was getting a headache. This was all way too deep and complicated for a guy as dedicated to the rush as he was. But while he was tackling the hard stuff, there was no sense stopping halfway.

"You didn't answer me, Mama. Are you sick?" He hesitated, and said softly, feeling the anguish of it, "Are you going to die?"

"Yes, *schatz,* sooner or later. We are all dying. From the very minute we are born, we are marching toward the other end. Why does everybody act surprised when it comes?

Why does everyone waste so much time, as if time is endless, when it is the most finite of all things?"

"I don't know," he said.

"Do something nice for Lucy. It will make you feel better. And send a card to your mother."

Mama patted his cheek, got up and went up the stairs.

Well, since he wasn't sending a card to his mother, that left doing something nice for Lucy. And he knew exactly what that was. She'd somehow lost sight of who she was. She was uncomfortable going to the yacht club! Hell, she should walk in there like the queen that she was!

He thought about her lips on his.

And wondered if Mama had any idea how complicated things could get.

CHAPTER SEVEN

LUCY WAS SITTING on her deck with her laptop. Her mother had sent her an email from Africa with a picture attached. Her mother looked happy. Her hair wasn't done, and she had a sunburn. It was odd, because Lucy didn't really recall her mother not having her hair done. And she was not what she would have ever called a happy person.

Her inbox had more RSVPs, two more from her old high-school crowd, saying no, they would not be able to attend the gala.

It didn't have quite the sting it had had previously. Of course, it was a beautiful mild spring day, the sun on the lake and her skin and in her hair. How could you feel bad on a day like this?

Was there a possibility she was able to dismiss negative things more easily and feel beautiful things more intensely since that kiss?

"Of course I'm not!" It was days ago! She hadn't, thank goodness, seen Mac since.

But think of the devil, and he will appear!

"Hey, Lucy Lin!" Mac was on the other side of her deck, peering through the slats of the deck railing at her. "Are you talking to yourself?"

Which would seem pathetic. Thankfully, she was not in her pajamas. It felt as if she was experiencing his sudden appearance intensely, too.

Her heart began to beat a little faster, her cheeks felt suddenly flushed. She was so aware of how incredibly handsome he was. And sexy. She was a little too aware of how his lips tasted.

He didn't wait for an answer.

"It doesn't look like you've made much progress on that paint."

"I'm not sure about the color anymore," she admitted a bit grumpily.

"Come and see what I found in Mama's shed."

She needed to pretend he wasn't there, go in her house and follow his suggestion of locking her doors.

But, of course, if she reacted like that, he

would *know* he was affecting her way too deeply.

She set her laptop aside, got up and reluctantly padded over and looked over the railing, bracing herself. With Mac it could be anything, from a snake to an antique washboard.

He grinned up at her, and she knew that was what she really needed to brace herself against.

That, and the fact Mac was holding the handlebars of a bicycle built for two. It might have been gold once, now it was mostly rust. The leather seats were cracked.

"If you promise to keep your lips off of me, I'll take you for a ride."

"Look, let's get something straight. I didn't kiss you because I find you in any way attractive."

"Hey! That was just plain mean."

"Not that you aren't." Oh! This was going sideways. "I kissed you as a way of saying thank you for caring so deeply about Mama."

"Well, I'm glad you cleared that up. Let's go for a ride."

She looked at him. She looked at the bike. She had cleared up the lip thing. Well, she hadn't really, but he had accepted her explanation. It was a beautiful day. An unexpected gift was being offered to her.

You are giving in to temptation, she told herself. "No," she told Mac.

"Look, princess, it's a bike ride or the Rolliepop. You owe me."

Her lips twitched. Once, for a few weeks, it had felt as if Macintyre Hudson was her best friend. She could tell him anything, be totally herself around him. In many ways, it felt as if she had found out what that meant—to be totally herself—around him.

She was aware of missing that.

Could they be friends? Without the complication of becoming lovers? What would it hurt to find out?

"You're even dressed for it," he said, sensing her weakening. "Aren't those things called pedal pushers?"

Those *things* were a pair of eighty-dollar trousers she had ordered well before her self-imposed austerity program. "It said capris when I ordered them online."

"Ah, well, you know, one born every minute."

And even though she had practiced saying

no to him over and over again in her mind, she might as well not have practiced at all.

Because he was in possession of a bicycle built for two, and she wasn't in the mood to eat a Rolliepop. Plus, she was wearing an eighty-dollar pair of pedal pushers. It seemed like it would be something of a waste not to try them out!

She came down off her deck, and they pushed the bike, which was amazingly heavy, up her steep driveway to the relative flatness of Lakeshore Drive above it.

"Hop on." He took the front.

She folded her arms over her chest. "Why would you automatically get the front?"

"I assumed it would be harder."

"I think you want control. That's where the brakes are. And the steering."

"Maybe *you* want control!"

"Maybe I do," she admitted.

He sighed as if she was really trying his patience. "If you want the front, you can have it. Look, you even have the bell." He rang a rusty old bell.

He surrendered the front, and she got on the bike. He got on the back. After a few false starts, they were off.

It felt as if she was pulling him. It was really the most awful experience. Because even though his handlebars were stationary and didn't move, he acted as if they did, and every time he wrenched on them the whole bicycle shook precariously.

"Quit trying to steer!"

"I can't help myself."

"Are you pedaling?" she gasped.

"With all my might. Ring the bell and wave, we're going by your neighbor gardening."

She giggled, rang the bell and waved. The bike veered, and he tried to correct it with his handlebars that didn't work. He nearly threw them both off the bicycle. Mrs. Feldman looked up, startled, and then smiled, unaware of the problems they were having, and waved back.

They rode by the houses with name plaques at the tops of the driveways. Her father had disapproved of naming the lake properties, saying he found it corny. But Lucy liked the names, ranging from whimsical: Bide Awhile, Pair-a-Dice, Casa Costallota, to the imposing: The Cliff House, Eagle's Rest, Thunder Mountain Manor. Sometimes you could catch a glimpse of the house from the road, other times lawns, gardens, trees, lake, the odd tennis court or swimming pool.

Had she been asked, Lucy would have said Lakeshore Drive was perfectly flat. Now, it was obvious that from her house toward town, it sloped substantially upward.

She was gasping for air. "Don't run over my tongue."

"Ready to trade places?"

She did, gladly.

Though the back position was slightly more relaxing than the front, the feeling of being out of control was terrible. She had to trust him.

"Hey, you got the easy part," she complained. The road that had been sloping upward crested, and began a gradual incline down.

"Woo-hoo! Look, no hands!"

"Put your hands back down."

"No, you put yours up. Come on, Lucy, fly!"

And so she did, and found herself shrieking with laughter as they catapulted down the hill, arms widespread, chins lifted.

His hands went back to the handlebars and so did hers.

"I think we need to slow down," she said. They were approaching the bottom of the rise, the road banked sharply to the right.

"You think I'm not trying?"

In horror, she leaned by him to see he was squeezing the handbrakes with all his might. Nothing was happening.

"Try pushing backwards on the pedals."

He did. She did. The bike did not slow. They were coming up to the last curve into Lindstrom Beach.

He put his feet down to slow them. She was afraid he would break his leg. What his feet did was alter the course of the bike. It veered sharply left as the road went right. Her yanking away on her handlebars did nothing for their perilous balance.

They flew off the road and into a patch of thick bracken fern. She flew over her handlebars into him, and together they tumbled through the ferns. She landed on top of him, and the bike landed on top of her.

He reached up, and with one hand tenderly cupped the side of her face.

"Are you okay, Lucy Lin?" he asked with such gentleness it made her ache.

"I am," she heard herself saying. "I am okay. I haven't been for a long, long time, but I am right now."

"That's good. That's perfect. Did I mention where we were going before we were so rudely interrupted?" Mac asked her.

"I didn't think we were going anywhere. For a bike ride."

He reached around and shoved the bike off them. She sat up, then got up. The capris were probably ruined, a dark oily-looking smudge across the front leg, a grass stain on the other side.

"Ah, actually, no. We were going to cocktail hour at the yacht club."

She glanced at him, realized he must be kidding. "You have to *dress,*" she reminded him, joking.

He was picking up the bike, inspecting it for damage. "We are dressed."

"That's not what she meant."

"Claudia had her opportunity to clarify and she didn't. So, we're dressed or we're naked. You pick."

She suddenly saw he was serious.

"I'm not going. I've scraped my knee. I think there are leaves in my hair."

He wheeled the bike over, picked the leaves out of her hair, bent down and inspected her knee. Then he kissed it.

"You're going," he said.

"There are smudges on the front of my pants."

"Well, there's one on your derriere, too."

"I am not going to the yacht club all disheveled and smudged, with leaves in my hair! What would they think of me?"

"Why do you care what they think of you?" he asked softly.

"I wish I didn't care, but I do, okay? So far, not one of them is coming to the Mother's Day Gala."

"Why not?"

"No one in this set has ever liked Mama. My father set the tone for that years ago. They're all for doing good on paper, but they don't do it in their backyard."

"That makes me all the more committed to attending their little cocktail hour."

"Not me," she said with a shiver.

"We are going," he said, firmly. "And you're

walking into that room like a queen. Do you understand me?"

She looked at him. He wasn't kidding.

"I don't want to go."

"Life's about doing lots of things you don't want to do. You're going."

And suddenly Lucy knew, with him beside her, she could do just what he had said. She could go. And she could hold her head high, too.

Suddenly, she knew he was absolutely right. She *had* to go.

She sighed. "I love it when you're masterful."

"Really? I'll have to try that more often. Back on the bike, wench."

And just like that she was riding toward what she had feared the most for a long, long time. Only, she didn't feel at all afraid.

They rode up on their now quite wobbly bicycle built for two. She would have left it at the back door, but Mac was in the control position, and he rode along the pathway that twisted to the front of the club, where it faced the lake. Some of the cocktail crowd were out on the deck.

There was a notable pause in the conversation as they parked the bike.

Mac threw his arm over her shoulder as they went up the steps, and she glanced at his face.

He had that smile on.

If you didn't know him, you might be charmed by it.

She said quiet hellos to people on the deck, sucked in her breath and, with Mac at her side, entered the yacht club.

"Macintyre Hudson!" Claudia squealed, just in case anyone hadn't recognized him, "I'm so glad you came. Look, folks—" she looped her arm through his "—Mac is back!"

If he cared that he was in shorts when every other man was in a sports jacket and slacks, you couldn't tell.

As always, he carried himself like a king.

And she took her cue from him. Claudia was pointedly ignoring her, so she pointedly ignored Claudia.

"Ellen!" she said, finding a familiar face, "I haven't seen you for ages. What's this I hear that you don't like my paint color on my house?"

"Don't you, Ellen?" Her husband, Norman, turned and looked at her. "I like it."

Claudia's mouth puckered and pointed down. "Let me get you a drink, Mac."

"I'll have lemonade. Lucy?"

"The same."

She grinned at Mac. He had Claudia fetching her a drink!

He winked at her.

And suddenly, in this crowd of people who had once been her friends, she felt lighthearted. Had she bumped her head on the bike?

Because all these people *had* once been her friends. The girls she had known and chummed with since kindergarten. They had stopped calling her. Looked the other way when she came into a room.

And suddenly, she really didn't care. Wasn't that more about them than her? Why hadn't she picked up the phone? When had she forgotten who she was?

They all seemed so stuffy! The atmosphere in this room seemed subdued and stifling. Mac's question came back to her. *What do you do for fun?*

"Why are we all inside?" Lucy asked. "It's a gorgeous day. And Mac and I brought a bicycle built for two!"

People were looking at her! Good!

"Anyone want to try the bike?" she asked.

Silence. It was obvious no one here was dressed for this. But even so, how could they be so young and still so set in their ways? Where were their kids, for heaven's sake? Didn't they like being with their kids? That made her feel almost sorry for them.

Lucy felt determination bubbling up in her. Not to change who they were. No, not that at all. But not to hide who she was, either. Not anymore.

"There will be a prize," she said, "It's trickier than it looks!"

Still, silence. They were going to reject her. She didn't care! She was stunned by the freedom of not caring!

"The prize is complimentary tickets to the Mother's Day Gala. I have a few left."

Some of them looked uncomfortable then!

"I might throw in a free canoe rental for an afternoon. Much more romantic than those power boats tied up at the dock. That's if I'm still in business."

She was throwing their snubs back in their faces, and loving it.

"Don't pass up on this! Mac is going to

serenade you with that famous song about a bicycle built for two while you ride."

She was aware of Mac giving her a side-long look, but also of a little smile tickling the edges of his mouth that was quite different from his devil-may-care smile.

"Well, that I can't resist!" And then quiet little Beth Adams, whom she had always liked, stepped forward. "I'll try it." She gave Lucy a quick, hard hug, and said quietly, "It is so good to see you."

It was so sincere that Lucy felt tears sting her eyes.

After that it was as if a dam had burst. People coming and hugging her, shaking Mac's hand, saying how good it was to see them both.

The party moved out onto the lawn as everyone lined up to watch Beth try the bike. Beth hitched up her skirt and kicked off her shoes. Lucy got on the backseat. There was laughter and encouragement as they wobbled down the path.

"Sing," Lucy ordered Mac.

He was a good sport.

"Ring the bell," Lucy called as they turned around at the parking lot and came back, the

assembled crowd scattering off the walkway. "Don't get going too fast, the brakes
are faulty."

Beth rang the bell, as Mac sang.

The way his eyes rested on her, it almost
felt as if he was singing to her. He looked so
proud of her!

Then Beth called her sister, Prue, to try it
with her. Prue gamely hitched up her dress
and tossed her shoes on the grass.

Mac started the song all over. Lucy sang
with him.

And then to her amazement, everyone was
singing.

Laughter flowed as others tried the bike,
first some of the women together, and then
couples.

It seemed everyone had to have a turn.

Mac nursed his lemonade, delivered to him
and Lucy on the lawn by a very sulky Claudia. He was glad to be out of the clubhouse
and back into the sunshine.

The yacht club had surprised him. Once,
it had seemed like *the* place that meant you'd
arrived, the exclusive enclave of the old and
wealthy Lindstrom Beach families. He'd

never been invited here when he lived here, nor had he attended the functions that had been open to the public, a kind of reverse snub.

Now, all these years later he'd been to places that were truly exclusive. Many of them.

And in comparison the Lindstrom Beach Yacht Club seemed like a three trying to be a nine. It had a "clubhouse" feel to it, but not in a good way. There was carpet, which was always a bad idea in a place close to water. The paneling was too dark and the paintings too somber.

He smiled as Lucy got everyone moving to the deck and then down on the lawn.

There was quite a gathering of people he'd gone to school with, some of them relatively unchanged, some changed for the worse. Most had arrived in the powerboats that were tied to the dock, and most of the women, at least, were "dressed," their opportunity to haul out the expensive cocktail dresses they normally wouldn't get a chance to wear.

Billy Johnson had aged poorly and had a tortured comb-over hairdo, and a potbelly.

Lucy was as he remembered her, finally.

At the heart of it all. Encouraging them to laugh and have fun. Just as in the old days, they thought they were so cool, but they were chirping along to that hokey old song.

In her smudged pants and sleeveless top, with her knee bashed up, he thought she did look like queen.

He loved how she was getting everyone on that bicycle.

He loved how they were all singing that song, Lucy waving her arms around like a bandleader.

He noticed Claudia simmering beside him.

"You and Billy should try it," he said.

"Why would I?" she snapped.

"Come on, Claudia," Billy said. "Everybody but us has tried it. We could win the prize!"

She had been getting drinks when Lucy had announced the prize so Mac had to bite back a shout of laughter.

Annoyed, Claudia nonetheless did not want to seem like the only spoilsport on the lawn.

And Billy still had a bit of the captain of the football team in him. Or a few too many drinks. Because where everyone else had gone up the path and around the parking lot a few times, Billy began to go up the long steep driveway that people used to get their boats into the water.

At the top, he and Claudia disappeared onto Lakeshore Drive.

"Riding to town," someone guessed.

"Had a wreck," someone else said. "Impaired driving!"

"Oh, here they come!"

They had just turned around somewhere on the road. Claudia had obviously missed the part about the brakes, Billy had possibly already had too many drinks to get it.

As they whirred down the hill on the ancient bicycle, the little crowd burst into song.

The bike was wobbling but picking up speed. Billy was yelling, happily, "Faster! Faster!" He put his head down, pedaled with fury.

Claudia, her cocktail dress flying in the wind behind her was shrieking to him to slow down.

The crowd sang boisterously, saluting the couple with their wineglasses.

The bike careened down the hill and past the crowd. It went down the cement ramp that allowed boats to be backed gently into the lake.

Mac wasn't sure that Billy even tried the brake.

In fact, he seemed to be yelling "Ta-da" as they entered the water in a great spray of foam.

Claudia, on the backseat, flew off and into him, just as he and Lucy had done earlier.

It was spectacular! They both plunged into the water with a great splash.

Claudia floundered and squealed until Billy picked her up and hauled her out of the water. People swarmed around them. Claudia's dress looked as if it was made out of soggy toilet paper. Her hair hung in horrible ropes. Her makeup was running.

Her husband whirled her around. "Now, honey, *that* was fun! Hey, Lucy, did we win the prize?"

"Oh, you sure did," Lucy said. She was doubled over with laughter.

"What prize?" Claudia sputtered.

Mac could not take his eyes from Lucy. This is what he remembered. At the very center of it all. Only, there was something about it that was even better.

Because before, there had been no shadows in her.

And now that there were, it was twice as gratifying to see them go away. And now that there were, it was like seeing the sun after weeks of rain.

Beautiful.

The most beautiful thing he had ever seen.

CHAPTER EIGHT

"I'VE GOT TO make some changes to the gala," Lucy panted. She was on the front of the bike, pedaling with all her might. They had left the yacht club and were on the final hill before her house. "I had it all wrong. It was like, when I was planning it, I was trying to win their approval. And none of them were even coming!"

"Well, they're all coming now," he said.

"That remains to be seen. They could all come to their senses before then."

"I think they just did come to their senses."

"I don't want it to be stuffy."

"Like cocktail hour was before you arrived?"

"Exactly. We need something more fun for the gala. I mean, still a dinner, and obviously it's too late to change the black-tie part, but what would you think of a comedian?"

"Lucy, please be quiet and pedal the bike!" She didn't even seem to be tired, bursting with a new energy. Mac wondered what the heck he had unleashed.

Since they knew the bike had no brakes, they walked the final decline in the road. Now that he had seen her light flicker back on, Mac felt honor bound to fan it to life, to keep it going, and it didn't take much.

Over the next few days, he did simple things. He brought a pack of hot dogs and some sticks to her place, and they roasted wieners over an open fire. And then cooked marshmallows, and ate them until their hands and faces were sticky.

He had the bike fixed and they rode it into town for ice cream.

He had one of his double kayaks sent up, and they began to explore the lake in the afternoons.

All this wholesome fun was great, but he wanted to show her more. He wanted to show her a bigger world than Lindstrom Beach. He wanted to show her he was more than the boy he had once been. That he had succeeded in a different place and moved in that place with comfort and confidence.

It occurred to him that his need to show her something more of himself was not strictly within the goal he had set for himself of showing Lucy some fun.

But since he already knew just how he would do it, he refused to ask the question whether he was going deeper than he had ever intended to go.

"Miss Lindstrom?" a deep voice, faintly muffled voice said.

"Yes?" Lucy shook herself awake, played along. She was still in bed. She looked at the clock. It was 6:00 a.m. A girl could live to wake up to the sound of his voice, even when he was trying to disguise it.

"You have won an all-expense-paid trip to Vancouver, B.C. Your flight is departing from the Freda dock in ten minutes."

That sounded so fun. And exciting. Lucy marveled at this woman she had become. But maybe they'd better set some limits.

"Mac!"

His voice became normal. "How did you guess?"

"You're the only one I know with a plane tied up at Mama's dock. I can't come—for goodness' sake, the gala is days away. This is no time to be taking off."

"Literally, taking off."

"Ha-ha."

"I'm coming over."

Something in her sighed. Mac coming over, them passing back and forth between houses as if it was the most natural thing in the world.

The truth was she couldn't wait to see him. Seeing him for the first time in a day always felt so wonderful. She told herself she had to stop this. She told herself she was playing with fire.

But she had set it off, all those days ago when he had shown up with the bicycle to see if they could be friends.

And it seemed as if they could.

Okay, so she yearned to taste him. To hold him. To kiss him. But no, that had ruined everything last time.

This time she was going to be satisfied with friendship.

She wrapped her housecoat around her and went to the door. Mac looked incredible, of course, in a nice shirt and khakis.

"You spend an awful lot of time in that housecoat, Lucy Lin."

"It's six in the morning."

He grinned wickedly. "So, what do you say? You want to come play?"

"One of us has to be a responsible adult! The gala—"

"Part of the reason for the trip," he said with sincerity.

She folded her hands over her chest, waiting to see how he was going to pull this off.

"Mama found out it's not just about Mother's Day. That it's in her honor. She's quite impressed that something at the yacht club is being held in her honor. She considers it *swanky.*"

"But it's supposed to be a surprise!"

"Come on. There are no secrets in Lindstrom Beach."

That, Lucy knew firsthand. "Did you tell her?"

He looked hurt. "No. Agnes Butterfield. It slipped out, apparently. Mama thinks it's a good thing she found out, because, according to her, she has nothing suitable to wear to such a *swanky* venue."

"Could you quit saying *swanky* like that?

As if we're a bunch of small town hicks putting on airs?"

"Consider swanky banned from my vocabulary. If you'll come."

Really? A fly-in shopping trip to the big city? How on earth could she refuse that? Apparently he still thought she was resisting, and it was fun to make him try and convince her to do something she'd already decided she wanted to do.

"Mama says a galoot-head like myself cannot be trusted to help her pick a dress."

He was pushing all the right buttons. "Mac, she has more dresses and matching hats than the queen." But she said it weakly.

The carefree look melted from his face. He turned from her and looked over the inky darkness of the lake. His voice was low when he spoke. "She told me nothing she owns fits, that she lost a lot of weight last winter."

Lucy felt that ripple of fear. "I never noticed that," she said, biting a nail.

"I didn't, either. I thought it was because I hadn't seen her for a while. She said it's because she walks more, now that she doesn't have a driver's license."

Lucy closed her eyes, tried to swallow the

fear and think rationally. She realized she was really dealing with two kinds of fear.

One, that something was wrong with Mama that had her losing weight and planning her own funeral.

And two, that Mac Hudson was standing on her back deck, and he still made her feel as though she was melting.

There was something quintessentially sexy about a man who could fly an airplane.

As if he knew she had given in, he said, "I told her I'd get her a new dress for her birthday. Lucy, we'll leave in a few minutes, shop, have a nice private birthday lunch with Mama and be home by early evening. It will be fun."

Oh, more fun. Didn't it seem like she was setting herself up for a heartbreak? Because he would leave and all the fun she was becoming so accustomed to would stop.

It was only a heartbreak if there was love involved she told herself. They were just friends. Besides, when was the last time she had just had a lighthearted shopping trip?

Come to think of it, Lucy realized, she was going to need a dress, too.

And come to think of it, she needed a dress that would show Mac she was not quite the stick-in-the-mud, fun-free creature he seemed to believe she was.

And maybe that she had come to believe she was, too!

Besides, wouldn't it be the best of exercises to prove that not only was she capable of embracing a spontaneous day of pure fun, but that she didn't have anything to fear from her reactions to Mac anymore?

She was a grown-up. So was he.

They could be friends. They had been proving that all week, with their strongest bond being their mutual caring for Mama Freda.

Still, this felt different than hanging out over a bonfire, eating marshmallows until they were sticky and sick.

Lucy found herself choosing what to wear very carefully. Finally, she settled on jeans, high heels, a white tailored shirt and a leather jacket. She'd finished with a dusting of makeup, a few curls in her too-short hair, and big gold hoop earrings. The look she was hoping for was casual but stunning.

And from the almost surprised male appreciation in his eyes, she had achieved it.

Mac helped Mama into the plane. Then it was her turn, and his hand closed around hers to hand her up. Given that the plane was bobbing on water, and they were stepping from the dock, this took more physical contact than Lucy had prepared herself for, but at least she didn't end up with his hand on her backside!

Her reaction to it, she told herself, was only evidence that it was time for her to stop being such a hermit.

Mama insisted on sitting in the back.

Apparently she was terrified of flying, a small detail that she was not going to allow to get in the way of a shopping trip and a new dress.

Mac leaned into the back to help her with her seat belt, but she refused the headset Mac passed to her. Instead, out of a gargantuan red handbag, she pulled a bulky eight-track tape player. After checking batteries, she plugged in an eight-track cassette. Then, she fished through the enormous purse, pulled out a book of word searches and a pencil and hunkered down in her seat.

"Mama, there's nothing to be worried about," Mac told her.

"Worried, schmurried," she muttered without looking up from the book.

He shrugged and grinned at Lucy, then

helped her buckle in, and adjusted her headset for her. There was something entirely too sexy about Mac at the controls of the plane. He was confident and professional, on a two-way radio filing a flight plan, going through a series of checks.

As the plane taxied along the lake, Lucy looked over her shoulder to see Mama jacking up the volume of her eight track and squinting furiously at her book.

"Is that Engelbert Humperdinck?" Mac asked.

"I'm sure that's what she's listening to." Lucy confirmed.

She thought she heard a sound from Mama, but when she turned around again it was to see Mama glance out the window at the lakeshore rushing by them, go pale and jack up the volume yet again.

The plane wrested itself from gravity, left water and found air. Lucy found herself holding her breath as the plane lifted over the trees at the far end of the lake and then banked sharply.

"Have you ever been in a small plane before?"

"No."

"Nervous?"

Lucy contemplated that. "No," she decided. "It's exhilarating."

Mac flew back over her house and she knew he had done that just for her. Her house from the air was so cute, like a little dollhouse, all the canoes lined up like toys on her dock.

She thought it looked very nice in white.

"Is the lavender going to be a mistake?" she said into the headset. Then, "No! No, it isn't!"

He smiled at her as if she had passed a test—not that devil-may-care smile that held people at a distance. But a real smile, so genuine she could feel tears smart behind her eyes.

She turned and tried to get Mama's attention so she could see her own house from the air, but Mama was muttering along to her music, licking her pencil furiously, and scowling at her word-puzzle book, determined not to look out that window.

"What's Caleb's House?" Mac asked.

She went from feeling safe and happy to feeling as if she was on very treacherous ground. Lucy felt her heart race. "What? Why do you ask?"

"That's the charity Mama told me she

wants the money from the fund-raiser to go to. I'd never heard of it. She said to ask you."

She was aware she could tell him now. That there was something about hearing him say Caleb's name that made her want to be free of carrying it all by herself.

But the time was not right, and it might never be right. He was here only temporarily. Why share the deepest part of her life with him? Why act as though she could trust him with that part of herself?

She had trusted him way too much once before. She had talked and talked until she had no secrets left. Now, she had a secret.

After he had left here, seven years ago, Lucy had found out she was pregnant. Terrified, she had confided in one friend.

Claudia.

Claudia had felt a need to tell her mother and father, who had told Lucy's mother and father, and maybe a few other members of their church, as well.

Lucy's decent, upstanding family had been beyond dismayed.

"How could you do this to us?" her mother had whispered. "I'll never be able to hold up my head again."

Her father's disgust had been visited on her in icy silence. Her plans for college had gone up in smoke. Her friends had abandoned her. She had been terrified and alone, an outcast in her own town.

She had never felt so lonely.

And still, that life that grew within her had not felt like an embarrassment to her. It felt like the love she had known was not completely gone. She whispered to her baby. When she found out it was a boy, she went and bought him the most adorable pair of sneakers, and a little blue onesie.

When it had ended the way it had, in a miscarriage, it was as if everyone wanted to pretend it had never happened.

But by then she had already named him, crooned his name to him to make him feel welcome in a world where he was not really welcome to anybody but her. That was the night she had run to Mama's in her bare feet, needing to be somewhere where it would be okay to feel, to grieve, to acknowledge she could never pretend it hadn't happened.

That was the night she had spoken out loud the name of the little baby who had not survived.

Caleb.

Lucy was careful to strip her voice of all emotion when she answered.

"It's a house for young girls who are pregnant," she said. "It's still very much in the planning stages."

"One thing about Mama," he said wryly. "There's never any shortage of causes in her world."

To him it was just a cause. One of many. She took a deep breath. Was it possible he had changed as much as she had?

"Mac," she said, "tell me about you."

Part of her begged for him to see it for what it was, an invitation to go deeper.

Maybe it was different this time. If it was, would she tell him about Caleb?

"Remember I built that cedar-strip canoe?"

She nodded.

"My first sales were all those kind of canoes. It was hard to make money at it, because they were so labor-intensive, but I loved doing it. I started getting more orders than I could keep up with, so I went into production. Pretty soon, I was experimenting with kayaks, too. Two things set me apart from others. Custom paint that no one had ever seen before—canoes were always green or red or yellow, some solid, nature-inspired palette, and I started doing crazy patterns on them. It appealed to a certain market."

As much as she genuinely enjoyed hearing about the building of his business, it hardly struck her as intimate.

"The other thing was, when you bought a canoe from me, you became part of a community. I kept in touch with people, put them in touch with other people who had purchased stuff from me. Eventually, it got big enough I had to do a newsletter and a website, a social-media page and all that stuff. I didn't realize I was setting something in place that was going to be marketing gold."

Was there something a little sad about him regarding the building of relationships as marketing gold?

"They didn't just buy a canoe. They belonged to something. They were part of Wild Side. Everybody wants to belong somewhere."

"It's kind of ironic," Lucy said. "Because you seemed like you didn't have that thing about belonging." *Even to me.*

"I guess I never found anything in Lindstrom Beach I wanted to belong to."

She looked swiftly out the window.

"I didn't mean that the way it sounded."

"No, it's okay," she said stiffly. "It was just a little summer fling. I'm sure you moved on to bigger and better things. I mean, that's obvious."

"It's true I've become a successful businessman. And it's true I seem to have found my niche in life. But I've never been good at the relationship thing, Lucy. I have not improved with time. People want something I can't give them."

Was it a warning or a plea? She turned back and looked at him.

"And what is that?" she asked.

"They want to connect on a deep and meaningful level," he said, and there was that grin, devil-may-care and dashing. "And I just want to have fun."

She was not sucked in by the smile. "That sounds very lonely to me."

He raised an eyebrow. "I'm looking for someone to rescue me," he said, rather seductively, teasing.

Lucy turned back to the window and studied the panoramic views, water, earth and sky. He had always been like this. As soon as it started to go a little too deep, he turned up the wattage of that smile, kidded it away.

"Aren't you going to try and rescue me, Lucy Lin?" he prodded her.

"No," she said, and then looked back at him. "I'm going to get you a cat."

"I killed my last three houseplants."

"Wow. That takes commitment phobia to a new level. You can't even care about a plant?"

"Just saying. The cat probably isn't your best idea ever."

She sighed. "Probably not." Then she realized they were in an airplane. It wasn't as if he could jump out. She could probe his inner secrets if she wanted to.

"You always seemed kind of set apart from everyone else. It seemed like a choice, almost as if you saw through all those superficial people and scorned them."

"I don't know if *scorn* is the right word," he said. "I've always liked being by myself. I'll still choose a tent in the woods beside a lake with not another soul around over just about anything else."

"It sounds to me like someone hurt you."

His face was suddenly remote.

"It sounds to me as if you don't trust anyone but yourself."

He didn't even glance at her, suddenly intently focused on the operation of the plane, and the instrument panel.

"I'm sure my father didn't help any. I'm sorry about the way Lindstrom Beach treated you. And especially my father. When you told me how he threatened you, said he was going to set you up as a thief, I was stunned. I was more stunned that you let it work. That you let him drive you away. I always figured you for the kind of guy who would stick around and fight for what you wanted."

"And I figured you would say something to your old man in my defense, but you never did, did you?"

All these years that she had nursed her resentment against Mac, and it had never once occurred to her that she had hurt him.

"That summer," he continued quietly, "I'd never felt like that with another person. So close. So connected. Not alone."

Lucy felt as if she couldn't breathe. It was the most Mac had ever said about how he was feeling.

"And the fact it was you, the rich girl, the

doctor's daughter, loving *me*. Only, it was like you weren't the rich girl, the doctor's daughter. You stepped away from that role. You were so real, so authentic. And so was I around you. Myself. Whatever that was."

"Why didn't you at least ask me to go with you, Mac?"

"When you didn't take a stand with your dad, I guess I already knew what you would tell me later. That in the end, you would never fall for a boy like me. It would be too big a stretch for you. And unfair even to ask it."

But she was surprised by the pain, ever so briefly naked in his face. He had trusted her, and she had let him down. She could see his trust had been a most precious gift.

Lucy tried to explain. "It was only when it was obvious you were going, and you weren't going to ask me to go, that it was not even an option you had considered, that I said that. *I could never fall for a boy like you.*"

He glanced at her, searching. "It cut me to the quick, Lucy. It made me so aware of everything that was different about us when I had been living and breathing everything that was the same. I guess before you said that, I thought we'd keep in touch. That I'd phone and write. And maybe come back to visit."

Now was the time to tell him that she hadn't meant it as in he wasn't worthy of her. She had meant it as in he was too closed, he couldn't be vulnerable with her.

"Mac, I'm so sorry."

But he suddenly looked uneasy, as if he had already revealed more about himself than he wanted to, been as vulnerable as he cared to get. Some things didn't change, and she did not feel she could repair that hurt caused all those years ago by trying to clarify it now.

He must have felt the same way.

"It's all a long time ago," he said with an uncomfortable shrug. "Look where it led me. Hey, and look where we are. We're almost there. Look out your window. We'll be passing right over the Pacific Ocean in two minutes, and then making our approach to the Vancouver Flight Centre at Coal Harbour."

His face was absolutely closed. If she pursued this any farther, she was pretty sure if he had a parachute tucked behind his seat he was going to strap it on and jump.

They still had the trip home! And maybe he needed a rescuer, even as he kidded about it. She didn't know how long he was going to stick around, but she had him for today.

Maybe, just for today, neither of them needed to be lonely.

"It's only been two hours! It takes four or five times that long to drive here from Lindstrom Beach!"

"I know. It's great, isn't it?"

"It is," she said, and suddenly felt a new willingness to let go, to embrace whatever surprises the day held for her, to embrace the fact that for some reason fate had thrown her back together with the man who had left her pregnant all those years ago. Who had hurt her.

And whom she had hurt, too. Were they being given a second chance? Could they just take it and embrace it without completely rehashing the past? Lucy found herself hoping.

"Are we landing?" Mama demanded from the back.

"Yes."

She put her puzzle book away and fished through her bag. She drew out her rosary beads.

"Hail Mary..."

Whether it was Mama's prayers or his expertise, or some combination of both they landed without incident and docked at one of the eighteen float-plane spaces at the dock.

A chauffeur-driven limousine was waiting for them, and it whisked them by the Vancouver Convention Centre to the amazing Pacific Centre Mall.

He pressed them into a very posh-looking store. The salesclerks in those kind of stores always recognized power and money, even when it came dressed as casually as Mac was.

"My two favorite ladies need to see your very best in evening wear," he said.

The clerk took it as a mission. Lucy and Mama were whisked back to private dressing rooms. Mac was settled in a leather chair and brought a coffee.

"Would you like something to read? I have a selection of newspapers."

He shook his head, but after Mama and Lucy had modeled the saleslady's first few selections, he wandered off. Lucy assumed he was restless, and didn't blame him.

Lucy had grown up with privilege, but even so, it had been Lindstrom Beach. She had never worn designer labels like these. She and Mama were in awe of how good clothes fitted, the fabric, the drape of them. Of course, even if she weren't on an austerity program, she would never be able to afford dresses like these. Even so, it was so much fun to try them on.

Mac came back, a dress over each arm. "The black for Mama, the red for you."

"Red," she said, and wrinkled her nose. "You know I'm not flashy, so you must be afraid of losing me in the parking lot. Do you have any idea what dresses like these cost?"

"The saleslady asked for my gold card before she'd even take those down for me."

"I shouldn't even try it on," she said, but heard the wistfulness in her own voice.

"You're trying it on."

"What can I say? You know I love it when you're masterful."

And so she did. She wasn't going to buy this dress, and she certainly wasn't going to allow him to buy it for her, but why not just give herself over to the experience?

Mama went first. Lucy and Mac had "oohed" and "aahed" over the selection of designer dresses that had been brought out for Mama so far, but the one he had chosen was the best. Simple, black, silk: it was classic.

Lucy and Mac applauded as Mama modeled, as if she had been on the runway all her life. She sauntered down the walkway between the change rooms, hand on her ample hip, turned, winked, flipped the matching scarf over her shoulder.

The salesclerk, Mac and Lucy applauded. Mama beamed. "This is it."

It was Lucy's turn. The clerk came into the fitting room with her to help slide the yards of red silk over her head.

Even before she looked in the mirror, Lucy could tell by the way she felt that this dress was the kind of dress a woman dreamed of.

The clerk stared at her. "That man has taste," she said.

Lucy turned and looked in the mirror. The dress had slender shoulder straps and a neckline that was a sensual V without being plunging. It had an empire waistline, tight under her breasts, and then it floated in a million pleats to the floor.

She came out of the dressing room.

"Walk like a queen," the clerk said.

That's what Mac had said, too, when he had forced her to go to the yacht club. *Walk like a queen.* In a dress like this it was easy enough to do.

When Mac saw her, his reaction was everything she could ever hope for.

She had never seen him look anything but in control, but suddenly he looked flustered.

"You," he said hoarsely, "are not a queen. Lucy Lin, you are a goddess."

She could not resist walking with swaying hips, spinning in a swirl of rich color, tossing a look over her shoulder. She licked her lips and winked.

She was trying to add a bit of levity, but Mac, for once, did not seem to find it funny.

After she had taken off the dress, Lucy came out of the dressing room, feeling oddly out of sorts. What woman tried on a dress like that and then felt okay when she walked away from it?

She went and waited outside the store while Mac bought Mama the black dress to wear at the gala.

Mama was hugging her package to her and chastising him in a mix of German and English about spending too much money on her. But they could both tell she was utterly thrilled.

They went for a fabulous lunch at a waterfront restaurant, and then, almost as if the whole thing had been a dream, they were back in the plane.

They were home before supper.

He helped her get down from the plane, then they watched Mama waddle happily across the yard with all her bags.

"Thank you for a beautiful day, Mac. It was like something out of a dream. Honestly."

He finished mooring the plane. He turned back to her.

"Okay," he said. "That's it. The whole show. I've shown you everything I do for fun. And you still haven't shown me. You said there was something."

"Oh." She felt doubtful. And then she decided to be brave. What if, by showing him, she eased that loneliness that he wore like a shield? Even for a few more hours?

"Let me make some phone calls. I'll call you in the morning."

"Phone calls to arrange fun," he said. "Sky-diving? Horseback riding? I've got it! Bungee jumping!"

"I'm afraid I'm going to be a big disappointment to you, Mac."

Or maybe to herself. Because once again, even though he had given nothing, she had made a decision to be vulnerable. She would show him that thing she did that made her feel so alive.

And he most likely wouldn't understand that there were ways a person could not feel lonely.

And how could that be anything but a good thing if he didn't understand how connected this one thing made her feel? She could have her world back the way it had been before he landed again.

Only, she had a feeling it was not going to be quite that simple.

Mac picked up the phone on the first ring in the morning.

"Are you ready for your big outing, Mr. Hudson?" Lucy asked. "Be ready in ten minutes."

"Should I be dressing for bungee jumping or horseback riding?"

"Actually, whatever you wear normally will be okay."

That could be anything from a wet suit to a suit suit, so Mac just put on some khakis and a sports shirt with the little kayak emblem on it.

He tried to take a clue from what Lucy was wearing and came to the conclusion it would be nothing too exciting. She might have been dressed for a day clerking at the bookstore. She was not the goddess he had seen in that dress yesterday.

And wasn't that a mercy?

Still, as they got in the car, he was so aware of her. Aware he liked being with her.

"We're going to Glen Oak."

They picked up coffees and conversation flowed freely between them. They talked of Mama and house repairs, the swiftly approaching gala and last-minute details, he made her laugh by doing an impression of Claudia receiving her free tickets to the gala, which he had delivered personally.

Having spent years in Lindstrom Beach, Mac was familiar with Glen Oak. Sixty miles from Lindstrom Beach, Glen Oak was the major city that serviced all the smaller towns around it. All the large chain stores had outlets there, there was an airport, hotels, golf courses and the regional hospital.

"Golfing," he guessed. "I have to warn you, I'm not much of a golfer. Too slow for me."

"That's okay, we're not golfing."

"Not even mini?" he said a little sadly as they passed a miniature golf course. He was aware he would like to go miniature golfing with her.

And horseback riding, for that matter. He wondered what it would take to talk her into bungee jumping.

He frowned as Lucy pulled into the hospital parking lot.

"We're going to a hospital for fun?" Mac asked. "Oh, boy, Lucy, you are in worse shape than I thought."

"I tried to warn you."

Perplexed, he followed her through the main doors. She did not stop at the main desk, but the receptionist gave her a wave, as if she knew her.

What if she was sick? What if that's what she was trying to tell him? Mac felt a wave of fear engulf him, but it passed as she pushed through doors clearly marked Neonatal.

She went to an office and a middle-aged woman smiled when she saw her and came out from behind her desk and gave her a heartfelt hug.

"My very favorite cuddler!" she said.

Cuddler?

"This is Macintyre Hudson, the man I spoke to you about this morning. Mac, Janice Sandpace."

"Nice to meet you, Mr. Hudson. Come this way."

And then they were in a small anteroom. Through a window he could see what he assumed were incubators with babies in them.

"These babies," Janice explained, "are premature. Or critically ill. Occasionally we get what is known as a crack baby. We instigated a cuddling program several years ago because studies have shown if a baby has physical contact it will develop better, grow better, heal better, and have a shorter hospital stay. It also relieves stress on parents to know that even if they can't be here 24/7, and many can't because they have other children at home or work obligations, their baby is still being loved."

Lucy had already donned a gown with bright ducks all over it, and she turned for Janice to do up the back for her.

"You'll have to gown up, Mr. Macintyre."

He chose a gown from the rack. It had giraffes and lions on it. Lucy was already donning a mask and covering her hair.

Her eyes twinkled at him from above the mask.

He followed suit, as did Janice. She showed him how to give his hands a surgical scrub.

"Today we have multiples," Janice told him from behind her mask. "Twins. Preemies."

She gestured to a rocking chair. Lucy was already settled in one.

Side by side in their rocking chairs.

And then Janice brought Lucy the tiniest little bundle of life he had ever seen. Tightly swaddled in a pink blanket, the baby was placed in Lucy's arms. It stared up at her with curious, unblinking eyes.

"Amber," Janice said, smiling.

In seconds, Lucy was lost in that world. It was just the baby and her. She crooned to it. She whispered in its tiny little ear. She rocked.

This was what she did for fun.

Only, the look on her face said it wasn't just fun.

What Lucy did had gone way beyond fun.

Her eyes on that baby had a light in them that was the most joyous thing he had ever seen.

Suddenly fun seemed superficial.

Lucy glanced at him. Even though she had a mask on, he could tell she was smiling. More than smiling—she was radiant.

"This is Sam," Janice said.

He looked up at her. His panic must have been evident.

"Don't worry," she said. "I'll walk you through it. Support his neck. See how Lucy is holding the baby?"

And then Mac found a baby in his arms. It looked up at him, eyes like buttons in the tiniest wrinkled face he had ever seen.

"Talk to him," Janice suggested.

"ET, call home," he said softly. If he was not mistaken, the baby sighed. "I was just kidding. You look more like Yoda. A very handsome Yoda."

He looked over at Lucy, crooning away as if she'd been born to this.

He didn't know what to say.

And then he did.

He sang softly.

It felt as if they had been there for only seconds when Janice came back in and took the now sleeping baby from him. "Thank you," she said.

"No, thank you."

And he meant it.

They were quieter on the way home. When she drove by the mini-golf course, he didn't feel like playing anymore.

Seeing her with that baby, he had known. He had known what he had wanted his whole life and had been so afraid of never being able to have that he had pretended he didn't want it at all.

She drove into her driveway. "I have so much to get done for the gala!"

But he wasn't letting her go that easily. "Is that a charitable organization, the baby thing?" he asked Lucy.

"Yes. It's called Cuddle-Hugs."

"Why aren't we doing Mama's fund-raiser in support of that?"

"Of course they need money to operate, but that's not what Mama chose."

"I'll talk to Corporate this afternoon. I'll have them call Janice. Anything they want. Anything. They'll get it."

"That's not why I took you there, to solicit a donation."

"I know. And we didn't go to Vancouver to buy you a dress, but I bought it for you anyway."

"You bought me that dress?" she gasped.

"So, what do you think now, Lucy Lin? Could you fall for a boy like me now?"

CHAPTER NINE

IT WAS ALL wrong. It was not what he had wanted to say at all.

Mac could have kicked himself. He didn't know where the question had come from. It certainly hadn't been on his agenda to ask something like that. That certainly hadn't been the reason for his donation, the reason for the fly-in shopping trip yesterday. He hadn't done it to impress her.

It was all just a gift to her. He had found his better side after all.

But now somehow he'd gone and spoiled it all by bringing up the past. Over the past few days Mac had convinced himself that they had pretty much put the past behind them.

But really, wasn't it was always there, the past? Wasn't that why he'd made her go to the yacht club and stand up for herself? Wasn't it true that he could not look at her without seeing her younger self, without remembering the joy of her trust in him, the way she had felt in his arms, the way her heated kisses had felt scattering across his face?

She took a startled step back from him. "Oh, Mac," she said, "when I said that all those years ago, it was never about what you had or didn't have."

He gave her his most charming smile. "It wasn't? You could have fooled me."

"I guess I did fool you. Because I didn't want you to know how deeply it hurt me that you never, ever told me a single thing about you. Not one single thing about you that mattered. And then when you left, you didn't even ask me to go with you. It seems nothing has changed. Even these gifts, so wonderful and grand, are like a guard you put up. That smile you are smiling right now? That's the biggest defense of all."

"You want to know why I never asked you to go with me, Lucy? It wasn't because I wasn't willing to fight for you. It was because you loved this place more than me. It was because I could see your family being torn up and your friends looking at you sideways as if you'd lost your mind. I gave you your life back. The part I don't get is that you didn't take it back. At all."

"No," she said, quietly, "I didn't."

"Why?"

"This isn't how it works, Mac, with you keeping everything to yourself, while I spill my guts."

"You know what? I've had about as much of Lindstrom Beach as I can handle. I wish I had never come back here."

"I wish you hadn't, either!"

He watched, stunned, as she walked away, went into her house and closed the door behind her.

With a kind of soft finality.

"Mama," he said a few minutes later, "something's come up. I have to go back to Toronto. I bought that dress for Lucy. Will you give it to her?"

"Give it to her yourself," Mama said, and went up the stairs. He heard her bedroom door slam.

Both the women he loved were mad at him.

Wait a minute! He loved Lucy? Then he was getting out of here just in the nick of time....

* * *

Lucy listened to Mac's plane take off.

"I don't care if he's gone," she told her cat. "I don't. I always knew he wasn't staying."

She had a gala to finish organizing. She had her dream of Caleb's House to hold tight to.

She burst into tears.

When the phone rang, she rushed to it. Maybe it was him. Could he phone her from the plane? Was he telling her he was turning around?

"Hello from Africa, Lucy!"

Her mother was brimming with excitement. She'd seen an elephant that day. She'd seen a lion. Somehow, Lucy didn't remember her mother like this.

"Anyway," her mother said, "I know you'll be busy on Mother's Day, so I thought I'd phone today. I didn't want you having to track me down adding an extra stress to your day."

That was unusually thoughtful for her mother. It made Lucy feel brave.

"Mom," she said, "do you mind if I paint the house purple? I mean, it's not purple, exactly, a kind of lavender."

It was kind of a segue to *Do you mind if*

I turn our old family home into a house for unwed mothers?

"Lucy! I don't care what color you paint the house. It's your house!"

"Mom, did you give me this house because you felt sorry for me? Because you thought I'd never get my life together without help from you?"

"No, Lucy, not at all. I gave you that house because I hated it."

"What?"

"It was the perfect house, I was the perfect doctor's wife and you were the perfect doctor's daughter."

"Until I ruined everything," Lucy said.

"It's only in the last while that I've seen how untrue that is, Lucy. When you got pregnant, it blew a hole in the facade. When you miscarried, I thought we could patch up the hole. That everything would be the same. That you would be the same.

"But you didn't come back. You didn't want what you had always wanted anymore. I think, at first, we were all angry with you for not coming back to your old life. Me, certainly. Your friend Claudia, too.

"Now I can see how we were really all

prisoners in that house. Trying to live up to your father's expectations of us. Which was a nearly impossible undertaking. Everything always had to look so good. But keeping it that way took so much energy—without my even knowing it, had sucked the life force out of me.

"That hole you blew in all our lives? I glimpsed freedom out that hole. If your dad hadn't died, I would have left him."

Lucy was stunned.

"Lucy, paint the house purple. Swim naked in the moonlight. Dream big and love hard. I'm glad you didn't marry James. He was like your father—in every way, if you get my drift. He was cold and withholding and a control freak. And he was a philanderer."

"Mom? Mac came back." Somehow this was the talk she had always dreamed of having with her mother.

"And?"

"I love him!" she wailed. "And he left again!"

"Sweetie, I can't be there. If I was I would take you on my lap and hold you and comb your hair with my fingers until you had no tears left. That's what I wish I had done all those years ago. The night the baby died."

A baby. Not a fetus. "Thanks, Mom."

"Life has a way of working out the way it's supposed to, Lucy. I am living proof of that. I love you."

"You, too, Mom. I'll be thinking of you on Mother's Day."

"Now, go eat two dishes of chocolate ice cream. Then go and skinny-dip in the lake!"

Lucy was laughing as she hung up the phone. Her mother was right. Everything would work out the way it was supposed to.

Mac was gone.

But she still had Mama, and the gala, and the babies to cuddle. Sometime, somewhere, she had become a woman who would paint her house purple, and who had a dream that was bigger than she was.

And he was part of that. Loving him was part of that.

He hadn't ruined her life. Her mother had made her so aware of that. He had given her a gift. He had broken her out of the life she might have had. He had made her see things differently and want things she had not wanted before.

That's what love did. It made people better. Even if it hurt, it was worth the pain.

Lucy was going to cry. And eat the ice cream. She'd skip the dip in the lake. She was going to feel every bit of the glorious pain.

Because it meant she had loved. And her mother was right. Love, in the end, could only make you better. Not worse.

Mac was aware he was cutting things very close to the wire. He'd gone back to Toronto. His life had seemed empty and lonely, and no amount of adrenaline had been able to take the edge off his pain.

He loved her. He loved Lucy. He always had.

He had to give that a chance. He had to. And if it required more of him, then he had to dig deep and find that.

He was aware he was cutting things close. He arrived back in Lindstrom Beach the night before the gala.

He had never felt fear the way he felt it when he crossed back over those lawns and knocked on Lucy's door.

"Can I come in?"

When she saw it was him, Lucy looked scared to open that door. And he didn't blame her. But hope won out. She stood back from the door.

"You're in your housecoat," he said.

"It *is* nighttime." She scanned his face. "Come sit down, Mac."

The room was beautiful at night. She had a small fire burning in the hearth, and it cast its golden light across fresh tulips in a vase, a cat curled up on the rug in front of it, a book open on its spine on the arm of the chair. What would it be like to have a life like this?

Not a life of adrenaline rush after adrenaline rush, but one of quiet contentment?

A life of Lucy sharing evenings with him?

He couldn't think about that. Not until she knew the full truth. He sat on the couch, she took the chair across from him, tucked those delectable little toes up under her folded legs.

"Lucy, if you care to listen, I'm going to tell you some things I've never told anyone. Not even Mama."

Why was he doing this?

But he knew why. He could see it all starting again. She loved him. She wanted more from him. She always had.

She was leaning toward him, and he could see the hope shining in her face.

He considered himself the most fearless of men. No raging chute of white water ever put fear into his heart, only anticipation.

But wasn't this what he had always feared? Being vulnerable? Opening up to another? Tackling a foaming torrent of raging water was nothing in comparison to opening your heart. Nothing in comparison to letting someone see all of you.

But once she knew all his secrets would she still love him? Could she? Now seemed like the time to find out.

Mac took a deep breath. It was time. It was time to let it all go. It was time to tell someone. It involved the scariest thing of all. It involved trust. Trusting her.

He hesitated, looking for a place to start. There was only one starting point.

"When I was five, my mom left my dad and me. I remember it clearly. She said, I'm looking for something. I'm looking for something *more*.

"As an adult, I can understand that. We didn't have much. My dad was a laborer on a construction crew in a small town, not so different from Lindstrom Beach. He didn't make a pile of money, and we lived pretty humbly in a tiny house. As I got older I realized it was different from my friends' houses. No dishwasher, no computer, no fancy stereo, no big-screen TV. We heated with a wood heater, the furniture was falling apart and we didn't even have curtains on the windows.

"To tell you the truth, I don't know if he couldn't afford that stuff, or if it just wasn't a priority for him. My dad loved the outdoors. Since I could walk, I was trailing him through the woods. In retrospect, I think he thought of *that* as home. Being outside with his rifle or his fishing rod or a bucket for picking berries. And me.

"Mom left in search of something *more,* and I don't remember being traumatized by it or anything. My dad managed pretty well for a guy on his own. He got me registered for school, he kept me clean, he cooked simple meals. When I was old enough, he taught me how to help out around the place. We were a team.

"My mom called and wrote, and showed up at Christmas. She always had lots of presents and stories about her travels and adventures. She was big on saying 'I love you.' But even that young, I could tell she *hated* how my dad lived, and maybe even hated him for being content with so little.

"When she left, there was always a big screaming match about his lack of ambition and her lack of responsibility. I was overjoyed when she came, and guiltily glad when she left.

"Then she found her something *more*. Literally. She found a very, very rich man. I was eight at the time, and she came and got me and took me to Toronto for a visit with her and the new man. Walden, her husband, had a mansion in an area called the Bridle Path, also called Millionaire's Row. They had a swimming pool. She bought me a bike. There was a computer in every room. And a theater room.

"That first time I went for a visit with them, I couldn't wait to get home. But what I didn't know was that the visit there was the opening shot in a campaign.

"My mom started phoning me all the time. Every night. Why didn't I come live with them? They could give me so much *more*.

"I love you. I love you. I love you.

"What I didn't really get was how she had started undermining my dad, how she was working at convincing me only her kind of love was good. She would ask questions about him and me and how we lived, and then find flaws. She'd say, in this gentle, concerned tone, *'Little boys should not have to cook dinner.'* Or do laundry. Or cut wood. Or she'd say, mildly shocked, *'He did what? Oh, Macintyre, if he really cared about you, you would have gotten that new computer you wanted. Didn't you say he got a new rifle?'*

"In one particularly memorable incident, I told her my dad wouldn't let me play hockey because he couldn't afford it.

"She expressed her normal shock and dismay over his priorities, and then told me she would pay for hockey. I was over the moon, and I ran and told my dad as soon as I hung up the phone.

"I can play hockey this year. My mom's going to pay for it!"

"You know, I'd hardly ever seen my dad really, really mad, but he just lost it. Throwing things around and breaking them. Screaming, 'She's never paid a dentist's bill or for school supplies, but she's going to pay for hockey? She's never coughed up a dime when you need new sneakers or a present to bring to a birthday party, but she's going to pay for hockey? What part of hockey? The fee to join the team? The equipment? The traveling? The time I have to take off work?' And then the steam just went out of him, and he sat down and put his head in his hands and said, 'Forget it. You are not playing hockey.'

"This went on for a couple of years. Her planting the seeds of discontent, literally being the Disneyland Mama while my dad was slugging it out in the trenches.

"When I was twelve, I went and spent the summer with her and Walden. I made some friends in her neighborhood. I had money in my Calvin Klein jeans. I was swimming in my own pool. She bought me a puppy. She didn't have rules like my dad did. It was kind of anything goes. She actually let me have wine with dinner, and the odd beer.

"And when summer was over, she sat down on the side of my bed and wept. She loved me so much, she couldn't bear for me to go back to *that* man. She told me I didn't have to go back. She said I didn't have to think about my dad or his feelings. I should have seen the irony in that—that my dad's feelings counted for nothing, but hers were everything, but I didn't.

"I was twelve, nearly thirteen. At home, my dad made me work. By then, I was in charge of keeping our house supplied with firewood. I did a lot of the cooking. Sometimes he took me to work with him and handed me a shovel. I was allowed to go out with my friends only if I'd met all my obligations at home.

"And here she was offering me a life of frolic. And ease. I saw all the *stuff* I could ever want. I could be one of the rich, privileged kids at school instead of Digger Dan's son.

"I phoned my dad and told him I was staying. I could hear his heart breaking in the silence that followed. But she had convinced me that didn't matter. Only *I* mattered.

"And that's what I acted like for the next few months. Like only I mattered. She encouraged that. When my dad called, sometimes I blew him off. I was supposed to spend Christmas with him, but I didn't want to miss my best friend's New Year's Eve party, so I begged off going to be with him."

Mac took a deep shuddering breath. "Do

you remember, a long time ago, I told you I killed a man?"

"With your bare hands," she whispered.

"Not with my bare hands. With my self-centeredness. With my callousness. With my utter insensitivity.

"He died. My dad died on Christmas Day."

"Oh, Mac," she whispered.

"At home, all by himself. He managed to call for help, but by the time they got there he was gone. They said it was a massive heart attack, but I knew it wasn't. I knew I'd killed him."

"Oh, Mac."

"Killed that man who had been nothing but good to me. He might not have been big on words. I don't think I heard him say 'I love you' more than twice in my whole life. But he was the one who had been there when no one else was, who had stepped up to the plate, who had done his best to provide, who had taught me the value of hard work and honesty. I had traded everything he taught me for a superficial world, and I hated myself for it.

"And her. My mother. I hated her. When she told me she didn't see the point in me going to the funeral, that was the last straw.

I ran away and went back. To his funeral, to sort through our stuff.

"I never lived with her again. I couldn't. When they tried to make me go back to her, I ran away. That's how I ended up in foster care.

"I haven't spoken to her in fourteen years. I doubt I ever will again. I can see right through her clothes and her makeup, her perfect hair and her perfect house. She plays roles. For a while I was the role and she could play at being the fun-loving, cool mom, because it filled something in her. It relieved her of any guilt she felt about leaving me when I was little.

"But underneath that veneer she was mean-spirited and manipulative, and basically the most selfish and self-centered person ever born. She was using me to meet her needs, and I was done with her.

"I went through a series of foster homes, crazy with grief and guilt. And then I came here. To Mama Freda.

"And Mama saw the broken place in me, and didn't even try to fix it. She just loved me through it.

"I owe Mama my life."

The silence was so long. There, Lucy had it all. She knew the truth about him. He was the man who had killed his own father.

"When you told me, all those years ago, that you had killed a man, I thought you were blowing me off," Lucy whispered.

When had she moved beside him? When had her hand come to rest on his knee?

"I started to tell you. Back then. I saw the look on your face and retreated to the default defense. I always told people that when I was trying to drive them away, protect myself. I added the part about *with my bare hands* because it seemed particularly effective."

"You feel as if you killed your father," she said, looking at him. The firelight reflected off her face. In her eyes he saw the same radiance he had seen when she held the baby.

It hadn't been pity for the baby. And it wasn't pity for him.

It was love. It was the purest love he'd ever seen.

"I did kill my father," he whispered, daring her to love him anyway.

"No," she said, firmly, with almost fierce resolve. "You didn't."

Three words. So simple. *No. You. Didn't.*

Her hand came to his face, and her eyes were so intent on his.

It felt like absolution. It felt as if, by finally naming it out loud, the monster that had lived in the closet was forced to disappear when exposed to light.

He'd been a teenage boy who did what teenage boys do, so naturally. He had been selfish and thoughtless and greedy. He'd thought only of himself.

It didn't have to be who he was today. It wasn't who he was today.

"You're terrified of love," she said.

"Terrified," he whispered, and knew he had never spoken a truer word.

And she didn't try to fix him. Or convince him. She laid her head on his chest, and wrapped her arms hard around him. He felt her tears warm, soaking through his shirt, onto the skin of his breast.

Her tenderness enveloped him.

And he knew another truth.

That she would see him through it.

Mama's love had carried him so far. Now it was time to go the distance. If he was strong enough to let her. If he was strong enough to say yes to something he had said no to for the past fourteen years.

Love.

He suddenly felt so tired. So very tired. And with her arms wrapped around him, with his head on her breast, he slept, finally, the sleep of a man who did not have to go to his dreams to do battle with his guilt.

When he awoke in the morning, she was gone. The coffee was on, and there was a note.

"Sorry, three zillion things to do. The gala is tonight!"

He went back over to Mama's. Overnight the population there had exploded. Her many foster children wandered in and out, many of them with children of their own. There were tents on the lawn and inflatable mattresses on the floor.

"You stayed with Lucy?" Mama asked, in a happy frenzy of cooking.

"Not in the way you think. Mama, come outside with me for a minute." He found a spot under the trees, and took a deep breath. "Lucy asked some of your foster children to speak at the gala tonight. She chose a few. I was one of them and I've said no. But I think, with your permission, I'll change my mind. But only if you'll allow me to share that story you told me all those years ago."

"*Ach.* For what purpose, *schatz?*"

"For the same purpose you told it to me. To let everyone know that in the end, if you hold tight, love wins."

Her eyes searched his. She nodded.

The gala was sold out. He had seen Lucy flitting around in her red dress. He had told her he would speak.

But it seemed to him strange that with the big day here, the day that she had given her heart and soul to, she seemed wan.

"Are you not feeling well?" he asked her.

"Oh," she said. "No. I'm fine. I thought my doing this…" Her voice faltered. "Mother's Day is hard on me."

"Why? Because your own mother is so far away?"

"I'm just being silly," she said. "Sorry. I think I'm a little overwhelmed."

"Everything looks incredible. The silent auction is racking up bids."

She smiled, but it still seemed wan, disconnected.

He had the awful thought it might be because of what he had shared with her last night.

"I think the custom-painted Wild Ride kayak is going to be the high earner of the night."

"It will be. I keep pushing up the bid on it."

He expected her to laugh. She ran a hand through her hair, looked distracted.

"Oh," she said brightening slightly. "He's here."

"Who?"

"I couldn't find a comedian on such short notice. I found something Mama will like even better. An Engelbert impersonator."

He waited for her to smile. But she didn't. She looked as if she was going to cry.

"Later," she said, and walked away.

After dinner, some of Mama's foster children spoke. Ross Chillington talked about his parents being killed in an accident and about coming to Mama's house, how she was the first one who ever applauded his skill in acting.

Michael Boylston told how Mama had given him the courage and confidence to take on the world of international finance and how now he lived a life beyond his wildest dreams in Thailand.

Reed Patterson told of a drug-addicted mother and a life of pain and despair before Mama had made him believe he could take on the world and win.

And then it was his turn. But he didn't talk about himself.

"A long time ago," he said, "in a world most of us in this room had not yet been born into, there was a terrible war." And then he told Mama's story.

When he finished, the room was as silent as it had been that day fourteen years ago when he had first heard this story.

Into the silence he laid his next words with tenderness, with care.

"Mama spent the rest of her life finding that soldier. She found him over and over again. She found him in every lost boy she took into her home. She found him and she saved him. She saved him before the great evil had a chance to overcome him.

"I am one of those boys," he said quietly, proudly. "I am one of the boys who benefited from Mama's absolute belief in redemption, in second chances.

"I am one of those boys who was saved by love. Who was redeemed by it. And as a result, finally, was able to love back.

"Mama." He looked right at her. "I love you."

The words felt so good. She was weeping. As was most of the audience. His eyes sought Lucy. It wasn't hard to find her in her bright red dress. She had her face buried in her hands, crying.

Mac realized right then that he had a new mission in life. He had not killed his father. But it was possible that he had contributed to his death.

He could not change that. But he could try to redeem himself. He could spend the rest of his life on that. Make up for every wrong he had ever done by loving Lucy. And their children. By believing all that love was a light, and when it grew big enough it would envelop the darkness. Obliterate it.

Lucy still didn't look right. She was in her element, surrounded by people. She had just pulled off something incredible. But she was still crying.

And suddenly she spun around and went into the night.

He waited for her to come back, especially when the Engelbert impersonator geared up and the tables were cleared away for dancing.

Mama stood right in front of the stage. She took off her scarf and threw it at the man's feet.

He picked it up and wiped his sweaty brow, and tossed it back to Mama, who looked as if she was going to die of happiness. Michael Boylston came and asked her to dance. Mac watched and shook his head.

If Mama was unwell, there was no sign of that now. None.

It occurred to Mac that there was something of the miraculous in this evening.

Those foster kids who had grown into adults seemed to be the first to take to the floor, having embraced so much of Mama's enthusiasm and joy for life. They were asking others to dance with them, and, in some instances, were dancing with the people who had once snubbed them as the riffraff from Mama's house.

Claudia was trying to get Ross to sign a movie poster with him on it. Over in the corner, Billy was drinking too much and talking football with Reed Patterson.

Lucy had done what she always did best. She had brought people together.

It hit him out of nowhere.

Things on her dining-room table she didn't want him to see.

Rezoning that had the neighbors in an uproar.

Caleb's House: a home for unwed mothers.

Finding joy in holding little babies.

Mother's Day is hard on me.

It hit him out of nowhere: all her plans had been altered. Claudia feeling superior to her. Her friends not being her friends anymore. No college. Moving away from here. And coming back. Changed.

"Oh my God," he said out loud, and he headed for the door.

There was still, thankfully, a little light in the evening sky. If it had been darker, he might not have been able to see her.

But as it was, her red dress was like a beacon in the thick greenery above her house.

Mac went toward that beacon as if he was a sailor lost at sea. There was a trail, well-traveled along the side of her house, that led him to her.

She was in a small clearing above her house,

sitting on a small stone bench. There was a little flower bed cut from the thick growth. In the center of that bed was a stone, hand-painted in the curly cursive handwriting of a girl.

Caleb.

He went and sat beside her on the bench. "There was a baby," he said, and it was a statement not a question. His mouth had the taste of dust in it.

"They said not to name him," she choked. "They said he wasn't even a baby yet. A fetus. They wouldn't let me bury him. He was disposed of as medical waste."

She was sobbing, and he felt a grief as deep as anything he had ever felt.

"He was mine, wasn't he?"

"Yes, Mac, he was yours."

So many questions, and all of them poured out, one on top of the other. "Why didn't you tell me? Were you planning on telling me? Would you have told me if he lived?"

"Mac, I was at the scared-out-of-my-mind stage. I knew Mama would know where you were. I'd decide to tell you. I'd even cross the lawn to Mama's house. And then I'd talk myself out of it. I felt that you would come back—not for love, but because I'd trapped you into it."

"I had a right to know."

"Yes," she said softly, ever so softly, "Yes, you did. And I think, eventually, I would have finished that million-mile journey across her lawn. But then the baby was gone, and the pain was so bad that the last person I was thinking of was you."

Mac was silent. He could feel that pain unfurling in him. *His baby. His and hers.* It made life as he had lived it so far seem unreal. How would he have been different if he had known?

"When were you going to tell me?" he finally asked.

"Soon," she whispered. "I hoped to get through Mother's Day. If you hadn't come back I was going to call you. I knew it was time. To trust you with it."

He looked at her, and knew it was true. And he knew something else. That he had to rise to the fragile trust she was handing him. This had been her secret, her intensely personal grief, but it was no longer. This pain would be an unbreakable bond between them.

Something that they, and they alone, would know the full depth of.

In this instant he sat beside her and felt her grief, and he felt his own. He felt a momentary hurt that he had been excluded from one of the biggest events of his own life.

And yet looking into her eyes, he felt his hurt dissolve and he was taken by the bravery he saw in her. Her hands were clutched around something, and he unfolded them from around it.

It was a small box.

"I bring it with me when I come here."

"May I look?" His voice sounded gruff, hoarse with unshed emotion.

Lucy nodded through her tears, her eyes on his face, begging him.

Inside was a tiny pair of sneakers. A blue onesie with a striped bear embossed on it. And an ultrasound picture.

Begging him to what? To love her anyway, when everyone else had stopped? That was a given.

He touched the little sneakers to his lips. He had not wept since his father died. But he wept now, on Mother's Day, for the baby who would have been his son.

And that's when he saw what she was really begging him for. Someone to share this love with him. The love she had carried alone for too long.

He vowed to himself she would not be alone with it anymore. Not ever.

He saw so clearly what was being given to them both. A chance at redemption. A chance to make good come from bad.

A chance for love to grow from this garden where there had been sorrow.

A long time later they sat in silence, their hands intertwined. The sounds from the party below them grew more boisterous.

The sounds of "I Can't Take My Eyes Off You" floated up through the air.

"You know we would have never made it if I'd asked you to come with me all those years ago."

"I know."

"But I think we could make it now."

She turned to him, her eyes wide with love and hope.

Mac felt now what he could never have felt

back then, as a callow youth. The complexity of loving someone.

"I'm asking you to marry me, Lucy Lin, I'm half crazy all for the love of you."

"Yes," she whispered, and then stronger, "Yes."

"You know, Lucy," he said, softly, his voice still gruff with emotion, "it won't all be a bicycle built for two. There are going to be hurts. And misunderstandings. I have places in me that are so tender they will bruise if you try to touch them. It's going to be a lifelong exercise in building trust."

She leaned her head on his shoulder. "I know what I'm getting into."

He watched the moonlight in her eyes and saw that the light coming from them was radiant.

"I do believe you do, Lucy Lin."

Mac took Lucy in his arms, and her soft warmth melted into him and he thanked God for second chances.

EPILOGUE

MACINTYRE HUDSON SIGHED AS a rush of girl-ish laughter filled the air. Mother's Day was still a whole week away, but Caleb's House, next door to this one, was filled to capacity. There were two trucks with campers on them parked up on the road. No doubt Claudia would be by shortly to complain about that.

There was no official Mother's Day celebration at Caleb's House, but they always came back, those girls, turned into young women, who had stayed there.

They came back whether they had kept their babies or given them up for adoption.

They were drawn back there as if by a spell. Every year, at the same time, they came.

Some came with families—mothers and fathers they had reconciled with, or young husbands who had accepted their history and stepped up to the plate for their future. They came with new young babies and toddlers.

They joined whoever was in residence now, and pretty soon the giggling started and carried across the lawns of that beautiful lavender house to this one.

Mama's house was long since gone. He'd torn it down, and he and Lucy had built a new one. It had what was called a mother-in-law suite, but they moved back and forth between the two living spaces seamlessly. Mama particularly liked their kitchen with all its shiny stainless-steel appliances, even though she didn't make *apfelstrudel* very often anymore.

But it was still *her* house, and ever since the gala, so many of those children Mama had fostered came back on Mother's Day weekend. Came back to the place where they had learned the meaning of home.

Right now, this part of Lakeshore Drive looked like a carnival.

"Did you see this?" Lucy came up behind him.

The funeral-planning kit was out on the table, where they could not miss it.

"Do you know what it's about?" she asked, that cute little worry line puckering her forehead.

"She was staring out the window the other day, lamenting the fact she might not see our children before she dies."

"I guess we should tell her, hmm?" Lucy said.

"No! I don't want her thinking every time she produces that brochure we're going to have a baby for her. Aren't there enough of them next door?"

"Ach," Lucy said, imitating Mama, "a baby is always a blessing."

Those words were a motto, and hung on a smaller sign right below the one that read Caleb's House.

Lucy wrapped her arms around him from behind, nestled into him for a moment and sighed with utter contentment. Then she went to the fridge and took out a jar of Rolliepops.

She popped one in her mouth.

"Those things can't be good for the baby."

"Who are you kidding? You hate kissing me after I've had one. Can't help it. Cravings." She removed a large stainless-steel bowl of potato salad.

"Potluck at Caleb's tonight," Lucy said. "Between Mama's kids and my kids, I think there must be a hundred people out there. Have you seen my mom?"

"She went through here with Donald on her hip a while ago, muttering about diapers." Donald was the baby she had brought back from Africa.

Next year there would be one more added to this amazingly diverse, huge and loving family Mac found himself a part of.

"Are you coming?" Lucy asked. "They'll be starting in a few minutes."

"Give me a minute."

Funny how even after all this time, the sound of his son's name, the son whom had never been born and who he had never known, still squeezed at his heart.

Mac went back to the table. Beside the funeral-planning kit, Mama had set out a card.

He picked it up. On the front it said, "Happy Mother's Day." Inside was completely blank. He set it back down, then went and stood at the window and looked over the familiar sparkling waters of Sunshine Lake.

His own child would be coming into this world soon.

It would require more of him.

Love required more of him. He had thought

it would be a lifetime exercise to build trust, but he had never been so wrong.

He trusted Lucy implicitly. He trusted himself to be the man she and Mama believed he was. He trusted in life. Hadn't it become joyous and sweet beyond his wildest dreams?

Mac fished through the junk drawer until he found a pen, and then he went and sat down at the old kitchen table that they could never replace. It was the *apfelstrudel* table. He stared at the card for a long time, and then opened it.

How to start?

And so he started like this.

Dear Mom,

Not too much. A few lines. That she would be a grandmother soon. That she had not met his wife yet. That maybe they could get together the next time he was down east.

He signed it, licked the envelope, addressed it and put a stamp on. Maybe, just maybe, they would have a chance to redeem themselves.

Mama waddled in and went right to the fridge. "Where's the potato salad? My German one. Not like the stuff they call potato salad here."

"Lucy took it already."

"Are you coming, my galoot-head? Listen. They're singing grace."

All those voices raised in a joyous song of thanks. His Lucy would be at the very center of it, where she belonged.

"I'll be along in minute. I'm going to run up to the mailbox first."

Mama's eyes shot to the table, where the card had been.

Mac thought you could live for moments like this: a heart filled with love, the sound of gratitude drifting in the window and a smile like the one Mama gave him.

* * * * *

Her Royal Wedding Wish

CHAPTER ONE

JAKE RONAN TOOK a deep, steadying breath, the same kind he would take and hold right before the shot or the assault or the jump.

No relief. His heart was beating like a deer three steps ahead of a wolf pack. His palms were slick with sweat.

He was a man notorious for keeping his cool. And in the past three years that notoriety had served him well. He'd taken a hijacked plane back from the bad guys, jumped from ten thousand feet in the dead of night into territory controlled by hostiles, rescued fourteen schoolchildren from a hostage taking.

But in the danger-zone department nothing did him in like a wedding. He shrugged, rolled his shoulders, took another deep breath.

His old friend, Colonel Gray Peterson, recently retired, the reason Ronan was here on the tiny tropical-island paradise of B'Ranasha, shifted uneasily beside him. Under his breath he said a word that probably had never been said in a church before. "You don't have your *sideways* feeling, do you?" Gray asked.

Ronan was famous among this tough group of men, his comrades-in-arms, for the *feeling,* a sixth sense that warned him things were about to go wrong, in a big way.

"I just don't like weddings," he said, keeping his voice deliberately hushed. "They make me feel uptight."

Gray contemplated that as an oddity. "Jake," he finally said reassuringly, his use of Ronan's first name an oddity in itself, "it's not as if you're the one getting married. You're part of the security team. You don't even know these people."

Ronan had never been the one getting married, but his childhood had been littered with his mother's latest attempt to land the perfect man. His own longing for a normal family, hidden under layers of adolescent belligerence, had usually ended in disillusionment long before the day of yet another elaborate wedding ceremony, his mother exchanging

starry-eyed "I do's" with yet another temporary stepfather.

Ronan had found a family he enjoyed very
much when he'd followed in his deceased father's footsteps, over his mother's strenuous
and tear-filled protests, and joined the Australian military right out of high school. Finally, there had been structure, predictability
and genuine camaraderie in his life.

And then he'd been recruited for a multina-
tional military unit that was a first-response
team to world crises. The unit, headquartered
in England, was comprised of men from the
most elite special forces units around the
world. They had members from the British
Forces SAS, from the French Foreign Legion,
from the U.S. SEALs and Delta Force.

His family became a tight-knit brotherhood
of warriors. They went where angels feared
to go; they did the work no one else wanted
to do; they operated in the most dangerous
and troubled places in the world. As well as
protecting world figures at summits, confer-
ences, peace talks, they dismantled bombs,
gathered intelligence, took back planes, rescued hostages, blew up enemy weapons
caches. They did the world's most difficult

work. They did it quickly, quietly and anonymously. There were few medals, little acknowledgment, no back-patting ceremonies.

But there was: brutal training, exhausting hours, months of deep cover and more danger than playing patty-cake with a rattlesnake.

When Ronan had been recruited, he had said a resounding yes. A man knew exactly when his natural-born talents intersected with opportunity, and from his first day in the unit, code-named Excalibur, he had known he had found what he was born to do.

A family, other than his brothers in arms, was out of the question. This kind of work was unfair to the women who were left at home. A man so committed to a dangerous lifestyle was not ready to make the responsibilities of a family and a wife his priority.

Which was a happy coincidence for a man who had the wedding *thing* anyway. Ronan's most closely guarded secret was that he, fearless fighting man, pride of Excalibur, would probably faint from pure fright if he ever had to stand at an altar like the one at the front of this church as a groom. As a man waiting for his bride.

So far, no one was standing at it, though on

this small island, traditions were slightly reversed. He'd been briefed to understand that the bride would come in first and wait for the groom.

Music, lilting and lovely, heralded her arrival, but above the notes Ronan heard the rustle of fabric and slid a look down the aisle of the church. A vision in ivory silk floated slowly toward them. The dress, the typical wedding costume of the Isle of B'Ranasha, covered the bride from head to toe. It was unfathomable how something so unrevealing could be so sensual.

But it was. The gown clung to the bride's slight curves, accentuated the smooth sensuality of her movements. It was embroidered in gold thread that caught the light and thousands of little pearls that shimmered iridescently.

The reason Ronan was stationed so close to the altar was that this beautiful bride, Princess Shoshauna of B'Ranasha, might be in danger.

Since retiring from Excalibur, Gray had taken the position as head of security for the royal family of B'Ranasha. With the upcoming wedding, he'd asked Ronan if he wanted to take some leave and help provide extra security. At first Gray had presented the job as a bit of a lark—beautiful island, beautiful women, unbeatable climate, easy job, lots of off-time.

But by the time Ronan had gotten off the plane, the security team had intercepted a number of threats aimed directly at the princess, and Gray had been grim-faced and tense. The colonel was certain they were generating from within the palace itself, and that a serious security breach had developed within his own team.

"Look at the lady touching the flowers," Gray said tersely.

Ronan spun around, amazed by how much discipline it took to take his eyes off the shimmering vision of that bride. A woman at the side of the church was fiddling with a bouquet of flowers. She kept glancing nervously over her shoulder, radiating tension.

There it was, without warning, that sudden downward dip in his stomach, comparable to a ten-story drop on a roller coaster.

Sideways.

Surreptitiously Ronan checked his weapon, a 9mm Glock, shoulder holstered. Gray noticed, cursed under his breath, tapped his own hidden weapon, a monstrosity that members of Excalibur liked to call the Cannon.

Ronan felt himself shift, from a guy who hated weddings to one hundred percent warrior. It was moments exactly like this that he trained for.

The bride's gown whispered as she walked to the front.

Gray gave him a nudge with his shoulder. "You're on her," he said. "I'm on the flower lady."

Ronan nodded, moved as close to the altar as he could without drawing too much attention to himself. Now he could smell the bride's perfume, tantalizing, as exotic and beautiful as the abundant flowers that bloomed in profusion in every open space of this incredible tropical hideaway.

The music stopped. Out of the corner of his eye, he saw the flower lady duck. *Now,* he thought, and felt every muscle tense and coil, *ready.*

Nothing happened.

An old priest came out of the shadows at the front of the chapel, his golden face tranquil, his eyes crinkled with good humor and acceptance. He wore the red silk robe of a traditional B'Ranasha monk.

Ronan felt Gray's tension beside him. They exchanged glances. Gray's hand now rested inside his jacket. His facade of complete calm did not fool Ronan. His buddy's hand was now resting on the Cannon. Despite the unchanging expression on Gray's face, Ronan felt the shift in mood, recognized it as that *itching* for action, battle fever.

The sideways feeling in Ronan's stomach intensified. His brain did a cool divide, right down the middle. One part of him watched the priest, the bride. The groom would arrive next. One part of him smelled perfume and noted the exquisite detail on her silk dress.

On the other side of the divide, Ronan had become pure predator, alert, edgy, ready.

The bride lifted her veil, and for just a split second his warrior edge was gone. Nothing could have prepared Jake Ronan for the fact he was looking into the delicate, exquisite perfect features of Princess Shoshauna of B'Ranasha.

His preparation for providing security for the wedding had included learning to recognize all the members of the royal families, especially the prospective bride and groom, but there had never been any reason to meet them.

He had been able to view Shoshauna's photographs with detachment: young, pretty, pampered. But those photos had not prepared him for her in the flesh. Her face, framed by a shimmering black waterfall of straight hair, was faintly golden and flawless. Her eyes were almond shaped, tilted upward, and a shade of turquoise he had seen only once before, in a bay where he'd surfed in his younger days off the coast of Australia.

She blinked at him, then looked to the back of the room.

He yanked himself away from the tempting vision of her. It was very bad to lose his edge, his sense of mission, even for a split second. A warning was sounding deep in his brain.

And in answer to it, the back door of the church whispered open. Ronan glanced back. Not the prince. A man in black. A hood over his face. A gun.

Long hours of training had made Ronan an extremely adaptable animal. His mission instantly crystallized; his instincts took over.

His mission became to protect the princess.

In an instant she was the focus of his entire existence. If he had to, he would lay down his life to keep her safe. No hesitation. No doubt. No debate.

The immediate and urgent goal: remove Princess Shoshauna from harm's way. That meant for the next few minutes, things were going to get plenty physical. He launched himself at her, registered the brief widening of those eyes, before he shoved her down on the floor, shielding her body with his own.

Even beneath the pump of pure adrenaline, a part of him *felt* the exquisite sweetness of her curves, felt a need beyond the warrior's response trained into him—something far more primal and male—to protect her fragility with his own strength.

A shot was fired. The chapel erupted into bedlam.

"Ronan, you're covered," Gray shouted. "Get her out of here."

Ronan yanked the princess to her feet, put his body between her and the attacker, kept his hand forcefully on the fragile column of her neck to keep her down.

He got himself and the princess safely behind the relative protection of the stone altar, pushed her through an opening into the priest's vestibule. There Ronan shattered the only window and shoved Princess Shoshauna through it, trying to protect her from the worst of the broken glass with his own arm.

Her skirt got caught, and most of it tore away, which was good. Without the layers of fabric, he discovered she could run like a deer. They were in an alleyway. He kept his hand at the small of her back as they sprinted away from the church. In the background he heard the sound of three more shots, screams.

The alley opened onto a bright square, postcard pretty, with white stucco storefronts, lush palms, pink flowers the size of basketballs. A cabdriver, oblivious to the backdrop of firecracker noises, was in his front seat, door open, slumbering in the sun. Ronan scanned the street. The only other vehicle was a donkey cart for tourists, the donkey looking as sleepy as the cabdriver.

Ronan made his decision, pulled the unsuspecting driver from his cab and shoved the princess in. She momentarily got hung up on the gearshift. He shoved her again, and she plopped into the passenger seat. He then jumped in behind her, turned the key and slammed the vehicle into gear.

Within seconds the sounds of gunfire and the shouted protests of the cabdriver had faded in the distance, but he kept driving, his brain pulling up maps of this island as if he had an Internet search program.

"Do you think everyone's all right back there?" she asked. "I'm worried about my grandfather."

Her English was impeccable, her voice a silk scarf—soft, sensual, floating across his neck as if she had actually touched him.

He shrugged the invisible hand away, filed it under *interesting* that she was more worried about her grandfather than the groom. And he red-flagged it that the genuine worry on her face made him feel a certain unwanted softness for her.

Softness was not part of his job, and he liked to think not part of his nature, either, trained out of him, so that he could make clinical, precise decisions that were not emotionally driven. On the other hand he'd been around enough so-called important people to be able to appreciate her concern for someone other than herself.

"No one was hit," he said gruffly.

"How could you know that? I could hear gunfire after we left."

"A bullet makes a different sound when it hits than when it misses."

She looked incredulous and skeptical. "And with everything going on, you were listening for that?"

"Yes, ma'am." Not listening for that *exactly,* but listening. He had not heard the distinctive *ka-thunk* of a hit, nor had he heard sounds that indicated someone badly hurt. Details. Every member of Excalibur was trained to pay attention to details that other people missed. It was amazing how often something that seemed insignificant could mean the difference between life and death.

"My grandfather has a heart problem," she said softly, worried.

"Sorry." He knew he sounded insincere, and at this moment he was. He only cared if one person was safe, and that was her. He was not risking a distraction, a misdirection of energy, by focusing on anything else.

As if to challenge his focus, his cell phone vibrated in his pocket. He had turned it off for the wedding, because his mother had taken to leaving him increasingly frantic messages that she had *big* news to share with him. Big news in her life always meant one thing: a new man, the proclamation it was *different* this time, more extravagant wedding plans.

Some goof at Excalibur, probably thinking it was funny, had given her his cell number against his specific instructions. But a glance at the caller ID showed it was not his mother but Gray.

"Yeah," he answered.

"Clear here."

"Here, too. Aurora—" he named the princess in Sleeping Beauty, a reference that was largely cultural, that might not be understood by anyone listening "—is fine."

"Excellent. We have the perp. No one injured. The guy was firing blanks. He could have been killed. What kind of nutcase does that?"

He contemplated that for a moment and came up with *one who wants to stop the wedding.* "Want me to bring her back in? Maybe they could still go ahead with the ceremony."

Details. The princess flinched ever so slightly beside him.

"No. Absolutely not. Something's wrong

here. Really wrong. Nobody should have been able to penetrate the security around that wedding. It has to be someone within the palace, so I don't want her back here until I know who it is. Can you keep her safe until I get to the bottom of it?"

Ronan contemplated that. He had a handgun and two clips of ammunition. He was a stranger to the island and was now in possession of a stolen vehicle, not to mention a princess.

Despite circumstances not being anywhere near perfect, he knew in his business perfect circumstances were in short supply. It was a game of odds, and of trust in one's own abilities. "Affirmative," he said.

"I can't trust my phone, but we can probably use yours once more to give you a time frame and set a rendezvous."

"All right." He should have hung up, but he made the mistake of glancing at her pinched face. "Ah, Gray? Is her grandfather all right?"

"Slamming back the Scotch." Gray lowered his voice, "Though he actually seems a little, er, pleased, that his granddaughter didn't manage to get married."

Ronan pocketed his phone. "Your grand-father's fine."

"Oh, that's wonderful news! Thank you!"

"I can't take you back just yet, though."

Some finely held tension disappeared from her shoulders, as if she allowed herself to start breathing after holding her breath.

Eyes that had been clouded with worry, suddenly tilted upward when she smiled. If he was not mistaken, and he rarely was, given his gift with details, a certain mischief danced in their turquoise depths.

She did not inquire about the groom, and now that her concerns for her grandfather had been relieved, she didn't look anything like a woman who had just had her wedding cer-emony shattered by gunfire, her dress shred-ded. In fact, she looked downright happy. As if to confirm that conclusion, she took off her bridal headdress, held it out the window and let the wind take it. She laughed with delight as it floated behind them, children chasing it down the street.

The wind billowing through the open win-dow caught at the tendrils of her hair, and she shook it all free from the remaining pins that held it, and it spilled down over the slenderness of her shoulders.

If he was not mistaken, Princess Shoshauna was very much enjoying herself.

"Look, Your Highness," he said, irritated. "This is not a game. Don't be throwing anything else out the window that will make us easy to follow or remember."

She tossed her hair and gave him a look that was faintly mutinous. Obviously, because of her position, she was not accustomed to being snapped at. But that was too bad. There was only room for one boss here, and it wasn't going to be her.

With the imminent danger now at bay, at least temporarily, his thought processes slowed, and he began to sort information. His assessment of the situation wasn't good. He had been prepared to do a little wedding security, not to find himself in possession of a princess who had someone trying to kill her.

He didn't know the island. He had no idea where he could take her where it would be secure. He had very little currency, and at some point he was going to have to feed her, and get her out of that all-too-attention-grabbing outfit. He had to assume that whoever was after her would be sophisticated enough to trace credit card use. Ditto for his cell phone. They could use it once more to arrange a time and place for a rendezvous and then he'd have to pitch it. On top of that, he had to assume this vehicle had already been reported stolen; it would have to be ditched soon.

On the plus side, she was alive, and he planned to keep it that way. He had a weapon, but very little ammunition.

He was going to have to use the credit card once. To get them outfitted. By the time it was traced, they could be a long way away.

"Do you have any enemies?" he asked her. If he had one more phone call with Gray, maybe he could have some information for him. Plus, it would help him to know if this threat was about something personal or if it was politically motivated. Each of those scenarios made for a completely different enemy.

"No," she said, but he saw the moment's hesitation.

"No one hates you?"

"Of course not." But again he sensed hesitation, and he pushed.

"Who do you think did this?" he asked. "What's your gut feeling?"

"What's a gut feeling?" she asked, wide-eyed.

"Your instinct."

"It's silly."

"Tell me," he ordered.

"Prince Mahail was seeing a woman before he asked me to marry him. She's actually a cousin of mine. She acted happy for me, but—"

Details. People chose to ignore them, which was too bad. "Your instincts aren't silly," he told her gruffly. "They could keep you alive. What's her name?"

"I don't want her to get in trouble. She probably has nothing to do with this."

The princess wasn't just choosing to ignore her instincts, but seemed *determined* to. Still, he appreciated her loyalty.

"She won't be in trouble." *If she didn't do anything.* "Her name?"

"Mirassa," she said, but reluctantly.

"Now tell me how to find a market. A small one, where I can get food. And something for you to wear."

"Oh," she breathed. "Can I have shorts?" She blinked at him, her lashes thick as a chimney brush over those amazing ocean-bay eyes.

He tried not to sigh audibly. Wasn't that just like a woman? Even a crisis could be turned into an opportunity to shop!

"I'm getting what draws the least attention to you," he said, glancing over at her long legs exposed by her torn dress. "I somehow doubt that's going to be shorts."

"Am I going to wear a disguise?" she asked, thrilled.

She was determined not to get how serious this was. And maybe that was good. The last thing he needed was hysteria.

"Sure," he said, going along, "you get to wear a disguise."

"You could pretend to be my boyfriend," Princess Shoshauna said, with way too much enthusiasm. "We could rent a motorcycle and blend in with the tourists. How long do you think you'll have to hide me?"

"I don't know yet. Probably a couple of days."

"Oh!" she said, pleased, determined to perceive this life-and-death situation as a grand adventure. "I have always wanted to ride a motorcycle!"

The urge to strangle her was not at all in keeping with the businesslike, absolutely emotionless attitude he needed to have around her. That attitude would surely be jeopardized further by pretending to be her boyfriend, by sharing a motorcycle with her. His mind went there—her pressed close, her crotch pressed into the small of his back, the bike throbbing underneath them.

Buck up, soldier, he ordered himself. *There's going to be no motorcycle.*

"I'll cut my hair," she decided.

It was the first reasonable idea she had presented, but he was aware he wasn't even considering it. Her hair was long and straight, jet-black and glossy. Her hair was glorious. He wasn't letting her cut her hair, even if it would be the world's greatest disguise.

He knew he was making that decision for all the wrong reasons, and that his professionalism had just slipped the tiniest little notch. There was no denying the *sideways* feeling seemed to have taken up permanent residence in his stomach.

Shoshauna slid the man who was beside her a look and felt the sweetest little dip in the region of her stomach. He was incredibly good-looking. His short hair was auburn, burnt brown with strands of red glinting as the sun struck it. His eyes, focused on the road, were topaz colored, like a lion's. As if the eyes were not hint enough of his strength, there was the formidable set of his lips, the stubborn set of his chin, the flare of his nostrils.

He was a big man, broad and muscled, not like the slighter men of B'Ranasha. When he had thrown her onto the floor of the chapel, she had felt the shock first. No man had ever touched her like that before! Technically, it had been more a tackle than a touch. But then she had become aware of the hard, unforgiving lines of him, felt the strange and forbidden thrill of his male body shielding hers.

Even now she watched as his hands found their way to his necktie, tugged impatiently at it. He loosened it, tugged it free, shoved it in his pocket. Next, he undid the top button of his shirt, rubbed his neck as if he'd escaped the hangman's noose.

"What's your name?" she asked. It was truly shocking, considering how aware she'd felt of him, within seconds of marrying someone else. She glanced at his fingers, was entranced by the shape of them, the faint dusting of hair on the knuckles. Shocked at herself, she realized she could imagine them tangling in her hair.

Of course, she had led a somewhat sheltered life. This was the closest she had ever been, alone, to a man who was not a member of her own family. Even her meetings with her fiancé, Prince Mahail of the neighboring island, had been very formal and closely chaperoned.

"Ronan," he said, and then had to swerve to miss a woman hauling a basket of chickens on her bicycle. He said a delicious-sounding word that she had never heard before, even though she considered her English superb. The little shiver that went up and down her spine told her the word was naughty. Very naughty.

"Ronan." She tried it out, liked how it felt on her tongue. "You must call me Shoshauna!"

"Your Highness, I am not calling you Shoshauna." He muttered the name of a deity under his breath. "I think it's thirty lashes for calling a member of the royal family by their first name."

"Ridiculous," she told him, even though it was true: no one but members of her immediate family would even dare being so familiar as to call her by her first name. That was part of the prison of her role as a member of B'Ranasha's royal family.

But she'd been rescued! Her prayers had been answered just when she had thought there was no hope left, when she had resigned herself to the fact she had agreed to a marriage to a man she did not love.

She did not know how long this reprieve could possibly last, but despite Ronan telling her so sternly this was not a game, Shoshauna intended to make the very most of it. Whether she had been given a few hours or a few days, she intended to be what she might never be again. Free. To be what she had always wanted most to be.

An ordinary girl. With an ordinary life.

She was determined to get a conversation going, to find out as much about this intriguing foreigner as she could. She glanced at his lips and shivered. Would making the most of the gift the universe had handed her include tasting the lips of the intriguing foreigner?

She knew how *wrong* those thoughts were, but her heart beat faster at the thought. How was it that imagining kissing Ronan, a stranger, could fill her with such delirious curiosity, when the thought of what was supposed to have happened tonight, between her and the man who should have become her husband, Prince Mahail, filled her with nothing but dread?

"What nationality are you?"

"Does it matter? You don't have to know anything about me. You just have to listen to me."

His tone, hard and cold, did not sound promising in the kiss department! Miffed, she wondered how he couldn't know that when a princess asked you something, you did not have the option of not answering. Even though she desperately wanted to try life as an ordinary girl, old habit made her give him her most autocratic stare, the one reserved for misbehaving servants.

"Australian," he snapped.

That explained the accent, surely as delicious sounding as the foreign phrase he had uttered so emphatically when dodging the chicken bicycle. She said the word herself, out loud, using the same inflection he had.

The car swerved, but he regained control instantly. "Don't say that word!" he snapped at her, and then added, a reluctant after-thought at best, "Your Highness."

"I'm trying to improve my English!"

"What you're trying to do is get me a one-way ticket to a whipping post for teaching the princess curse words. Do they still whip people here?"

"Of course," she lied sweetly. His expression darkened to thunder, but then he looked hard at her, read the lie, knew she was having a little fun at his expense. He made a cynical sound deep in his throat.

"Are women in Australia ever forced to marry men they don't love?" she asked. But the truth was, she had not been *forced*. Not technically. Her father had given her a choice, but it had not been a *real* choice. The weight of his expectation, her own desperate desire to please him, to be of *value* to him had in-fluenced her decision.

Plus, Prince Mahail's surprise proposal had been presented at a low point in her life, just days after her cat, Retnuh, had died.

People said it was just a cat, had been shocked at her level of despair, but she'd had Retnuh since he was a kitten, since she'd been a little girl of eight. He'd been her friend, her companion, her confidante, in a royal household that was too busy to address the needs of one insignificant and lonely little princess.

"Turn here, there's a market down this road."

He took the right, hard, then looked straight ahead.

"Well?" she asked, when it seemed he planned to ignore her.

"People get married all over the world, for all kinds of reasons," he said. "Love is no guarantee of success. Who even knows what love is?"

"I do," she said stubbornly. It seemed her vision of what it was had crystallized after she'd agreed to marry the completely wrong man. But by then it had been too late. In her eagerness to outrun how terrible she felt about her cat, Shoshauna had allowed herself to get totally caught up in the excitement—preparations underway, two islands celebrating, tailors in overtime preparing gowns for all members of both wedding parties, caterers in overdrive, gifts arriving from all over the world—of getting ready for a royal wedding.

She could just picture the look of abject

disappointment on her father's face if she had gone to him and asked to back out.

"Sure you do, Princess."

His tone insinuated she thought love was a storybook notion, a schoolgirl's dream.

"You think I'm silly and immature because I believe in love," she said, annoyed.

"I don't know the first thing about you, what you believe or don't believe. And I don't want to. I have a job to do. A mission. It's to keep you safe. The less I know about you *personally* the better."

Shoshauna felt stunned by that. She was used to interest. Fawning. She could count on no one to tell her what they really thought. Of course, it was all that patently insincere admiration that had made her curl up with her cat at night, listen to his deep purring and feel as if he was the only one who truly got her, who truly loved her for exactly what she was.

If even one person had expressed doubt about her upcoming wedding would she have found the courage to call it off? Instead, she'd been swept along by all that gushing about how wonderful she would look in the dress, how handsome Prince Mahail was, what an excellent menu choice she had made, how exquisite the flowers she had personally picked out.

"There's the market," she said coldly.

He pulled over, stopped her as she reached for the handle. "You are staying right here."

Her arm tingled where his hand rested on it. Unless she was mistaken, he felt a little jolt, too. He certainly pulled away as though he had. "Do you understand? Stay here. Duck down if anyone comes down the road."

She nodded, but perhaps not sincerely enough.

"It's not a game," he said again.

"All right!" she said. "I get it."

"I hope so," he muttered, gave her one long, hard, assessing look, then dashed across the street.

"Don't forget scissors," she called as he went into the market. He glared back at her, annoyed. He hadn't said to be quiet! Besides, she didn't want him to forget the scissors.

She had wanted to cut her hair since she was thirteen. It was too long and a terrible nuisance. It took two servants to wash it and forever to dry.

"Princesses," her mother had informed her,

astounded at her request, "do not cut their hair."

Princesses didn't do a great many things. People who thought it was fun should try it for a day or two. They should try sitting nicely through concerts, building openings, ceremonies for visiting dignitaries. They should try shaking hands with every single person in a receiving line and smiling for hours without stopping. They should try sitting through speeches at formal dinners, being the royal representative at the carefully selected weddings and funerals and baptisms and graduations of the *important* people. They should try meeting a million people and never really getting to know a single one of them.

Shoshauna had dreams that were not princess dreams at all. They were not even big dreams by the standards of the rest of the world, but they were her dreams. And if Ronan thought she wasn't taking what had happened at the chapel seriously, he just didn't get it.

She had given up on her dreams, felt as if they were being crushed like glass under her slippers with every step closer to the altar that she had taken.

But for some reason—maybe she had wished hard enough after all, maybe Retnuh was her protector from another world—she had been given this reprieve, and she felt as if she had to try and squeeze everything she had ever wanted into this tiny window of freedom.

She wanted to wear pants and shorts. She wanted to ride a motorcycle! She wanted to try surfing and a real bathing suit, not the swimming costume she was forced to wear at the palace. A person could drown if they ever got in real water, not a shallow swimming pool, in that getup.

There were other dreams that were surely never going to happen once she was married to the crown prince of an island country every bit as old-fashioned and traditional as B'Ranasha.

Decorum would be everything. She would wear the finest gowns, the best jewels, her manners would have to be forever impeccable, she would never be able to say what she really wanted. In short order she would be expected to stay home and begin producing babies.

But she wanted so desperately to sample life before she was condemned to that. Shoshauna wanted to taste snow. She wanted to go on a toboggan. She felt she had missed something essential: a boyfriend, like she had seen in movies. A boyfriend would be fun— someone to hold her hand, take her to movies, romance her. A husband was a totally different thing!

For a moment she had hoped she could talk Ronan into a least pretending, but she now saw that was unlikely.

Most of her dreams were unlikely.

Still, a miracle had happened. Here she was beside a handsome stranger in a stolen taxicab, when she should have been married to Prince Mahail by now. She'd known the prince since childhood and did not find him the least romantic, though many others did, including her silly cousin, Mirassa.

Mahail was absurdly arrogant, sure in his position of male superiority. Worse, he did not believe in her greatest dream of all.

Most of all, Shoshauna wanted to be educated, to learn glorious things, and not be restricted in what she was allowed to select for course material. She wanted to sit in classrooms with males and openly challenge the

stupidity of their opinions. She wanted to
learn to play chess, a game her mother said
was for men only.

She knew herself to be a princess of very
little consequence, the only daughter of a
lesser wife, flying well under the radar of
the royal watchdogs. She had spent a great
deal of time, especially in her younger years,
with her English grandfather and had thought
one day she would study at a university in
Great Britain.

With freedom that close, with her dreams
so near she could taste them, Prince Mahail
had spoiled it all, by choosing her as his bride.
Why had he chosen her?

Mirassa had told her he'd been captivated
by her hair! Suddenly she remembered how
Mirassa had looked at her hair in that moment, how her eyes had darkened to black,
and Shoshauna felt a shiver of apprehension.

Before Mahail had proposed to Shoshauna,
rumor had flown that Mirassa was his chosen bride. He had flirted openly with her on
several occasions, which on these islands
was akin to publishing banns. Shoshauna
had heard, again through the rumor mill,
that Mirassa had asked to see him after he

had proposed to Shoshauna and he had humiliated her by refusing her an appointment. Given that he had encouraged Mirassa's affection in the first place, he certainly could have been more sensitive. Just how angry had Mirassa been?

Trust your instincts.

If she managed to cut her hair off before her return maybe Prince Mahail would lose interest in her as quickly as he had gained it and Mirassa would stop being jealous.

Being chosen for her hair was insulting, like being a head of livestock chosen for the way it looked: not for its heart or mind or soul!

The prince had taken his interest to her father, and she had felt as if her father had noticed her, *really* seen her for the very first time. His approval had been drugging. It had made her say yes when she had needed to say no!

Ronan came back to the car, dropped a bag on her lap, reached in and stowed a few more on the backseat. She noticed he had purchased clothing for himself and had changed out of the suit he'd worn. He was now wearing an open-throated shirt that showed his arms: rippling with well-defined muscle, peppered with hairs turned golden by the sun. And he was wearing shorts. She was not sure she had ever seen such a length of appealing male leg in all her life!

Faintly flustered, Shoshauna focused on the bag he'd given her. It held clothing. A large pair of very ugly sunglasses, a hideous hat, a blouse and skirt that looked like a British schoolmarm would be happy to wear.

No shorts. She felt like crying as reality collided with her fantasy.

"Where are the scissors?" she asked.

"Forgot," he said brusquely, and she knew she could not count on him to make any of her dreams come true, to help her make the best use of this time she had been given.

He had a totally different agenda than her. To keep her safe. The last thing she wanted was to be safe. She wanted to be *alive* but in the best sense of that word.

She opened her car door.

"Where the hell are you going?"

"I'm going the *hell* in those bushes, changing into this outfit, as hideous as it is."

"I don't think princesses are supposed to change their clothes in the bushes," he said.

"Or say *hell,* for that matter. Just get in the car and I'll find—"

"I'm changing now." *And then I'm going into that market and buying some things I want to wear.* "And then I'm going into that market and finding the restroom."

"Maybe since you're in the bushes anyway, you could just—"

She stopped him with a look. His mouth snapped shut. He scowled at her, but even he, as unimpressed with her status as he apparently was, was not going to suggest she go to the bathroom in the bushes.

"Don't peek," she said, ducking into the thick shrubbery at the side of the road.

"Lord have mercy," he muttered, whatever that meant.

CHAPTER TWO

RESIGNED, RONAN HOVERED in front of the bushes while she changed, trying to ignore the rustling sound of falling silk.

When she emerged, even he was impressed with how good his choices had been. Princess Shoshauna no longer looked like a member of the royal family, or even like a native to the island.

The women of B'Ranasha had gorgeous hair, their crowning glory. It swung straight and long, black and impossibly shiny past their shoulder blades, and was sometimes ornamented with fresh flowers, but never hidden.

The princess had managed to tuck her abundant locks up under that straw hat, the sunglasses covered the distinctive turquoise of those eyes, and she'd been entirely correct about his fashion sense.

The outfit he'd picked for her looked hideous in exactly the nondescript way he had hoped it would. The blouse was too big, the skirt was shapeless and dowdy, hanging a nice inch or so past her shapely knees. Except for the delicate slippers that showed off the daintiness of her tiny feet, she could have passed for an overweight British nanny on vacation.

As a disguise it was perfect: it hid who she really was very effectively. It worked for him, too. He had effectively covered her curves, made her look about as sexy as a refrigerator box. He knew the last thing he needed was to be too aware of her as a woman, and a beautiful one at that.

He accompanied her across the street, thankful for the sleepiness of the market at this time of day. "Try not to talk to anyone. The washrooms are at the back."

His cell phone vibrated. "Five minutes," he told her, checked the caller ID, felt relieved it was not his mother, though not a number he recognized, either. He watched through the open market door as she went straight to the back, then, certain of her safety, turned his attention to the phone.

"Yeah," he said cautiously, not giving away his identity.

"Peterson."

"That's what I figured."

"How did Aurora take the news that she's going to have to go into hiding?"

"Happily waiting for her prince to come," he said dryly, though he thought a less-true statement had probably never been spoken.

"Can you keep her that way for Neptune?"

Neptune was an exercise that Excalibur went on once a year. It was a week-long training in sea operations. Ronan drew in his breath sharply. A week? Even with the cleverness of the disguise she was in, that was going to be tough on so many levels. He didn't know the island. Still, Gray would never ask a week of him if he didn't absolutely need the time.

Surely the princess would know enough about the island to help him figure out a nice quiet place where they could hole up for a week?

Which brought him to how tough it was going to be on another level: a man and a woman holed up alone for a week. A gorgeous woman, despite the disguise, a healthy man, despite all his discipline.

"Can do." He let none of the doubt he was feeling creep into his tone. He hoped the colonel would at least suggest where, but then realized it would be better if he didn't, considering the possibility Gray's team was not secure.

"We'll meet at Harry's. Neptune swim."

Harry's was a fish-and-chips-style pub the guys had frequented near Excalibur headquarters. The colonel was wisely using references no one but a member of the unit would understand. The Neptune swim was a grueling session in ocean swimming that happened at precisely 1500 hours every single day of the Neptune exercise. So, Ronan would meet Gray in one week, at a British-style pub, or a place that sold fish and chips, presumably close to the palace headquarters at 3 p.m.

"Gotcha." He deliberately did not use communication protocol. "By the way, you need to check out a cousin. Mirassa."

"Thanks. Destroy the phone," the Colonel said.

Every cell phone had a global positioning device in it. Better to get rid of it, something

Ronan had known all along he was going to have to do.

"Will do."

He hung up the phone and peered in the market. The princess had emerged from the back, and was now going through racks of tourist clothing, in a leisurely manner, hangers of clothing already tossed over one arm. Thankfully, despite the darkness of the shop, she still had on the sunglasses.

He went into the shop, moved through the cluttered aisles toward her. If he was not mistaken, the top item of the clothing she had strung over her arm was a bikini, bright neon green, not enough material in it to make a handkerchief.

A week with that? He was disciplined, yes, a miracle worker, no. This was going to be a challenging enough assignment if he managed to keep her dressed like a refrigerator box!

He went up beside her, plucked the bikini off her arm, hung it up on the closest rack. "We're not supposed to attract attention, Aurora. That doesn't exactly fit the bill."

"Aurora?"

"Your code name," he said in an undertone.

"A code name," she breathed. "I like it. Does it mean something?"

"It's the name of the princess in 'Sleeping Beauty.'"

"Well, I'm not waiting for my prince!"

"I gathered that," he said dryly. He didn't want to feel interested in what was wrong with her prince. It didn't have anything to do with getting the job done. He told himself not to ask her why she dreaded marriage so much, and succeeded, for the moment. But he was aware he had a whole week with her to try to keep his curiosity at bay.

"Do you have a code name?" she asked.

He tried to think of the name of a celibate priest, but he wasn't really up on his priests. "No. Let's go."

She glanced at him—hard to read her eyes through the sunglasses—but her chin tilted in a manner that did not bode well for him being the boss. She took the bikini back off the rack, tossed it back over her arm.

"I don't have to wear it," she said mulishly. "I just have to have it. Touch it again, and I'll make a scene." She smiled.

He glanced around uneasily. No other customers in the store, the single clerk, thankfully, far more interested in the daily racing form he was studying than he was in them.

"Let's go," he said in a low voice. "You have enough stuff there to last a year."

"Maybe it will be a year," she said, just a trifle too hopefully, confirming what he already knew—this was one princess not too eager to be kissed by a prince.

"I've had some instructions. A week. We need to disappear for a week."

She grabbed a pair of shorty-shorts.

"We have to go."

"I'm not finished."

He took her elbow, glanced again at the clerk, guided her further back in the room. "Look, Princess, you have a decision to make."

She spotted a bikini on the rack by his head. "I know!" she said, deliberately missing his point. "Pink or green?"

Definitely pink, but he forced himself to remain absolutely expressionless, pretended he was capable of ignoring the scrap of material she was waving in front of his face. Unfortunately, it was just a little too easy to imagine her in that, how the pink would set off the golden tones of her skin and the color of her eyes, how her long black hair would shimmer against it.

He took a deep breath.

"This is about your life," he told her quietly. "Not mine. I'm not going to be more responsible for you than you are willing to be for yourself. So, if you want to take chances with your life, if you want to make my life difficult instead of cooperating, I'll take you back to the palace right now."

Despite the sunglasses, he could tell by the tightening of her mouth that she didn't want to go back to the palace, so he pressed on.

"That would work better for me, actually," he said. "I kind of fell into this. I signed up for wedding security, not to be your bodyguard. I have a commanding officer who's going to be very unhappy with me if I don't report back to work on Tuesday."

He was bluffing. He wasn't taking her back to the palace until Gray had sorted out who was responsible for the attack at the church. And Gray would look after getting word back to his unit that he had been detained due to circumstances beyond his control.

But she didn't have to know that. And if he'd read her correctly, she'd been relieved that her wedding had been interrupted, delirious almost. The last thing she wanted to do was go back to her life, pick up where she'd left off.

He kept talking. "I'm sure your betrothed is very worried about you, anxious to make you his wife, so that he can keep you safe. He's probably way more qualified to do that than I am."

He could see, *clearly,* that he had her full attention, and that she was about as eager to get back to her prince as to swim with crocodiles.

So he said, "Maybe that's the best idea. Head back, a quick secret ceremony, you and your prince can get off the island, have your honeymoon together, and this whole mess will be cleared up by the time you get home."

His alertness to detail paid off now, because her body language radiated sudden tension. He actually felt a little bit sorry for her. She obviously didn't want to get married, and if she had feelings for her fiancé they were not positive ones. But again he had to shut down any sense of curiosity or compassion that he felt. That wasn't his problem, and in protection work, that was the priority: to re-

member his business—the very narrow pe-
rimeters of keeping her safe—and to not care
anything about what was her business.

Whether she was gorgeous, ugly, unhappy
at love, frustrated with her life, none of that
mattered to him. Or should matter to him.

Still, he did feel the tiniest little shiver of
unwanted sympathy as he watched her getting paler before his eyes. He was glad for her
sunglasses, because he didn't want to see her
eyes just now. She put the pink bikini back,
thankfully, but turned and marched to the
counter as if she was still the one in charge,
as if he was her servant left to trail behind
her—and pay the bills.

Apparently paying had not occurred to her.
She had probably never had to handle money
or even a credit card in her whole life. She
would put it on account, or some member of
her staff would look after the details for her.

She seemed to realize that at the counter,
and he could have embarrassed her, but there
was no point, and he certainly did not want
the clerk to find anything memorable about
this transaction.

"I got it, sweetheart," he said easily.

Though playing sweethearts had been her

idea, she was flustered by it. She looked ev-erywhere but at him. Then, without warning, she reached up on tiptoe and kissed him on the cheek.

"Thanks, Charming," she said huskily, ob-viously deciding he needed a code name that matched hers.

But a less-likely prince had never been born, and he knew it.

He hoped the clerk wouldn't look up, be-cause there might be something memorable about seeing a man blushing because his sup-posed lady friend had kissed him and used an odd endearment on him.

Ronan didn't make it worse by looking at her, but he felt a little stunned by the sweet-ness of her lips on his cheek, by the utter soft-ness, the sensuality of a butterfly's wings.

"Oh, look," she said softly, suddenly breath-less. She was tapping a worn sign underneath the glass on the counter.

"Motorcycles for rent. Hour, day, week."

It would be the last time he'd be able to use this credit card, so maybe, despite his ear-lier rejection of the idea, now was the time to change vehicles. Was it a genuinely good idea or had that spontaneous kiss on the cheek rattled him?

He'd already nixed the motorcycle idea in his own mind. Why was he revisiting the decision?

Was he losing his edge? Finding her just too distracting? He had to do his job, to make decisions based solely on what was most likely to bring him to mission success, which was keeping her safe. Getting stopped in a stolen car was not going to do that. Blending in with the thousands of tourists that scootered around this island made more sense.

Since talking to Gray, he wondered if the whole point of the threats against the princess had been to stop the wedding, not harm her personally.

But he knew he couldn't let his guard down because of that. He had to treat the threat to her safety as real, or there would be too many temptations to treat it lightly, to let his guard down, to let her get away with things.

"Please?" she said softly, and then she tilted her sunglasses down and looked at him over the rims.

Her eyes were stunning, the color and depth of tropical waters, filled at this moment with very real pleading, as if she felt her life depended on getting on that motorcycle.

Half an hour later, he had a backpack filled with their belongings, he had moved the car off the road into the thick shrubs beside it and he was studying the motorcycle. It was more like a scooter than a true motorcycle.

He took a helmet from a rack beside the motorcycles.

"Come here."

"I don't want to wear that! I want to feel the wind in my hair."

He had noticed hardly anyone on the island did wear motorcycle helmets, probably because the top speed of these little scooters would be about eighty kilometers an hour. Still, acquiring the motorcycle felt a bit like giving in, and he was done with that. His job was to keep her safe in every situation. Life could be cruelly ironic, he knew. It would be terrible to protect her from an assassin and then get her injured on a motorbike.

"Please, Charming?" she said.

That had worked so well last time, she was already trying it again! It served him right for allowing himself to be manipulated by her considerable charm.

She took off her sunglasses and blinked at him. He could see the genuine yearning in her eyes, but knew he couldn't cave in. This was a girl who was, no doubt, very accustomed to people jumping to make her happy, to wrapping the whole world around her pinky finger.

"Charming isn't a good code name for me," he said.

"Why not?"

"Because I'm not. Charming. And I'm certainly not a prince." To prove both, he added, sternly, "Now, come here and put on the helmet."

"Are you wearing one?"

He didn't answer, just lifted his eyebrow at her, the message clear. She could put on the helmet or she could go home.

Mutinously she snatched the straw hat from her head.

He tried not to let his shock show. In those few unsupervised minutes while he had talked to Gray on the phone, she had gone to the washroom, all right, but not for the reason he had thought or she had led him to believe. Where had she gotten her hands on a pair of scissors? Or maybe, given the raggedness of the cut, she had used a knife.

She was no hairdresser, either. Little chunks of her black hair stood straight up on her head, going every which way. The bangs were crooked. Her ears were tufted. There wasn't a place where her hair was more than an inch and a half long. Her head looked like a newly hatched chicken, covered in dark dandelion fluff. It should have looked tragic.

Instead, she looked adorable, carefree and elfish, a rebel, completely at odds with the conservative outfit he had picked for her. Without the distraction of her gorgeous hair, it was apparent that her bone structure was absolutely exquisite, her eyes huge, her lips full and puffy.

"Where's your hair?" he asked, fighting hard not to let his shock show. He shoved the helmet on her head quickly, before she had any idea how disconcerting he found her new look. His fingers fumbled on the strap buckle, he was way too aware of her, and not at all pleased with his awareness. The perfume he'd caught a whiff of at the wedding tickled his nostrils.

"I cut it."

"I can clearly see that." Thankfully, the mysteries of the helmet buckle unraveled, he

tightened the strap, let his hands fall away.
He was relieved the adorable mess of her hair
was covered. "What did you do with it after
you cut it?"

Her contrite expression told him she had
left it where it had fallen.

"So, you did it for nothing," he said sternly.
"Now, when we're traced this far, and we will
be, they'll find out you cut your hair. And
they'll be looking for a bald girl, easier to
spot than you were before."

"I'm not bald," she protested.

"I've seen better haircuts on new recruits,"
he said. She looked crestfallen, he told himself he didn't care. But he was aware he did,
just a little bit.

"I'll go back and pick up my hair," she said.

"Never mind. Hopefully no one is going
to see you."

"Does it look that bad?"

He could reassure her it didn't, but that
was something Prince Charming might do.
"It looks terrible."

He hoped she wasn't going to cry. She put
her sunglasses back on a little too rapidly. Her
shoulders trembled tellingly.

Don't be a jerk, he told himself. But then

he realized he might be a lot safer in this situation if she did think he was a jerk.

When had his focus switched from her safety to his own?

Rattled, he pushed ahead. "I need you to think very carefully," he said. "Is there a place on this island we can go where no one would find us for a week?"

He tried not to close his eyes after he said it. A week with her, her new haircut and her new green bikini stuffed in the backpack. Not to mention the shorty-shorts, and a halter top that had somehow been among her purchases.

He could see in her eyes she yearned for things that were forbidden to her, things she might not even be totally aware of, things that went far beyond riding on motorcycles and cutting her hair.

Things her husband should be teaching her. Right this minute. He had no right to be feeling grateful that she had not been delivered into the hands of a man she'd dreaded discovering those things with.

Instead she'd been delivered into his hands. One mission: keep her safe. Even from himself.

Still, he was aware he was a warrior, not a

saint. The universe was asking way too much of him.

He turned from her swiftly, got on the motorcycle, persuaded it to life. He patted the seat behind him, not even looking at her.

But not looking at her didn't help. She slid onto the seat behind him. The skirt hiked way up. Out of his peripheral vision he could see the nakedness of her knee. He glanced back. The skirt was riding high up her thigh.

It was a princess like no one had ever seen, of that he was certain. On the other hand, no one would be likely to recognize her looking like this, either.

"Hang on tight," he said.

And then he felt her sweet curves pull hard against him. Oh, sure. For once she was going to listen!

"I know a place," she called into his ear. "I know the perfect place."

His cell phone vibrated in his pocket. He slowed, checked the caller ID. His mother. He wrestled an impulse to answer, to yell at her, Don't do it! Instead he listened to her leave yet another voice mail.

"Ronan, call me. It's so exciting."

They were crossing over a bridge, rushing

water below, and he took the phone and flung it into the water.

He was in the protection business; sometimes it felt as if the whole world was his responsibility. But the truth was he could not now, and never had been able to, protect his own mother from what she most needed protecting from.

Herself.

Shoshauna pressed her cheek up against the delicious hardness of Ronan's shoulder. His scent, soapy and masculine, was stronger than the scent of the new shirt.

Alone with him for a week. In a place where no one could find them. It felt dangerous and exciting and terribly frightening, too. She pressed into him, feeling far more endangered than she had when the gun had gone off in the chapel.

Some kind of trembling had started inside her, and it was not totally because he had hurt her feelings telling her her hair looked terrible. It wasn't totally because of the vibration of the motorbike, either!

"Go faster," she cried.

He glanced over his shoulder at her.

"It doesn't go any faster," he shouted back at her, but he gave it a hit of gas and the little bike surged forward.

Her stomach dropped, and she squealed with delight.

He glanced back again. His lips were twitching. He was trying not to smile. But he did, and his smile was like the sun coming out on the grayest of days. That glimpse of a smile made her forget she had only a short time to squeeze many dreams into, though a week was more than she could have hoped for.

Still, it was as if his smile hypnotized her and made her realize maybe there was one dream he could help make come true. A dream more important than wearing shorts or riding astride or touching snow. A dream that scorned people who pretended all the time.

She had only a few days, and she wanted to be with someone who was real, not kowtowing. Not anxious to please. Not afraid of her position. Someone who would tell her the truth, even if it hurt to hear it.

I'm not going to be more responsible for you than you are willing to be for yourself, he had told her. She shivered. In that simple statement, as much as it had pained her to hear it, was the truth about how her life had gone off track so badly. Could Ronan somehow lead her back to what was real about herself?

When she was younger, there'd been a place she had been allowed to go where she had felt real. Relaxed. As if it was okay to be herself.

Herself—something more and more lost behind the royal mask, the essential facades of good manners, of duty. Something that might be lost forever when she was returned to Prince Mahail as his bride.

"There's an island," she called over the putter of the engine. "My grandparents have a summer place on a small island just north of the mainland. No one is ever there at this time of year."

"No one? No security? No grounds-keeper?"

"It's a private island, but not the posh kind. You'd have to know my grandfather to understand. He hates all the royal fuss-fuss as he calls it. He likes simplicity.

"The island is almost primitive. There's no electricity, the house is like a cottage, it even has a thatched roof."

"Fresh water, or do we have to bring our own?"

"There's a stream." Ronan thought like a soldier, she realized. All she could think about was it would be such a good place to try on her new bikini, such a wonderful place to rediscover who she really was! But, given the strange trembling inside her, how wise would that be? Given the reality of his smile, the pure sexiness of it, was it possible she was headed into a worse danger zone than the one she was leaving?

"Bedding? Blankets?"

His mind, thankfully, a million miles from bikinis, on the more practical considerations. "I think so."

"How do you get to it?"

"My grandfather keeps a boat at the dock across the bay from it."

"Perfect," he said. "Show me the fastest way to the boat dock."

But she didn't tell him the shortest way. She directed him the longest way possible, because who knew if she would ever ride a motorcycle again, her arms wrapped so intimately around a man with such an incredible, sexy smile?

She *loved* the motorcycle, even if she had been deprived of feeling the fingers of the wind playing with her hair. She could still feel the island breeze on her face, playing with the hem of her skirt, touching her legs. She could feel the kiss of warm sunshine. She had a lovely sensation of being connected to everything around her. The air was perfumed, birds and monkeys chattered in the trees. She didn't feel separate from it, she felt like a part of it.

And she could feel the exquisite sensation of being connected to him—her arms wrapped around the hard-muscled bands of his stomach, her cheek resting on the solid expanse of his back, her legs forming a rather intimate vee around him.

Her mother, she knew, would have an absolute fit. And her father wouldn't be too happy with her, either. She could only imagine how Mahail would feel if he saw her now!

Which only added to the delectable sense of dancing with danger that Princess Shoshauna was feeling: free, adventurous, as if anything at all could happen.

Just this morning her whole life had seemed to be mapped out in front of her, her fate inescapable. Now she had hair that Prince Mahail would hate, and she didn't think he'd like it very much that she had spent a week alone with a strange man, either!

"Can you go faster?' she called to Ronan over the wind.

The slightest hesitation, and then he did, opening the bike up so that they were roaring down the twisting highway, until tears formed in her eyes and she could feel the thrill to the bottom of her belly.

She refused to dwell on how long it would last, or if this was the only time she would ever do this.

Instead she threw back her head and laughed out loud for the sheer joy of the moment, at her unexpected encounter with the most heady drug of all—freedom.

CHAPTER THREE

RONAN CUT THE engine of the motorboat, letting it drift in to the deserted beach. He glanced at the princess, asleep in the bottom of the boat, exhausted from the day, and decided there was no need for both of them to get wet. He stood up, stepped off the hull into a gentle surf. The seawater was warm on his legs as he dragged the boat up onto the sand.

It was night, but the sky was breathtaking, star-studded. A full moon frosted each softly lapping wave in white and painted the fine beach sand a bewitching shade of silver.

From a soldier's perspective, the island was perfect. Looking back across the water, he could barely make out the dark outline of the main island of B'Ranasha. He could see the odd light flickering on that distant shore.

He had circled this island once in the boat, a rough reconnaissance. It was only about eight kilometers all the way around it. Better yet, it had only this one protected bay, and only the one beach suitable for landing a boat.

Everywhere else the thick tropical growth, or rocky cliffs, came right to the water's edge. The island was too small and bushed in to land a plane on. It would be a nightmare to parachute in to, and it would be a challenge to land a helicopter here. Planes and helicopters gave plenty of warning they were arriving, anyway.

It was a highly defensible position. Perfect from a soldier's perspective.

But from a personal point of view, from a man's perspective, it couldn't be much worse. It was a deserted island more amazing than a movie set. The sand was white, fine and flawless, exotic birds filled the night air with music, a tantalizing perfume rode the gentle night breeze. Palm trees swayed in the wind, ferns and flowers abounded.

At the head of the beach was a cottage, palm-frond roof, screened porch looking out to the sea. It was the kind of retreat people came to on holidays and honeymoons, not to hide out. Which was a good thing. He highly doubted anyone would think to look for the princess here.

He gave the rope attached to the boat another pull, hauled it further up on the sand until he was satisfied it would be safe, even from the tide, which, according to the tide charts he had purchased at a small seaside village, would come up during the night.

Only then did he peer back at Aurora, his very own Sleeping Beauty. The princess, worn down from all the unscheduled excitement of her wedding day, was curled up in the bottom of the boat, fast asleep on a bed of life jackets.

The silver of the moon washed her in magic, though he felt the shock of her shorn head again, followed by a jolt of a different kind—the short hair did nothing but accentuate her loveliness. Right now he was astonished by the length and fullness of her lashes, casting sooty shadows on the roundness of her cheeks. Her lips moved, forming words in her sleep, something in her own language, *ret-nuh*.

He'd insisted on a life jacket, but the skirt was riding high up her legs, he caught a glimpse of bridal white panties so pure he could feel a certain dryness in his mouth. He reached out and gave the skirt a tug down, whether to save her embarrassment or to save himself he wasn't quite sure.

A deserted island. A beautiful woman. A week. He was no math whiz, but he knew a bad equation when he came across it.

He'd done plenty of protection duty, and though it wasn't his favorite assignment, Ronan prided himself on doing his work well. He'd protected heads of states and their families, politicians, royalty, CEOs.

The person being protected was known amongst the team as the "principal." The team didn't even use personal names when they discussed strategy, formulated plans. The cardinal rule, the constant in protection work, was maintaining a completely professional, arm's-length relationship. Emotional engagement compromised the mission, period.

But the very circumstances of those other assignments made maintaining professionalism easy. The idea of forming any kind of deeper relationship or even a friendship, with the principal had been unthinkable. There was always a team, never just one person.

There was always an environment conducive to maintaining preordained boundaries.

Ronan was in brand-new territory, and he didn't like it. So, before he woke her up, he looked to the stars, gathered his strength, reminded himself of the mission, the boundaries, the *rules*.

"Hey," he called softly, finally, "wake up."

She stirred but didn't wake, and he leaned into the boat and nudged her shoulder with his hand. She was slender as a reed, the roundness of her shoulder the epitome of feminine softness.

"Princess." It would be infinitely easy to reach in and scoop her up, to carry her across the sand to that cottage, but that brief contact with her shoulder was fair warning it would be better not to add one little bit of physical contact to the already volatile combination.

A bad time to think of her lips on his cheek earlier in the day, her slight curves pressed hard against him on that motorcycle.

"Wake up," he said louder, more roughly.

She did, blinked—that blank look of one who couldn't quite place where they were. And then she focused on him and smiled in a way that could melt even the most professional soldier's dedication to absolute duty.

She sat up, looked around and then sighed with contentment. She liked being here. She had liked the entire day way too much! He had not been nearly as immune to her laughter and her arms wrapped around him as he had wanted to be, but thankfully she didn't have to know that!

She shrugged out of the life jacket and then stretched, pressing the full sensuous roundness of her breasts into the thin fabric of the ill-fitting blouse. Then she stood up. The boat rocked on the sand, and the physical contact he wanted so badly not to happen, happened anyway. He caught her, steadied her as the boat rocked on the uneven ground. She took one more step, the boat pitched, and she would have gone to her knees.

Except his hands encircled her waist nearly completely, the thumb and index finger of his right hand nearly touching those of his left. He lifted her from the boat, swung her onto the sand, amazed by her slightness. She didn't weigh any more than a fully loaded combat pack.

"You're strong!" she said.

He withdrew from her swiftly, not allowing himself to preen under her admiration. A week. They had to make it a week.

"It's beautiful, isn't it?" she asked, hugging herself, apparently oblivious to his discomfort. "I love it here. My grandfather called it Naidina Karobin—it means something like *my heart is home*."

Great.

"Isn't that pretty?"

"Yeah, sure." Real men didn't use words like *pretty*. Except maybe in secret, when they looked at a face like hers, washed in moonlight, alive with discovery. *Mission.*

He reached into the boat and grabbed the knapsack. As he followed her across the sand toward the cottage, he noted that the trees in the grove around it were loaded with edible fruits, coconuts, bananas, mangos.

He'd landed in the Garden of Eden. He only hoped he could resist the apple. *Boundaries.*

As they got closer, the princess jacked her skirt up and ran, danced really, across the sand. She looked like some kind of moonlit nymph, her slender legs painted in silver. *Rules, duty, professionalism.*

He followed her more slowly, as if he could

put off the moment when they set up house-keeping together and everything intensified yet more.

Becoming part of Excalibur, Ronan's endurance, physical strength, intellectual assets, ability to cope with stress had all been tested beyond normal limits. One man in twenty who was recruited for that unit made it through the selection process. Membership meant being stronger, faster, tougher in mind and spirit than the average man.

And yet to share the space of that cottage on this island with a real-live sleeping beauty seemed as if it would test him in ways he had never been tested before.

Ronan had been in possession of the princess for less than twenty-four hours and he already felt plenty tested!

He drew a deep breath as he followed her up wide steps to the screen door that he thought had been a screened-in veranda. As his eyes adjusted to the lack of moonlight inside, he saw he had been mistaken.

It was not a screened porch, but a screened-in house. A summer house, she'd said, obviously designed so that it caught the breeze from every angle on hot summer nights. The huge overhang of the roof would protect it from the rare days of inclement weather these islands experienced.

White, sheer curtains lifted and fell in the breeze, making the inside of the house enchanting and exotic. The main room had dark, beautiful wooden floors, worn smooth from years of use, moonlight spilling across them. Deeply cushioned, colorful rattan furniture was grouped casually around a coffee table, a space that invited conversation, relaxation.

Intimacy.

At the other end of the room was a dining area, the furniture old, dark, exquisitely carved and obviously valuable. That such good furniture would be left out in an unlocked cottage should have reassured him how safe the island was. But Ronan was a little too aware that the dangers here could come from within, not without.

The screens as walls gave a magnificent illusion of there being no separation between the indoor living space and the outdoors.

He spied a hurricane lamp and lit it, hoping the light would chase away the feeling of enchantment, but instead, in the flickering golden light, the great room became down-right romantic, soft, sultry, sensual.

The light was soft on her face, too, her expression rapt as she looked around, her eyes glowing with the happiness of memories.

Ronan would have liked it a lot better if she was spoiled rotten, complaining about spider-webs and the lack of electricity.

To distance himself from the unwanted *whoosh* of attraction he felt, Ronan went hurriedly across the room to investigate a door at the back of it. It led to an outdoor kitchen, and he went out. The outdoor cooking space was complete with a huge wood-fired oven and a grill. Open shelves were lined with canned goods. A person could camp out here, on this island, comfortably, for a year.

Beyond that, in a flower- and fern-encir-cled grove was an open-air shower, and the *whoosh* he'd been trying to outrun came back.

He reentered the house reluctantly, thankful he didn't see her right away. He finished his inventory of the main house: there were two rooms off the great room, and he entered the first. It was the main bedroom, almost entirely taken up by a huge bed framed with soaring rough timbers, dark with age, more sheer white curtains flowing around the bed, surrounding it. Again the screens acting as outer walls made the bed seem to be set right amongst the palms and mango trees. The perfume of a thousand different flowers tickled his nose. There was no barrier to sound, either. The sea whispered poetry. He backed hastily out of there.

Princess Shoshauna was in the smaller of the bedrooms, looking around and hugging herself.

"This is where I always stayed when I was a child! Look how it feels as if you are right outside! My grandfather designed this house. He was an architect. That's how he came to be on B'Ranasha. I'll have this room."

He would have much preferred she take the bigger room, act snotty and entitled so he could kill the *whoosh* in his stomach.

"I think you should take the bigger room," he suggested. "You are the princess."

"Not this week I'm not." She smiled, delighted to have declared herself not a princess.

If she wasn't a princess, if she was just an ordinary girl…he cut off the train of his thought. It didn't matter if she was a wandering gypsy. She was still the *principal,* and it was still his mission to protect her.

He reached into his pocket, took out a pocketknife and cut the cord that kept the mattress rolled up. He found the bedding in a tightly closed trunk under the bed. A floral sachet had been packed with it, and the white linen sheets smelled exotic.

He laid them quickly on the bed, then watched, bemused, when she eyed the pile of bedding as though it were an interesting but baffling jigsaw puzzle.

"You don't know how to make a bed," he guessed, incredulous, then wondered why it would surprise him that a princess had no idea how to make a bed.

The truth was, it would be way too easy to forget she was a princess, especially with her standing there with shorn hair, and in a badly rumpled and ill-fitting dress.

But that was exactly what he had to remember, to keep his boundaries clear, his professionalism unsullied, his duty foremost in his mind. She was a princess, a real one. He was a soldier. Their stations in life were millions of miles apart. And they were going to stay that way.

"My mother would never have allowed it," she said, sadly. "She had this idea that to do things that could be done by servants was *common*. Of course, she was a commoner, and she never quite overcame her insecurity about it."

She didn't know how to make a bed.

Every soldier had been tormented, at one time or another, with making a bed that could satisfy a drill sergeant who had no intention of being satisfied. Ronan could make a bed—perfectly—anywhere, anytime.

To focus on the differences between them would strengthen his will. To perceive her as pampered and useless would go a long way in erasing the memory of her slender curves pressed into his back as they rode that motorcycle together.

"I'd be happy to make it for you, Princess," he said.

She glared at him. "I don't want you to make it for me! I want you to show me how to make it."

He was tired. He had not had the benefit of a two hour nap in the bottom of the boat. She had slept for an hour or so before that, as well, while they had waited, hidden, for it to get dark enough to take her grandfather's boat from the dock and cross the water without being seen.

It would be easier for him to make the bed himself, but he had to get through a full week, and that wasn't going to be easy if he argued with her over little things.

His eyes went to the full puffiness of her lips, and he felt his own weariness, his resolve flickering.

He had to get though a full week without kissing her, too.

Making a bed together didn't seem like a very good starting point for keeping things professional and distant. Neither did fighting with her.

He had the uneasy feeling he'd better adjust to being put in no-win positions by the princess.

He separated the sheets from the blankets, found the bottom sheet and tossed it over the mattress.

"First you tuck this under the mattress," he said.

"I'll do it!" she said, when he reached out to demonstrate.

He held up his hands in surrender, stood

back, tried not to wince at her sloppy corners, the slack fabric in the center of the bed. He didn't offer to help as she grunted over lifting the corners of the mattress.

He handed her the second sheet, tried to stay expressionless as she shoved it under the bottom of the mattress in such a bunched-up mess that the mattress lifted.

She caught the tip of her tongue between her teeth as she focused with furious concentration on the task at hand. He folded his arms firmly over his chest.

She inserted the pillows in the cases with the seams in the wrong places and fluffed them. Then he handed her the top blanket, which she tossed haphazardly on top of the rest of her mess.

The bed was a buck private's nightmare, but she smiled with pleasure at her final result. To his eye, it looked more like a nest than a well-made bed.

"See?" she said. "I can do ordinary things."

"Yes," he said, deadpan. "I can clearly see that."

Something in his tone must have betrayed him, because she searched his face with grave suspicion.

A drill sergeant would have had the thrill of ripping it apart and making her do it again, but he wasn't a drill sergeant. In fact, at the moment he was just an ordinary guy, trying to survive.

"Okay," he said, "if you have everything—"

"Oh, I'll make yours, too. For practice."

"What do you need practice making a bed for?" he asked crankily. He didn't want her touching his bedding.

He was suddenly acutely aware of how alone they were here, of how the dampness of the sea air was making the baggy dress cling to her, of how her short hair was curling slightly from humidity, and there seemed to be a dewy film forming on her skin. He was aware of how her tongue had looked, caught between her teeth.

Ignoring him, she marched right by him into his room. He trailed behind her reluctantly, watched as she opened the trunk where the linens were kept and began tossing them on his bed.

"I'm going to do all kinds of ordinary things this week," she announced.

"Such as?" He didn't offer to help her make

the bed, just watched, secretly aghast at the mess she was making.

"Cooking!" she decided.

"I can hardly wait."

He got the suspicious look again.

"Washing dishes. Doing laundry. You can show me those things, can't you?"

She sounded so enthused he thought she must be pulling his leg, but he could tell by the genuine eager expression on her face she really wasn't.

How did a man maintain professional distance from a princess who wanted nothing more than to be an ordinary girl, who was enthralled at the prospect of doing the most ordinary of things?

He nodded cautiously.

"I would like to learn how to sew on a button," she decided. "Do you know how to do that?"

Sewing buttons, insignia, pant hems, was right up there with making beds in a soldier's how-to arsenal, but she didn't wait for him to answer.

"And I can't wait to swim in the ocean! I used to swim here when I was a child. I love it!"

He thought of that bikini in their backpack, closed his eyes, marshaling strength.

"You don't happen to know how to surf, do you?" she asked him. "There used to be a surfboard under the cottage. I hope it's still there!"

His boyhood days had been spent on a surfboard. It was probably what had saved him from delinquency, his love of the waves, his *need* to perfect the dance with the extraordinary, crashing power of them.

"This bay doesn't look like it would ever get much in the way of surf," he told her. "It's pretty protected."

She looked disappointed, but then brightened. "There's snorkeling equipment under there, too. Maybe we can do that."

We, as if they were two kids together on vacation. Now would be the time to let her know he had no intention of being her playmate, but he held his tongue.

She gave his bed a final, satisfied pat. "Well, good night Ronan. I can't wait for tomorrow." She blew him a kiss, which was only slightly better than the one she had planted on his cheek earlier in the day.

He rubbed his cheek, aggravated, as if the kiss had actually landed, an uncomfortably whimsical thought for a man who prided himself on his pragmatic nature. He listened for her to get into her own bed, then went on silent feet and checked each side of the cabin.

The night was silent, except for the night birds. The ocean was dark and still, the only lights were from the moon and stars, the few lights on the mainland had winked out.

He went back into his bedroom. He knew he needed to sleep, that it would help him keep his thinking clear and disciplined. He also knew he had acquired, over the years, that gift peculiar to soldiers of sleeping in a state of readiness. Any sound that didn't belong would awaken him instantly. His highly developed sixth sense would guard them both through the night.

He shrugged out of his shirt but left the shorts on. He certainly didn't want her to ever see him in his underwear, and he might have to get out of bed quickly in the night. He climbed into bed. It had to be his imagination that her perfume lingered on the sheets. Still, tired as he was, he tossed and turned until finally, an hour later, he got out of the bed, remade it *perfectly*. He got back in and slept instantly.

Shoshauna awoke to light splashing across her bed, birdsong, the smell and sound of the sea.

She remembered she was on her grandfather's island and thought to herself, my heart *is* home. She remembered her narrow escape from marriage, the unexpected gifts yesterday: riding the motorcycle, buying the daring bathing suit and shorty-shorts.

Kissing Ronan on the cheek. Feeling the muscles of his back as they shared the motorcycle, feeling his hands encircle her waist.

Ronan was a gloriously made man, all hard muscle, graceful efficiency of movement, easy, unconscious strength, a certain breathtaking confidence in his physical abilities. Add to that the soft, firm voice, his accent. And his eyes! A soldier's eyes to be sure, stern, forbidding even. But when the mask slipped, when they glinted with laughter, she felt this uncontrollable—and definitely wicked—shiver of pure wanting. He made her feel such an amazing mixture of things: excited and shy, aggravated, annoyed, *alive*.

Shoshauna knew it was wrong to be thinking like that. She was promised to another. And yet…if you could pick a man to spend a week on a deserted island with, you would pick a man like Ronan.

She gave her head a shake at the naughty direction of her own thoughts and realized her head felt unnaturally light and then remembered she had cut her hair.

She had glimpsed her hair in the mirror of the motorcycle. Now she hopped out of bed and had a good look in the mirror above the dressing table.

"Oh!" she said, touching her fingers to it. It looked awful, crushed in places from sleep, standing straight up in others. Despite that, she decided she loved it. It made her look like a girl who would never back down from an adventure, not a princess who had spent her life in a tower, at least figuratively speaking! In fact, she felt in love with life this morning, excited about whatever new gifts the day held. Excited about a chance to get to know Ronan better.

But wasn't that a betrayal of the man she was promised to?

Not necessarily, she told herself. This was her opportunity to be ordinary!

She realized she had not felt this way—happy, hopeful—since she had said yes to Prince Mahail's proposal. Up till now she had woken up each and every morning with a knot in her stomach that shopping for the world's most luxurious trousseau could not begin to undo. She had woken each morning with a growing sense of dread, a prisoner counting down to their date with the gallows.

Her stomach dipped downward, reminding her that her reprieve was probably temporary at best.

But she refused to think of that now, to waste even one precious moment of her freedom.

Ronan had left the backpack in her room, and she pawed through it, found the shorty-shorts and a red, spaghetti-strapped shirt that hugged her curves. She put on the outfit and twirled in front of the mirror, her sense of being an *ordinary* girl increased sweetly.

Her mother would have hated both the amount of leg showing and the skimpiness of the top, which made Shoshauna enjoy her outfit even more. She liked the way lots of bare skin against warm air felt: free, faintly sensual and very comfortable.

She went out her door, saw his bedroom was already empty. She stopped when she saw his bed was made, hesitated, then went in and inspected it. The bedding was crisp and taut. She backed out when she realized the room smelled like him: something so masculine and rich it was nearly drugging.

She went back to her own room, tugged the rumpled bedding into some semblance of order, declared herself and the room perfectly wonderfully ordinary and went in search of Ronan.

He was at the outdoor kitchen, a basket of fruit beside him that he was peeling and cutting into chunks. She watched him for a moment, enjoying the pure poetry of him performing such a simple task, and then blushed when he glanced at her and lifted an eyebrow. He had known she stood there observing him!

Still, there was a flash of something in his eyes as he took in her outfit, before it was quickly veiled, a barrier swiftly erected. And there was no hint of that *flash* in his voice.

"Princess," he said formally, "did you sleep well?"

It was several giant steps back from the man who had laughed with her yesterday. She wanted to break down the barrier she saw in his eyes. What good was being an ordinary girl if it was as if she was on this island alone? If her intrigue with this man was not shared?

"You must call me Shoshauna," she said.

"I can't."

She glared at him. "I command it."

He actually laughed out loud, the same laugh that had given her her first glimpse yesterday of just how real he could be, making her yearn to know him, know someone real.

"Command away, Princess. I'm not calling you by your first name."

"Why?"

"It's too familiar. I'm your bodyguard, not your buddy."

She felt the sting of that. Her disappointment was acute. He wanted the exact opposite of what she wanted! She wanted to feel close to another human being, he wanted to feel distant. She wanted to use this time together to explore his mysteries, he was just as determined to keep them secret.

It was frustrating! Her mother would approve of his attitude, a man who knew his *place* and was so determined to keep their different positions as a barrier between them.

But so would her grandmother love him. Her grandmother said soldiers made the best husbands, because they already knew how to obey. Not that he was showing any sign of obeying Shoshauna!

And not that she wanted to be thinking of this handsome man and the word *husband* in the same sentence. She had just narrowly missed making marriage her fate.

Still, she wanted him to participate in the great adventure she was on. How could she forget she was a princess, forget her obligations and duties for a short while, if he was going to insist on reminding her at every turn by using a formal title?

"How about my code name, then?" she asked.

He hesitated, glanced at her, shrugged. She couldn't tell if it was agreement or appeasement, though whichever it was, she sensed it was a big concession from him, he suddenly refused to look at her, took an avid interest in the fruit in front of him.

"I'll do that," she said, moving up beside him. Did he move a careful step away from her? She moved closer. He moved away again and without looking at her, passed her a little tiny knife and a mango.

"Don't cut your fingers off," he said dryly.

She watched for a moment as his own fingers handled the knife, removed a fine coil of peel from the fruit. He caught her watching him, *again,* put down the knife and turned away from her to put wood in the oven.

"What are we going to make in there?" she asked eagerly.

"*I'm* going to make biscuits."

"I want to learn!"

"What for?"

"It seems like it would be a useful skill," she said stubbornly.

"It is a useful skill. For someone like me, who frequently finds himself trying to make the best of rough circumstances. But for a princess?" He shook his head.

"I want to know useful things!"

"What is useful in your world and what is useful in mine are two very different things," he said almost gently.

Rebelliously she attacked the mango with

her knife. Ten minutes later as she looked at the sliver of fruit in front of her, what was left of her mango, she realized he was probably right. Domestication at this late date was probably hopeless. She felt sticky to the elbow, and had managed to get juice in her eye. The mango was mangled beyond recognition.

She cast him a look. Ronan was taking golden-brown biscuits off a griddle above the stove. The scent of them made her mouth water.

"Here," she said, handing him the remnants of her mango. He took it wordlessly, his face a careful blank, and added it to the plate of fruit he had prepared.

She thought they'd take the food inside to the dining table, but he motioned her over to a little stone bench, set the plate down between them, lifted his face to the morning sun as he picked up a piece of fruit.

She followed his example and picked up a slice of fruit and a biscuit with her fingers.

Shoshauna had dined on the finest foods in the world. She had eaten at the fanciest tables of B'Ranasha, using the most exquisite china and cutlery. But she felt as if she had never tasted food this fine or enjoyed flavor so much.

She decided she loved everything, absolutely everything, about being an ordinary girl. And she hadn't given up on herself in the domestic department yet, either!

CHAPTER FOUR

AFTER A FEW minutes Shoshauna couldn't help but notice that her pleasure in the simplicity of the breakfast feast seemed to be entirely one-sided.

Ronan, while obviously enjoying the sunshine and eating with male appetite, seemed pensive, turned in on himself, as anxious not to connect with her as she *was* to connect with him.

"Are you enjoying breakfast?" she asked, craving conversation, curious about this man who had become her protector.

He nodded curtly.

She realized she was going to have to be more direct! "Tell me about yourself," she invited.

He shot her a look, looked away. "There's nothing to tell. I'm a soldier. That means my life is ninety-nine percent pure unadulterated boredom."

She supposed you didn't learn to make a bed like that if you led a life of continuous excitement, but she knew he was fudging the truth. She could tell, from the way he carried himself, from the calm with which he had handled things yesterday that he dealt with danger as comfortably as most men dealt with the reading of the morning paper.

"And one percent what?" she asked when it became apparent he was going to add nothing voluntarily.

"All hell breaking loose."

"Oh!" she said genuinely intrigued. "All hell breaking loose! That sounds exciting."

"I wish you wouldn't say that word," he said, ignoring her implied invitation to share some of his most exciting experiences with her.

"Hell, hell, hell, hell, hell," she said, and found it very liberating both to say the word and to defy him. Her society prized meekness in women, but she had made the discovery she was not eager to be anyone's prize!

He shot her a stern look. She smiled back. He wasn't her father! He didn't look more than a few years older than she was. He couldn't tell her how to behave!

He sighed, resigned, she hoped, to the fact he was not going to control her. She'd been controlled quite enough. This was her week to do whatever she wanted, including say *hell* to her heart's content.

"What's the most exciting thing that ever happened to you?" she pressed, when he actually shut his eyes, lifted his chin a bit higher to the sun, took a bite of biscuit, apparently intent on pretending he was dining alone and ignoring her questions.

He thought about it for a minute, but his reluctance to engage in this conversation was palpable. Finally he said, without even opening his eyes, "I ran into a grizzly bear while in Canada on a mountain survival exercise."

"Really?" she breathed. "What happened?" It was better than she could have hoped. Better than a movie! She waited for him to tell her what she could picture so vividly—Ronan wrestling the primitive animal to the ground with his bare hands...

"It ran one way and I ran the other."

She frowned, sharply disappointed at his

lack of heroics. "That doesn't sound very exciting!"

"I guess you had to be there."

"I think I would like to go to the mountains in Canada." Yes, even with bears, or maybe because of bears, it sounded like an adventure she'd enjoy very much. "Are the mountains beautiful? Is there snow?"

"Yes, to both."

"What's snow like?" she asked wistfully.

"Cold."

"No, what does it *feel* like." Again, he was trying to disengage, but he was the only person she'd ever met who had experienced snow, and she *had* to know.

"It's different all the time," he said, giving in a little, as if he sensed her needing to know. "If it's very cold the snow is light and powdery, like frozen dust. If it's warmer it's heavy and wet and sticks together. You can build things with it when it's like that."

"Like a snowman?"

"Yeah, I suppose. I built a snow cave out of it."

"Which kind is better for sledding?"

"The cold, dry kind. What do you know about that?"

"Nothing. I've seen it on television. I've always had a secret desire to try it, a secret desire to see different things than here, more beautiful."

"I don't know if there's anything more beautiful than this," he said. "It's a different kind of beauty. More rugged. The landscape there is powerful rather than gentle. It reminds a person of how small they are and how big nature is." He suddenly seemed to think he was talking too much. "I'm sure your husband will take you there if you want to go," he said abruptly.

It was her turn to glare at him. She didn't want to be reminded, at this moment, that her life was soon going to involve a husband.

"I'm fairly certain Prince Mahail," she said, "is about as interested in tobogganing in snow as he is in training a water buffalo to tap dance."

"He doesn't like traveling? Trying new things?" He did open his eyes then, lower his chin. He was regarding her now with way too much interest.

She felt a sensation in her stomach like panic. "I don't know what he likes," she said, her voice strangled. She felt suddenly like crying, looked down at her plate and blinked back the tears.

Her life had come within seconds of being linked forever to a man who was a stranger to her. And despite the fact the heavens had taken pity on her and granted her a reprieve, there was no guarantee that linking would not still happen.

"Hey," Ronan said, "hey, don't cry."

After all the events of yesterday, including being shot at, this was the first time she'd heard even the smallest hint of panic in that calm voice!

"I'm not crying," she said. But she was. She scrubbed furiously at the tear that worked its way down her cheek. She didn't want Ronan to be looking at her like that because he felt sorry for her!

She reminded herself she was supposed to be finding out about Ronan, not the other way around!

"What made you want to be a soldier?" she asked, trying desperately for an even tone of voice, to change the subject, to not waste one precious second contemplating all the adventures she was not going to have once she was married to Mahail.

Something flickered in his eyes. Sympathy? Compassion? Whatever it was, he opened up to her just the tiniest little bit.

"I had a lousy home life as a kid. I wanted routine. Stability. Rules. I found what I was looking for." He regarded her intently, hesitated and then said softly, "And you will, too. Trust me."

He would be such an easy man to trust, to believe that he had answers.

"Isn't it a hard life you've chosen?" she asked him, even though what she really wanted to say was *how? How will I ever find what I'm looking for? I don't even know where to look!*

He shrugged, tilted his chin back toward the sun. "Our unit's unofficial motto is Go Hard or Go Home. Some would see it as hard. I see it as challenging."

Was there any subtle way to ask what she most wanted to ask, besides *How will I ever find what I'm looking for?* It was inappropriate to ask him, and too soon. But still, she was not going to find herself alone on a deserted island with an extremely handsome man ever again.

She had to know. She had to know if he

was available. Even though she herself, of course, was not. Not even close.

"Do you have a girlfriend?" She hoped she wasn't blushing.

He opened his eyes, shot her a look, closed them again. "No."

"Why not?"

His openness came to an abrupt end. That firm line appeared again around his mouth. "What is this? Twenty questions at the high school cafeteria?"

"What's a high school caff-a-ter-ee-a?"

"Never mind. I don't have a girlfriend because my lifestyle doesn't lend itself to having a girlfriend."

"Why?"

He sighed, but she was not going to be discouraged. Her option was to spend the week talking to him or talking to herself. At the moment she felt her survival depended on focusing on his life, rather than her own.

Maybe her desperation was apparent because he caved slightly. "I travel a lot. I can be called away from home for months at a time. I dismantle the odd bomb. I jump from airplanes."

"Meeting the grizzly bear wasn't the most

exciting thing that ever happened to you!" she accused.

"Well, it was the most exciting thing that I'm allowed to talk about. Most of what I do is highly classified."

"And dangerous."

He shrugged. "Dangerous enough that it doesn't seem fair to have a girlfriend or a family."

"I'm not sure," she said, thoughtfully, "what is unfair about being yourself?"

He looked at her curiously and she explained what she meant. "The best thing is to be passionate about life. That's what makes people really seem alive, whole, isn't it? If they aren't afraid to live the way they want to live and to live fully? That's what a girlfriend should want for you. For a life that makes you whole. And happy. Even if it is dangerous."

She was a little embarrassed that she, who had never had a boyfriend, felt so certain about what qualifications his girlfriend should have. And she was sadly aware that passion, the ability to be alive and whole, were the very qualities she herself had lost somewhere a long the way.

As if to underscore how much she had lost

or never discovered, he asked her, suddenly deciding to have a conversation after all, "So, what's the most exciting thing you've ever done?"

Been shot at. Cut my hair. Ridden a motorcycle.

All the most exciting events of her life had happened yesterday! It seemed way too pathetic to admit that, though it increased her sense of urgency, this was her week to live.

"I'm afraid that's classified," she said, and was rewarded when he smiled, ever so slightly, but spoiled the effect entirely by chucking her under her chin as if she was a precocious child, gathered their plates and stood up.

Shoshauna realized, that panicky sensation suddenly back, that she had to squeeze as much into the next week as she possibly could. "I'm putting on my bathing suit now and going swimming. Are you coming?"

He looked pained. "No. I'll look after the dishes."

"We can do the dishes later. Together. You can show me how."

He said another nice word under his breath.

She repeated it, and when he gave her *that*

look, the stern, forbidding, don't-mess-with-me look, she said it again!

When he closed his eyes and took a deep breath, a man marshaling his every resource, she knew beyond a shadow of a doubt that he was dreading this week every bit as much as she was looking forward to it.

"How about if we do the dishes now?" he said. "In this climate I don't think you want to leave things out to attract bugs. And then," he added, resigned, "if you really want, I'll show you how to make biscuits."

She eyed him suspiciously. He didn't look like a man who would be the least bothered by a few bugs. He'd probably eaten them on occasion! And he certainly did not look like a man who wanted to give out cooking lessons.

So that left her with one conclusion. He didn't like the water. No, that wasn't it. And then, for some reason, she remembered the look on his face when he'd put that pink bikini back on the rack in the store yesterday.

And she understood perfectly!

Ronan did not want to see her in a bikini. Which meant, as much as he didn't want to, he found her attractive.

A shiver went up and down her spine, and

she felt something she had not felt for a very long time, if she had ever felt it at all.

Without knowing it, Ronan had given her a very special gift. Princess Shoshauna felt the exquisite discovery of her own power.

"I'd love to learn to make biscuits instead of going swimming," she said meekly, the perfect B'Ranasha princess. Then she smiled to herself at the relief he was unable to mask in his features. She had a secret weapon. And she would decide when and where to use it.

"Hey," Ronan snapped, "cut it out."

The princess ignored him, took another handful of soap bubbles and blew them at him. Princess Shoshauna had developed a gift for knowing when it was okay to ignore his instructions and when it wasn't, and it troubled him that she read him so easily after four days of being together.

He had not managed to keep her out of the bathing suit, hard as he had tried. He'd taken her at her word that she wanted to learn things and had her collecting fruit and firewood. He'd taught her how to start a decent fire, showed her edible plants, a few rudimentary survival skills.

Ronan had really thought she would lose interest in all these things, but she had not. Her fingers were covered in tiny pinpricks from her attempts to handle a needle and thread, she was sporting a bruise on one of her legs from trying to climb up a coconut tree, she gathered firewood every morning with enthusiasm and without being asked. Even her bed making was improving!

He was reluctantly aware that the princess had that quality that soldiers admired more than any other. They called it "try." It was a never-say-die, never-quit determination that was worth more in many situations than other attributes like strength and smarts, though in fact the princess had both of those, too, her strength surprising, given her physical size.

Still, busy as he'd tried to keep her, he'd failed to keep her from swimming, though he'd developed his own survival technique for when she donned the lime-green handkerchief she called a bathing suit.

The bathing suit was absolutely astonishing on her. He knew as soon as he saw it that he had been wrong thinking the pink one he'd made her put back would look better, because nothing could look better.

She was pure, one-hundred-percent-female menace in that bathing suit, slenderness and curves in a head-spinning mix. Mercifully, for him, she was shy about wearing it, and got herself to the water's edge each day before dropping the towel she wrapped herself in.

His survival technique: he went way down the beach and spearfished for dinner while she swam. He kept an eye on her, listened for sounds of distress, kept his distance.

He was quite pleased with his plan, because she was so gorgeous in a bathing suit it could steal a man's strength as surely as Delilah had stolen Sampson's by cutting off his hair.

Shoshauna blew some more bubbles at him.

"Cut it out," he warned her again.

She chuckled, unfortunately, not the least intimidated by him anymore.

It was also unfortunately charming how much fun she was having doing the dishes. She had fun doing everything, going after life as if she had been a prisoner in a cell, marveling at the smallest things.

Hard as it was to maintain complete professionalism in the face of her joie de vivre, he was glad her mood was upbeat. There had been no more emotional outbursts after that single time she had burst into tears at the very mention of her fiancé, her husband-to-be.

Ronan could handle a lot of things, up to and including a mad mamma grizzly clicking her teeth at him and rearing to her full seven-foot height on her hind legs. But he could not handle a woman in tears!

Still he found himself contemplating that one time, in quiet moments, in the evenings when he was by himself and she had tumbled into bed, exhausted and happy. How could Shoshauna not even know if her future life partner liked traveling, or if he shared her desire to touch snow, to toboggan? The princess was, obviously, marrying a stranger. And just as obviously, and very understandably, she was terrified of it.

But all that fell clearly into the none-of-his-business category. The sense that swept over him, when he saw her shinny up a tree, grinning down at him like the cheeky little monkey she was, of being protective, almost furiously so, of wanting to rescue her from her life was inappropriate. He was a soldier. She was a princess. His life involved doing things he didn't want to do, and so did hers.

But marrying someone she didn't even really know? Glancing at her now, bubbles from head to toe, it seemed like a terrible shame. She was adorable—fun, curious, bratty, sexy as all get-out—she was the kind of girl some guy could fall head over heels in love with. And she deserved to know what that felt like.

Not, he told himself sternly, *that he was in any kind of position to decide what she did or didn't deserve. That wasn't part of the mission.*

He'd never had a mission that made him feel curiously weak instead of strong, as if things were spinning out of his control. He'd come to *like* being with her, so much so that even doing dishes with her was weakness, pure and simple.

It had been bad enough when she waltzed out in shorts every morning, her legs golden and flawless, looking like they went all the way to her belly button. Which showed today, her T-shirt a touch too small. Every time she moved her arms, he saw a flash of slender tummy.

It was bad enough that when he'd glanced over at her, hacking away at the poor defenseless mango or pricking her fingers with a needle, he felt an absurd desire to touch her hair because it had looked spiky, sticking up all over the place like tufts of grass but he was willing to bet it was soft as duck down.

It was bad enough that she was determined to have a friendship, and that even though he knew it was taboo, sympathy had made him actually engage with her instead of discouraging her.

I had a lousy home life as a kid. That was the most personal information he'd said to anyone about himself in years. He *hated* that he'd said it, even if he'd said it to try and make her realize good things could come from bad.

He hated that sharing with her that one stupid, small sentence had made him realize a loneliness resided in him that he had managed to outrun for a long, long time. He'd said he didn't have a girlfriend because of his work, but that was only a part truth. The truth was he didn't want anyone to know him so well that they could coax information out of him that made him feel vulnerable and not very strong at all.

He was a man who loved danger, who rose to the thrill of a risk. He lived by his unit's motto, Go Hard or Go Home, and he did it with enthusiasm. His life was about intensely masculine things: strength, discipline, guts, toughness.

After his mother's great love of all things frilly and froufrou, he had not just accepted his rough barracks existence, he had embraced it. He had, consciously or not, rejected the feminine, the demands of being around the female of the species. He had no desire to be kind, polite, gentle or accommodating.

But in revealing that one small vulnerability to Shoshauna, he recognized he had never taken the greatest risk of all.

Part of the reason he was a soldier—or maybe most of the reason—was he could keep his heart in armor. He'd been building that armor, piece by meticulous piece, since the death of his dad. But when he'd asked her, that first day together, "Who knows what love is?" he'd had a flash of memory, a realization that a place in him thought it knew exactly what love was.

There was a part of him that he most wanted to deny, that he had been very successfully denying until a few short days ago, but now it nibbled around the edges of his mind. Ronan secretly hoped there was a place a man could lay his armor down, a place he could be soft, a place where there was room to love another.

Shoshauna, without half trying, was bringing his secrets to the surface. She was way too curious and way too engaging. Luckily for him, he had developed that gift of men who did dangerous and shadowy work. He was taciturn, wary of any interest in him.

In his experience, civilians thought they wanted to know, thought a life of danger was like adventure movies, but it wasn't and they didn't.

But Shoshauna's desire to know seemed genuine, and even though she had led the most sheltered of lives, he had a feeling she could handle who he really was. More than handle it—embrace it.

But these were the most dangerous thoughts—the thoughts that jeopardized his mission, his sense of professionalism and his sense of himself.

But what had his choices been? To totally ignore her for the week? Set up a tent out back here? Pretend she didn't exist?

He was no expert on women, but he knew they liked to talk. It was in his own best interests to keep the princess moderately happy with their stay here. Hell, part of him, an unfortunately large part, *wanted* to make her happy before he returned her to a fate that he would not have wished on anyone.

Marriage seemed like a hard enough proposition without marrying someone you didn't know. Ask his mother. She'd made it her hobby to marry people she didn't really know.

A renegade thought blasted through his mind: if he was Shoshauna's prince, he'd take her to that mountaintop just because she wanted to go, just to see the delight in her face when she looked down over those sweeping valleys, to see her inhale the crispness of the air. He'd build snowmen with her and race toboggans down breathtakingly steep slopes just to hear the sound of her laughter.

If he was her prince? Cripes, he was getting in bigger trouble by the minute.

There had been mistakes made over the past few days. One of them had been asking her about the most exciting thing in her life. Because it had been so pathetically evident it had probably been that motorcycle ride and all of *this*.

From the few words she'd said about passion he'd known instantly that she regretted the directions of her own life, *yearned* for more. And he'd been taken by her wisdom, too, when he'd told her that the dangerous parts of his job kept him from a relationship.

Was there really a woman out there who understood that caring about someone meant encouraging her partner to pursue what made him whole and alive? Not in his experience there wasn't! Beginning with his mother, it was always about how *she* felt, what *she* needed to feel safe, secure, loved. Not that it had ever worked for her, that strangling kind of love that wanted to control and own.

The last thing he wanted to be thinking about was his mother! Even the bathing suit would be better than that. He was aware the thought of his mother had appeared because he had opened the door a crack when he admitted he had a lousy childhood. That was the whole problem with admissions like that.

He was here, on this island, with the princess, to do a simple job. To protect her. And that meant he did not—thank God—have the luxury of looking at himself right now.

Still, he knew he had to be very, very careful because he was treading a fine line. He'd already felt the uncomfortable wriggle of emotion for her. He didn't want to be rude, but he had to make it very clear, to himself and to her, this was his job. He wasn't on vacation, he wasn't supposed to be having fun.

He couldn't even allow himself to think the thoughts of a normal, healthy man when he saw her in that bathing suit every day.

But now he was wondering if he'd overrated that danger and underrated this one. Because in the bathing suit she was sexy. Untouchable and sexy, like a runway model or a film actress. He could watch her from a safe distance, up the beach somewhere, sunglasses covering his eyes so she would never read his expression.

With soap bubbles all over her from washing dishes, she was still sexy. But cute, too. He was not quite sure how she had managed to get soap bubbles all over the long length of her naked legs, but she had.

She put bubbles on her face, a bubble beard and moustache. "Look!"

"How old are you?" he asked, putting duty first, pretending pure irritation when in fact her enjoyment of very small things was increasingly enchanting.

"Twenty-one."

"Well, quit acting like you're six," he said.

Then he felt bad, because she looked so crestfallen. *Boundaries,* yes, but he was not going to do that again: try to erect them by hurting her feelings. He'd crossed the fine line between being rude and erecting professional barriers. Ronan simply expected himself to be a better man than that.

Against his better judgment, but by way of apology, he scooped up a handful of suds and tossed them at her. She tossed some back. A few minutes later they were both drenched in suds and laughing.

Great. The barriers were down almost completely, when he had vowed to get them back up—when he knew her survival depended on it. And perhaps his own, too.

Still, despite the fact he knew he was dancing with the kind of danger that put meeting a grizzly bear to shame, it occurred to him, probably because of the seriousness of most of his work, he'd forgotten how to be young.

He was only twenty-seven, but he'd done work that had aged him beyond that, stolen his laughter. The kind of dark, gallows humor he shared with his comrades didn't count.

Even when the guys played together, they

played rough, body-bruising sports, the harder hitting the better. He had come to respect strength and guts, and his world was now almost exclusively about those things. There was no room in it for softness, not physical, certainly not emotional.

His work often required him to be mature way beyond his years, required him to shoulder responsibility that would have crippled any but the strongest of men. Life was so often serious, decisions so often involved life and death, that he had forgotten how to be playful, had forgotten how good it could feel to laugh like this.

The rewards of his kind of work were many: he felt a deep sense of honor; he felt as if he made a real difference in a troubled world; he was proud of his commitment to be of service to his fellow man; the bonds he had with his brothers in arms were stronger than steel. Ronan had never questioned the price he paid to do the work before, and he absolutely knew now was not the time to start!

Sharing a deserted island with a gorgeous princess who was eager to try on her new bikini, was absolutely the wrong time to decide to rediscover those things!

But just being around her made him so aware of *softness,* filled him with a treacherous yearning. The full meltdown could probably start with something as simple as wanting to touch her hair.

"Okay," he said, serious, trying to be very serious, something light still lingering in his heart, "you want to learn how to make my secret biscuit recipe?"

Ronan had done many different survival schools. All the members of Excalibur prided themselves in their ability to produce really good food from limited ingredients, to use what they could find around them. He was actually more comfortable cooking over a fire than he was using an oven.

An hour later with flour now deeply stuck on her damp skin, she pulled her biscuit attempt from the wood-fired oven.

Ronan tried to keep a straight face. Every biscuit was a different size. Some were burned and some were raw.

"Try one," she insisted.

Since he'd already hurt her feelings once today and decided that wasn't the way to keep his professional distance, he sucked it up and took one of the better-looking biscuits.

He took a big bite. "Hey," he lied, "not bad for a first try."

She helped herself to one, wrinkled her nose, set it down. "I'll try again tomorrow."

He hoped she wouldn't. He hoped she'd tire soon of the novelty of working together, because it was fun, way more fun than he wanted to have with her.

"Let's go swimming now," she said. "Could you come with me today? I thought I saw a shark yesterday."

Was that pure devilment dancing in the turquoise of those eyes? Of course it was. She'd figured out he didn't want to swim with her, figured out her softness was piercing his armor in ways no bullet ever had. She'd figured out how badly he didn't want to be anywhere near her when she was in that bathing suit.

In other words, she had figured out his weakness.

He could not let her see that. One thing he'd learned as a soldier was you never ran away from the thing that scared you the most. Never. You ran straight toward it.

"Sure," he said, with a careless shrug. "Let's go."

He said it with the bravado of a man who

had just been assigned to dismantle a bomb and didn't want a single soul to know how scared he was.

But when he looked into her eyes, dancing with absolute mischief, he was pretty sure he had not pulled it off.

She was not going to be fooled by him, and it was a little disconcerting to feel she could see through him so completely when he had become such an expert at hiding every weakness he ever felt.

CHAPTER FIVE

SHOSHAUNA STARED AT herself in the mirror in her bedroom and gulped. The bathing suit was really quite revealing. It hadn't seemed to matter so much when Ronan was way down the shoreline, spearfishing, picking up driftwood, but today he was going to swim with her! Finally.

She could almost hear her mother reacting to her attire. "Common." Her father would be none to pleased with this outfit, either, especially since she was in the company of a man, completely unchaperoned.

But wasn't that the whole problem with her life? She had been far to anxious to please others and not nearly anxious enough to please herself. She had always dreamed of being bold, of being the adventurer, but in the end she had always backed away.

She remembered the exhilarating sense of

power she had felt when she realized Ronan
didn't want to see this bathing suit, when
she'd realized, despite all his determination
not to, he found her attractive. Suddenly she
wanted to feel that power again. She was so
aware of the clock ticking. They had been
here four days. There was three left, and then
it would be over.

Suddenly nothing could have kept her from
the sea, and Ronan.

At the last minute, though, as always, she
wrapped a huge bath towel around herself before she stepped out of the house.

Ronan waited outside the door, glanced at
her, his expression deadpan, but she was sure
she saw a glint of amusement in his eyes, as
if he *knew* she was really too shy to wear that
bikini with confidence, with delight in her
own power when there was a man in such
close quarters.

"Look what I found under the porch," he
said.

Two sets of snorkels and fins! No one could
look sexy or feel powerful in a snorkel and
fins! Still, she had not snorkeled since the last
time she had been here, and she remembered
the experience with wonder.

"Was the surfboard there?"

"Yeah, an old longboard. You want me to grab it? You could paddle around on it."

"No, thank you," she said. Paddle around on it, as if she was a little kid at the wading pool. She wanted to surf on it—to capture the power of the sea—or nothing at all. Just to prove to him she was not a little kid, *at all,* she yanked the towel away.

He dropped his sunglasses down over his eyes rapidly, took a sudden interest in the two sets of snorkels and fins, but she could see his Adam's apple jerk each time he swallowed.

She marched down the sand to the surf, trying to pretend she was confident as could be but entirely aware she was nearly naked and in way over her head without even touching the water. She plunged into the sea as quickly as she could.

Once covered by the blanket of the ocean, she turned back, pretending complete confidence.

"The water is wonderful," she called. "Come in." It was true, the water was wonderful, warm, a delight she had been discovering all week was even better against almost-naked skin.

Suddenly she was glad she'd found the

courage to wear the bikini, glad she'd left the towel behind, glad she was experiencing how sensuous it was to be in the water with hardly anything between it and her, not even fabric. Her new haircut was perfect for swimming, too! Not heavy with wetness, it dried almost instantly in the sun.

She looked again at the beach. Ronan was watching her, arms folded over his chest, like a lifeguard at the kiddy park.

She was going to get that kiddy-park look off his face if it killed her!

"Come in," she called again, and then pressed the button she somehow knew, by instinct, he could not stand to have pressed. "Unless you're scared."

Not of the water, either, but of her. She felt a little swell of that feeling, *power,* delicious, seductive, pure feminine power. She had been holding off with it, waiting, uncertain, but now the time felt right.

She watched as Ronan dropped the snorkeling gear in the sand, pulled his shirt over his head. She felt her mouth go dry. This was how she had hoped he would react to her. A nameless yearning engulfed her as she stared at the utter magnificence of his build.

He was pure and utter male perfection. Every fluid inch of him was about masculine strength, a body honed to the perfection of a hard fighting tool.

Shoshauna had thought she would feel like the powerful one if they swam together, but now she could see the power was in the chemistry itself, not in her, not in him.

There was a universal force that called when a certain woman looked at a certain man, when a certain man looked at a certain woman. It pulled them together, an ancient law of attraction, metal to magnet, a law irresistible, as integral as gravity to the earth.

Shoshauna became aware that the "power" she had so wanted to experiment with, to play with, was out of her control. She felt a kind of helpless thrill, like a child who had played with matches and was now having to deal with a renegade spark that had flared to flame.

Impossible to put this particular fire out. Ronan was all sleek muscle and hard lines, not an ounce of superfluous fat or flesh on his powerful male body. His chest was deep, his stomach flat, ridged with ab muscles, his shoulders impossibly broad. His legs were long, rippling with muscle.

He dove cleanly into the water, cutting it with his body. Two powerful strokes carried him to her, another beyond her. She watched, mesmerized, as his strong crawl carried him effortlessly out into the bay. He stopped twenty or thirty yards from her, trod water, shook diamond droplets of the sea from his hair.

Watching him, she realized what she had been doing could not even really be called swimming. She was paddling. No wonder he treated her as if she belonged in the kiddy pool! Bathing suit aside, in the water she was an elephant trying to keep pace with a cheetah!

Ronan flipped over on his back, spread his arms like a star and floated. It looked so comfortable, so relaxing that she tried it and nearly drowned. She came up sputtering for air.

"Are you okay?"

And what if she wasn't? Would he swim over here, gather her in his arms, maybe give her mouth-to-mouth resuscitation?

"I'm fine," she squeaked.

He did swim back over, but did not come too close. "You're about as deep as you should go," he told her. "I've noticed over the past few days you are not a very strong swimmer."

"In my mother's mind swimming in the ocean was an activity for the sons and daughters of fishermen."

"It seems a shame to live in a place like this, surrounded by water and not know how to swim. It seems foolish to me, unnecessarily risky, because with this much water you're eventually going to have an encounter with it." Hastily he added, "Not that I'm calling your mother foolish."

"Plus, she has this thing about showing skin." And that was with a *regular* bathing suit.

Ronan eyed her. "I take it she wouldn't approve of the bathing suit."

He *had* noticed.

"She'd have a heart attack," Shoshauna admitted.

"It's having just about the same effect on me," he said with a rueful grin, taking all her power away by admitting he'd noticed, a man incapable of pretense, *real,* just as she'd known he was.

"That's why your mom doesn't want you wearing stuff like that. Men are evil creatures, given to drawing conclusions from visual clues that aren't necessarily correct."

Back to the kiddy pool! He was going to turn this into a lecture. But he didn't. He left it at that, yet she felt a little chastened anyway.

As if he sensed that, he quickly changed the subject. "So, I've got you out here in the water. Want to—"

Was she actually hoping he was going to propose something a little evil?

"Want to learn how to swim a little better?"

She nodded, both relieved and annoyed by his ability to treat her like a kid, his charge, nothing more.

"You won't be ready to enter the Olympics after one lesson, but if you fall out of a boat, you'll be able to survive."

It had probably been foolish to suggest teaching Shoshauna to swim. But the fact of the matter was she lived on an island. She was around water all the time. It seemed an unbelievable oversight to him that her education had not included swimming lessons.

On the other hand, what did he know about what skills a princess needed? Still, he felt he could leave here a better man knowing that if she did fall off a boat, she could tread water until she was rescued.

Probably he was kidding himself that he was teaching her something important. If a princess fell overboard, surely ten underlings jumped in the water after her.

But somehow it was increasingly important to him that she know how to save herself. And maybe not just if she fell off a boat. All these things he had been teaching her this week were skills that made no sense for a princess.

But for a woman coming into herself, learning the power of self-reliance seemed vital. It felt important that if he gave her nothing else, he gave her a taste of that: what her potential was, what she was capable of doing and learning if she set her mind to it.

Because Ronan was Australian and had grown up around beaches and heavy surf, he had quite often been chosen to instruct other members of Excalibur in survival swimming.

Thankfully, he could teach just about anybody to swim without ever laying a hand on them.

She was a surprisingly eager student, more willing to try things in the water than many a seasoned soldier. Like the things she had been doing on land, he soon realized she had no fear, and she learned very quickly. By the end of a half hour, she could tread water for a few minutes, had the beginnings of a not bad front crawl and could do exactly two strokes of a backstroke before she sank and came up sputtering.

And then disaster struck, the kind, from teaching soldiers, he was totally unprepared for.

She was treading water, when her mouth formed a startled little *O*. She forgot to sweep the water, wrapped her arms around herself and promptly sank.

His mind screamed *shark* even though he had evaluated the risks of swimming in the bay and decided they were minimal.

When she didn't bob right back to the surface, he was at her in a second, dove, wrapped his arm around her waist, dragged her up. No sign of a shark, though her arms were still tightly wrapped around her chest.

Details. Part of him was trying to register what was wrong, when she sputtered something incomprehensible and her face turned bright, bright red.

"My top," she sputtered.

For a second he didn't comprehend what she was saying, and when he did he was pretty sure the heart attack he'd teased her about earlier was going to happen for real. He had his arms around a nearly naked princess.

He let go of her so fast she started to sink again, unwilling to unwrap her arms from around her naked bosom.

Somehow her flimsy top had gone missing!

"Swim in to where you can stand up," he ordered her sharply.

He knew exactly what tone to use on a frightened soldier to ensure instant obedience, and it worked on her. She headed for shore, doing a clumsy one-armed crawl— her other arm still firmly clamped over her chest—that he might have found funny if it was anyone but her. As soon as he made sure she was standing up on the ocean bottom, he looked around.

The missing article was floating several

yards away. He swam over and grabbed it, knew it was the wrong time to think how delicate it felt, how fragile in his big, rough hands, what a flimsy piece of material to be given so much responsibility.

He came up behind her. She was standing up to her shoulder blades in water and still had a tight wrap on herself, but there was no hiding the naked line of her back, the absolute feminine perfection of her.

"I'll look away," he said, trying to make her feel as if it was no big deal. "You put it back on."

Within minutes she had the bathing suit back on, but she wouldn't look at him. And he was finding it very difficult to look at her.

Wordlessly she left the water, spread out her towel and lay down on her stomach. She still wouldn't even look at him and he figured maybe that was a good thing. He put on the snorkeling gear and headed back out into the bay.

He began to see school after school of butterfly fish, many that he recognized as the same as he would see in the reefs off Australia: the distinctive yellow, white and black stripes of the threadfin, the black splash of color that identified the teardrop.

Suddenly, Ronan didn't want her to stay embarrassed all day, just so that he could be protected from his own vulnerability around her. He didn't want her to miss the enchantment of the reef fish.

Her embarrassment over the incident was a good reminder to him that she had grown up very sheltered. She had sensed the bikini would get his attention, but she hadn't known what to do with it when she succeeded.

In his world, girls were fast and flirty and knew exactly what to do with male attention. Her innocence in a bold world made him want to share the snorkeling experience with her even more.

They would focus on the fish, the snorkeling, not each other.

"Shoshauna! Put on a snorkel and fins. You have to see this."

He realized he'd called her by her first name, as if they were friends, as if it was *okay* for them to snorkel together, to share these moments.

Too late to back out, though. She joined him in the water, but not before tugging on her bathing suit strings about a hundred times to make sure they were secure.

And then she was beside him, and the magic happened. They swam into a world of such beauty it was almost incomprehensible. Fish in psychedelic colors that ranged from brilliant orange to electric blue swam around them. They saw every variety of damselfish, puffer fish, triggerfish, surgeonfish.

He tapped her shoulder. "Watch those ones," he said, pointing at an orange band. "It's a type of surgeonfish, they're called that because their spines are scalpel sharp."

Her wonder was palpable when a Moorish idol investigated her with at least as much interest as she was giving it! A school of the normally shy neon-green and blue palenose parrot fishes swam around her as if she was part of the sea.

He was not sure when he lost interest in the fish and focused instead on her reaction to them. Ronan was not sure he had seen anything as lovely as the awed expression on her face when a bluestripe snapper kissed her hand.

He was breaking all the rules. And somehow it seemed worth it. And somehow he didn't care. Time evaporated, and he was stunned when he saw the sun going down in the sky.

They went in to shore, dried the saltwater off with towels. He saw she was looking at him with a look that was both innocent and hungry.

"I'm going to cook dinner," he said gruffly. Suddenly breaking the rules didn't seem as great, it didn't seem worth it, and he did care.

He cared because he felt something, and he knew it was huge. He felt the desire to *know* someone. He *wanted* to know her better. He *wanted* things he had never wanted and that, in this case, he knew he could never have.

These four days together had created an illusion that they were just two normal people caught up together. These days had allowed him to see her as real, as few people had ever seen her. These days had allowed him to see her, and he had liked what he had seen. It was natural to want to know more, to explore where this affinity he felt for her could go.

But the island was a fantasy, one so strong it had diluted reality, made him forget reality.

He was a soldier. She was a princess. Their

worlds were a zillion miles apart. She was promised to someone else.

With those facts foremost in his mind, he cooked dinner, refusing her offer to help, and he was brusque with her when she asked him if he knew the name of a bright-yellow snout-nosed fish they had seen. She took the hint and they ate in blessed silence. Why did he miss being peppered with her questions? Did she, too, realize that a dangerous shift had happened between them?

Still, getting ready for bed, he was congratulating himself on what a fine job he'd done on reerecting the barriers, when he heard an unmistakable whimper from her room.

Surely she wasn't that embarrassed over her brief nude scene?

He knew he had to ignore her, but then she cried out again, the sound muffled, as if she had a blanket stuffed in her mouth. It was the sound being stifled that made him bolt from his room, and barge through her door.

She was alone, in bed. No enemy had crept up on him while he'd been busy playing reef guide instead of doing his job.

"What's the matter?" He squinted at her through the darkness.

The sheet was pulled up around her, right to her chin.

"I hurt so bad."

"What do you mean?"

He lit the hurricane lamp that had been left on a chair just inside her door, moved to the side of her bed and gazed down at her. She reluctantly pulled the sheet down just enough to show him her shoulders. That's why she had been quiet at dinner.

Not embarrassed, not taking the hint that he didn't want to talk to her, but in pain. Even in the light of the lantern he could clearly see she was badly sunburned. Cursing himself silently, he wondered how close she had come to heat exhaustion.

White lines where her bikini straps had been were in sharp contrast to her skin.

Because her skin tones were so golden it had never occurred to him she might burn. It had not seemed scorchingly hot out today. On the other hand he should have known breezes coming off the water could make it seem cooler than it was. It had never occurred to him that someone who lived in this island paradise might not avail themselves of the outdoors.

He remembered, too late, what she had said about her mother. "Has your skin ever seen the sun before?" he asked her.

She shook her head, contrite. "Not for a long time. I was allowed to come here until I was about thirteen, but then my mother thought I was getting to be too much of a tomboy. She thought skin darkened by the sun was—"

"Let me guess," he said dryly. "Common."

He was rewarded with a weak smile from her. Selfish bastard that he was he thought, *At least I'm not going to have to see her in a bikini again for the three days we have left here on the island.*

But there was another test he had to pass right now. He was going to have to administer first aid to her burns. She'd exposed her back to the sun while they snorkeled. The water beading on it had drawn the sun like a magnet. Though her shoulders were very red looking, most of that burn was going to be on her back where she couldn't reach it herself.

Having grown up in Australia, he was cautious of the sun, but his skin was also more acclimatized to sun than that of most of the people he worked with. He did not have fair coloring, his skin seemed to like the sun.

But many times after long training days in the sun, especially desert training, soldiers were hurting. Ronan had learned lots of ways to ease the sting with readily available ingredients: either vinegar or baking soda added to bath water could bring relief. Unfortunately, just as when he was in the field, they didn't have a bath here.

What they did have was aspirin, he had seen that in a cabinet in the outdoor kitchen, and powdered milk, an ingredient he'd used before to field dress a sunburn.

He knew, though, there was going to be a big difference between placing soothing dressings cooled with freshly made milk onto her back, and slapping it onto a fellow soldier's.

All day he'd struggled to at least keep the physical barriers between them up, since the emotional ones seemed to be falling faster than he could reerect them. When she'd lost the top, and he'd wrapped his arms around her to pull her back to the water's surface, he'd known he had to avoid going to that place again at all costs, skin against skin.

But here he was at that place again. It almost felt as if the universe was conspiring against him.

But she was his charge. He had no choice. He felt guilty that she'd gotten burned on his watch in the first place. It was proof, really, he could not be trusted with softer things, more tender things, things that required a gentle touch.

It was proof, too, that he was preoccupied, missing the details that he had always been so good at catching.

"Come on out to the kitchen," he said gruffly. "I'll put something on that that will make it feel better."

"I can't get dressed," she told him, and blushed. "My skin feels like its shrinking. I don't think I can move my arms. I don't want to put anything on that touches my skin."

Oh well, just run out there naked then.

He yanked the sheet out from the bottom of the bed and tucked it around her right up to her chin. "Come on."

She wobbled out behind him to the kitchen, the sheet draped clumsily over her, him uncomfortably and acutely aware that underneath it she was probably as naked as the day she was born. The outfit was somehow as dangerous—maybe more so—than the bikini had been.

And the night was dangerous—the stars like jewels in the night sky, the flowers releasing their perfume with a gentle and seductive vengeance.

"Sit," he said, swinging a chair out for her. He took a deep breath, prayed for strength and then did what had to be done. He lifted the sheet away from her back, forced himself to be clinical.

Her back looked so tender with burn that he forgot how awkward this situation was. The marks where her bikini strings had been tied up dissected it, at her neck and midback, white lines in stark contrast to the rest of her. Her skin was glowing bright red on top of her copper tones.

"I hate to be the bearer of bad news," he said, his sympathy genuine, his guilt acute even though he knew how hard it was to spot a burn as it was happening in the full sunlight, "but in the next few days your skin is going to be peeling. It may even blister."

"Really?" she asked.

She couldn't possibly sound, well, *pleased,* rather than distressed.

He had to make it a bit clearer. "Um, you could probably be lizard lady at the sideshow for a week or two."

"Really?" she said, again.

No doubt about it. Definitely pleased.

"Is there some reason that would make you happy?" he asked.

"Between my new hair and lizard lady, Prince Mahail will probably call off the wedding. Indefinitely."

Now there was no mistaking the pleasure in her voice.

Don't ask, Ronan. "Is he really that superficial?"

"He chose me for my hair!"

Well, he'd asked. Now he had to deal with the rush of indignation he felt. A man chose a wife for her *hair?*

It was primitive and tyrannical. It was not what she deserved. Wasn't he in the business of protecting democracy? Of protecting people's freedoms and right to choose? If she was being forced into this, then what? Cause an international incident by imposing his values on B'Ranasha, by rescuing the princess from her fate?

"Are you being forced to marry him?" he asked.

"Not exactly."

"What does that mean?"

"Nobody forced me to say yes, but there was enormous pressure, the weight of everybody's expectations."

He turned from her quickly to stave off the impulse to shake her. Here he'd been thinking he had to rescue her when the aggravating truth was she had not, as far as he could see, made a single move to rescue herself. She seemed to just be blindly trusting *something* was going to happen to get her out of her marriage. And much as he hated to admit it, so far that had worked not too badly for her.

But her luck was going to run out, and for a take-charge kind of guy, relying on luck to determine fate was about the worst possible policy.

Rather than share that with her, or allow her to see the fury he felt with her, Ronan busied himself mixing a solution of powdered milk and water in a big bowl. He tore several clean tea towels into rags and submerged them in the mixture.

Then, his unwanted surge of emotion under control, a gladiator who had no choice but the ring, he turned back to her, lifted the sheet off her back.

"Hold that up for me."

He laid the first of the milk-soaked rags flat on her naked back, smoothed it on with his hands. She seemed unbelievably delicate. Her skin was hot beneath the dressing. And, for now anyway, before the inevitable peeling, it felt incredibly smooth, flawless beneath his fingertips. He didn't know of any other way to bring her comfort, but touching her like this was intimate enough to make him feel faintly crazy, a purely primitive longing welling up within him.

He thought she might flinch, but instead she gave a little moan of pleasure and relief as the first cool, milk-soaked dressing adhered to her back, a sound that could have easily been made in another context.

"Oh," she breathed. "That feels so good. I don't think I've ever felt anything that good."

His wicked male mind wondered just how

innocent that made her. Plenty innocent. And it was his job to keep it that way.

He thought about a man he had never seen, whom he knew nothing about, becoming her husband, being trusted with her delicacy, and he felt another unwanted stab of strong emotion.

Not jealousy, he told himself, God forbid, not jealousy, just an extension of his job. Protectiveness.

But he knew it wasn't exactly a part of his job to wonder, was that man whom she had almost married, worthy of her? Would her prince be able to make her pleasure as important as his own when the time came? Would he be tender and considerate? Would he stoke the fire that burned in her eyes, or would he put it out?

Ronan, he reprimanded himself. *Stop it!* By her own admission, she was not being forced into anything. It was her problem not his.

Still, the feeling of craziness intensified, he felt a sudden primitive need to *show* her what it *should* feel like, all heat and passion, tenderness and exquisite pleasure. If she'd ever experienced what was *real* between a man and a woman she wouldn't accept a substitute, no matter how much pressure she thought she felt.

She was seriously going to pay with her life to relieve a little temporary pressure from her folks?

He gave himself a fierce mental shake. His thinking was ludicrous, totally unacceptable, completely corrupted by emotion. He had known her less than a full week, which really meant he did not know her at all!

He was not dating her, he was protecting her. Imagining his lips on her lips was not a part of the mission.

Who would have thought he would end up having to protect the princess from himself?

"Leave those dressings on there for twenty minutes," he said, his voice absolutely flat, not revealing one little bit of his inner struggle, the madness that was threatening to envelope him. "Unfortunately in this heat the residue of the milk will start to sour if you leave it on overnight. You're going to have to rinse off in the shower before you go back to bed." He passed her some aspirin and a glass of water.

"This will take the sting out." He sounded

as if he was reading from a first-aid manual. "Drink all the water, too, just in case you're a bit dehydrated. I think you'll sleep like a baby after all this."

She probably would, too, but he was wondering if he was ever going to sleep again!

Fixing her up had taken way too long, even with him trying to balance a gentle touch with his urgency to get this new form of torture over with.

"I'll head back to bed, I'll leave this lamp for you. You can peel those dressings off by yourself in twenty minutes or so. Don't forget to shower."

"All right."

"You should be okay for a few hours. If the pain comes back, starts bugging you, wake me up. We'll do it all again." He had to suck it up to even make that offer. He didn't want to touch her back again, have her naked under a sheet, the two of them alone in a place just a little too much like paradise.

No wonder Adam and Eve had gone for the apple!

"Ronan?" Her voice was husky. She touched his arm.

He froze, aware he was holding his breath,

scared of what could happen next, if she asked him to stay with her. Scared of the physical attraction, scared of the thoughts he had had earlier.

"What?" He growled.

"Thank you so much."

What was he expecting? She was burned to a crisp. The last thing on her mind was, well, the thing that was on his mind. Which was her lips, soft and pliable, and how they would feel underneath his, how they would taste.

"Just doing my job."

She glanced over her shoulder at him. Her eyes met his. There was no mistaking the heat and the hunger that changed their color from turquoise to a shade of indigo. He realized it wasn't the last thing on her mind after all. That one small push from the universe and they'd be all over each other, burn or no burn. The awareness that sizzled in the air between them put that burn on her back to shame.

He sucked in a deep breath, then ducked his head, turned abruptly and walked quickly away from her.

It took more discipline to do that than to do two hundred push-ups at the whim of a aggravated sergeant, to make a bed perfectly for the thousandth time, to jump out of an airplane from twenty thousand feet in the dead of the night. Way more.

He glanced at his watch to check the date. He had to get control over this situation before it deteriorated any more.

But when he thought of her shaking droplets of water from the jagged tips of her hair, laughing, the tenderness of her back underneath the largeness of his hands, he felt a dip in the bottom of his belly.

He focused on it, but it wasn't that familiar warning, his *sideways* feeling. It was a warmth as familiar as the sun and as necessary to life.

What had happened to his warning system? Had it become dismantled? Ronan wondered if he had lost some part of himself that he *needed* in the turquoise depths of her eyes.

Isn't that what he'd learned about love from his mother? That relationships equaled the surrender of power?

"You are not having a relationship with her," he told himself sternly, but the words were hollow, and he knew he had already crossed lines he didn't want to cross.

But tomorrow was a new day, a new battle. He was a warrior and he fully intended to recapture his lost power.

CHAPTER SIX

SHOSHAUNA TOOK A deep breath, slid a look at Ronan. He was intense this morning, highly focused, but not on her. She could not look at him—at the dark, neat hair, his face freshly shaven, the soft gold brown of his eyes, the sheer male beauty of the way he carried himself—without feeling a shiver, remembering his hands on her back last night.

"Are you mad at me?"

"Princess?" he asked, his voice flat, as if he had no idea what she was talking about.

"Yesterday you called me Shoshauna," she said.

He said nothing; he did not look at her. He had barely spoken to her all morning. She'd gotten up and managed to get dressed, a painful process given the sunburn. Still, she had been more aware of something hammering in her heart, a desire to see him again, to be with him, than of the pain of that burn.

But Ronan had been nowhere to be found when she had come out of her bedroom. He'd left a breakfast of fresh biscuits and cut fruit for her, not outside on the bench where she had grown accustomed to sharing casual meals with him, but at the dining room table, at a place perfectly set for one.

Shoshauna had rebelled against the formality of it and taken a plate outside. As she ate she could hear the thunk of an ax biting into wood in the distance. Just as she was finishing the last of the biscuits, he dragged a tree into their kitchen clearing.

Watching him work, hauling that tree, straining against it, that *awareness* tingled through her, the same as she had felt yesterday when she had watched him strip off his shirt before swimming. She felt as if she was vibrating from it. Ronan was so one hundred percent man, all easy strength and formidable will.

Even to her inexperienced eye it looked as if he was bringing in enough wood to keep the stove fired up for about five years.

"Good morning, Ronan." Good grief, she

could hear the *awareness* in her voice, a husky breathlessness.

She knew how much she had come to live for his smile when he withheld it. Instead, he'd barely said good morning, biting it out as if it hurt him to be polite. Then he was focusing on the wood he'd brought in. After using a handsaw to reduce the tree to blocks, he set a chunk on a stump chopping block, swung the ax over his head, and down into the wood.

The whole exercise of reducing the tree to firewood was a demonstration—entirely unconscious on his part—of pure masculine strength, and she could feel her heart skip a beat every time he lifted the ax with easy, thoughtless grace. She remembered again the strength in those hands, tempered last night, and shivered.

But today his strength was not tempered at all. He certainly *seemed* angry, the wood splintering into a thousand pieces with each mighty whack of the ax blade, tension bunching his muscles, his face smooth with a total lack of expression.

He had not even asked her how her sunburn felt, and it felt terrible. Could she be bold enough to ask him to dress it again? She felt as if she was still trembling inside from the way his hands had felt pressing those soothing cloths onto her back last night. But he looked angry this morning, remote, not the same man who had been so tender last night.

"Ronan?" she pressed, even though it was obvious he didn't want to talk. "Are you angry about something?"

Actually, something in him seemed to have shifted last night when he had questioned her about her marriage. He had gone very quiet after she had admitted she wasn't being forced to marry anyone.

"No, ma'am, I'm not angry. What's to be angry about?"

"Stop it!"

He set down the ax, wiped the sweat off his forehead with a quick lift of his shirt collar, then folded his arms over his chest, looked askance at her.

"I didn't mean chopping the wood," she said, knowing he had misunderstood her deliberately.

"What did you mean then, Princess?"

"Why are you being so formal? You weren't like this yesterday."

"Yesterday," he said tightly, "was a mistake. I forgot myself, and it's not going to happen again."

"Having fun, going snorkeling was forgetting yourself?"

"Yes, ma'am."

"If you call me ma'am one more time, I'm going to throw this coconut right at your large, overweight head!"

"I think you might mean my big, fat head."

"That's exactly what I meant!"

He actually looked as though he might smile, but if he was amused he doused it quickly.

"Princess," he said, his patience elaborate and annoying, "I'm at work. I'm on the clock. I'm not here to have fun. I'm not here to teach you to swim or to identify yellow tangs for you. My job is to protect you, to keep you safe until I can get you back to your home."

"I could have been assassinated while you were out there chopping down the jungle," she said, aware her tone was growing snippy with impatience. How could he possibly not want more of what they'd had yesterday?

Not just the physical touch, though that had filled her with a hunger that felt ravenous, a tiger that needed to be fed, but the laughter, the easy camaraderie between them. It was that she found herself craving even more. How could it be that he did not want the same things?

"I think," he said dryly, "if assassins had arrived on the island, I would have heard a boat. Or a helicopter. I was only a few seconds away."

He was deliberately missing the point! "Bitten by a snake, then!"

He didn't answer, and she hated that he was treating her like a precocious child, though for some reason his attitude was making her act like one.

"Eaten by a tiger," she muttered. "Attacked by a monkey."

He sent her one irritated look, went back to the wood.

"I'm making a point! There is no danger here. None. No assassins, no snakes, no tigers, no mad monkeys. It would be perfectly fine for you to relax your vigilance."

Crash. The wood splintered. He gathered the splinters, tossed them in a pile, wouldn't look at her. "I relaxed yesterday. You got a large, overweight sunburn because of it."

"You are not feeling responsible for that,

are you?" His lack of a response was all the answer she needed. "Ronan, it wasn't your fault. It's not as if it was life threatening, anyway. A little sunburn. I can hardly feel it today." Which was a lie, but if it got rid of that look from his face—a look of cool professional detachment—it would be a lie worth telling.

He said nothing, and she knew this was about more than a sunburn.

"Are you mad because I *agreed* to get married?"

Bull's-eye. Something hard and cold in his face shook her. "That falls squarely in the none-of-my-business category."

"That's not true. We're friends. I want to talk to you about it." And suddenly she did. She felt that if she talked to Ronan, all the chaos and uncertainty inside her would subside. She felt that the terrible loneliness that had eaten at her ever since she said yes to Prince Mahail would finally go away.

She felt as if she would know what to do.

"My cat died," she blurted out. "That's why I agreed to marry him."

It felt good to say it out loud, though she

could tell by the look on his face he now thought she was certifiably insane.

"But you have to understand about the cat," she said in a rush.

"No," he said, holding up his hand, a clear stop signal. "No, I don't have to understand about the cat. I don't want you telling me about your personal life. Nothing. No cat. No marriage. Not what is on or off your mother's approval list, though we both know that what isn't on it is cavorting in the ocean in a bathing suit top that is unstable with a man you barely know."

"I do know you," she protested.

"No you don't. We can't be friends," he said quietly. "Do you get that?"

She had thought they were past that, that they were already well on their way to being friends, and possibly even something more than friends. These last few days she had shared more with him than she could remember sharing with anyone. She had felt herself opening around him, like a flower opening to sunshine.

He made her discover things about herself that she hadn't known. Being around him made her feel strong and competent. And alive. It was *easy* to be herself with him. How could he say they could not be friends?

"No," she said stubbornly. "I don't get it."

"Actually," he said tersely, "it doesn't really matter if you get it or not, just as long as I get it."

She felt desperate. It was as if he was on a raft and she was on shore, and the distance between them was growing. She needed to bring him back, any way she could. "Okay, I won't tell you anything about me. Nothing."

He looked skeptical, so she rushed on, desperate. "I'll put a piece of tape over my mouth. But I can't go out in the sun today. I was hoping you'd teach me how to play chess. My mother felt chess was a very masculine game, that girls should not play it."

Even though he'd specifically told her not to mention her mother to him, she took a chance and believed she had been right to do so, because something flickered in his eyes.

He *knew* she'd be a good chess player if she got the chance, but if he'd realized that, he doused the thought as quickly as his smile of moments ago. He was silent, refusing the bait.

"Do you know how to play chess?" If she could just get him to sit down with her, spend time with her, soon it would be easy again and fun. She wanted to know so much about him. She wanted him to know so much about her. They only had a few days left! He couldn't spoil it. He just couldn't.

He took up the ax and put another piece of wood on the stump he was using as a chopping block. He hit it with such furious strength she winced.

"Are you going to ignore me?"

"I'm sure as hell going to try."

Shoshauna was a princess. She was not used to being ignored. She was used to people doing what she wanted them to do.

But this felt different. It felt as if she would die if he ignored her, if they could not get back to that place they had been at yesterday, swimming in the magical world of a turquoise sea and rainbow-hued fish, his hands on her back strong, cool, filled with confidence, the hands of a man who knew how to touch a woman in ways that could steal her breath, her heart, her soul.

Her sense of desperation grew. He was holding the key to something locked inside of her. How could he refuse to open that secret door? The place where she would, finally, know who she was.

"If I told my father you had done something inappropriate," she said coolly, "you'd spend the rest of your life in jail."

He gave her a look so fearless and so loaded with scorn it made her feel about six inches high. And that was when she knew he was immovable in his resolve. She knew it did not matter what she did—she could threaten him, try to manipulate him with sweetness—he was not going to do as she wanted. He had drawn his line in the sand.

And over such a ridiculously simple thing. She only wanted him to play chess with her!

Only, it wasn't really that simple, and he knew it, even if she was trying to deny it. Getting to know each other better would have complications and repercussions that could resound through both their lives.

But why worry about that today? They had so little time left. Couldn't they just go on as they had been? Couldn't they just pretend they were ordinary people in extraordinary circumstances?

But even as she thought it, she knew he would never like pretending. He was too real for that. And when she slid another look his way, she could tell by the determined set of his jaw that he intended to worry about *that* today, and she could tell something else by the set of his jaw.

She was completely powerless over him.

"I'm sorry I said that," she said, feeling utterly defeated, "about my father putting you in prison. It was a stupid thing to say, very childish."

He shrugged. "It doesn't matter." As if he *expected* her to say things like that, to act spoiled and rotten if she didn't get her own way. She had not done one thing—not one— to lead him to believe such things of her.

Unless you included saying yes to marrying a man she did not love.

That would speak volumes about her character to a man like Ronan, who wore his honor and his integrity as part of the armor around him.

"I would never do something so horrible as tell lies about you. I'm not a liar." But hadn't she lied to herself all along, about Mahail, her marriage, her life?

"I said it didn't matter," he said sharply.

"Now you really are mad at me."

He sighed heavily.

Shoshauna, looking at herself with the brutal assessment she saw in his eyes, burst into tears, ran into the house, slammed her bedroom door and cried until she had no tears left.

Shoot, Ronan thought, was she ever going to stop crying? Bastard. How hard would it have been to teach her to play chess?

It wasn't about teaching her how to play chess, he told himself sternly. It was about the fact that things were already complicated so much that she was in there crying over something as tiny as the fact he'd refused to teach her to play chess.

Though, dammit, when she had said her mother didn't want her to play chess, that it was *masculine,* something in him had just itched to give her the rudiments of the game. She had such a good mind. He bet she'd be a better-than-average player once she got the fundamentals down, probably a downright formidable one.

She didn't come out of that room for the rest of the day. When he told her he had lunch ready, she answered through the closed door, her voice muffled, that she wasn't hungry.

Now it was the same answer for supper. He should have been relieved. This was exactly what *he* needed to keep his vows. Distance. Space. Instead he felt worried about her, guilty about the pain he'd caused.

"Come on," he said, from the other side of the door, "you have to eat."

"Why? To make you feel like you've fulfilled your obligation to look after me? Is providing a nutritious menu part of protecting me? Go away!"

He opened the door a crack. She was sitting on her bed cross-legged in those shorty-shorts that showed way too much of her gorgeous copper-toned legs. She looked up when he came in, looked swiftly back down. Her eyes were puffy from crying. Her short, boyish hair was every which way. She'd taken her bra straps off her burned shoulders, and they hung out the arms of her T-shirt.

"I told you to go away."

"You should eat something." He stepped inside the door a bit.

"You know what? I'm not a little kid. You don't have to tell me to eat."

He was already way too aware she was not a little kid. He'd seen the damned bikini once too often! He'd seen what was under the bikini, too.

He was also aware this was becoming a failure of major proportions. He was going to take her back safe from threat but damaged nonetheless: hair chopped off, sunburned, starving, puffy-eyed from crying. Though they still had two days and a couple of hours to get through before he could cross back over that water with her, deliver her to Gray. She couldn't possibly cry that long.

His stomach knotted at the thought. Could she? He studied her to see if she was all done crying.

She'd found a magazine somewhere, and she was avoiding his eyes. The magazine looked as if it had been printed in about 1957, but she was studying it as intently as if she could read her future on the pages. Her eyes sparkled suspiciously. More tears gathering?

"Look," he said uncomfortably, shifting his weight from one foot to the other, "I'm not trying to be mean to you. I'm just telling you the way things have to be."

"Is that right?" she snapped, and threw

down the magazine. She regarded him with spitting eyes, and he could see clearly it was fury in them, not tears. "As it happens, I'm sick and tired of people telling me how it's going to be. Why are you the one who decides how it's going to be? Because you're a man?"

She had him there.

"Because I'm the one with the job to do," he said, but he heard the wavering of his own conviction. If ever a woman was born to be his equal it was this one.

She hopped off the bed. Instinct told him to get away from her. A stronger instinct told him to stay.

She stopped in front of him, regarded him with challenge. He, foolishly, held his ground.

She reached up on tiptoe, and she took his lips with her own.

He was enveloped in pure and sweet sensation. Her kiss was as refreshing and clean as rainwater. Her lips told him abut the polarities within her: innocence and passion, enthusiasm and hesitancy, desire and doubt.

He had heard there were drugs so strong a man could be made helpless by them after one taste.

He had never believed it until this moment.

He willed himself not to respond, but he did not have enough will to move away from her, from the sweetness of her quest.

The hesitancy and the doubt suddenly dissolved. Her arms reached out, tangled themselves around his neck, drew him closer to her. Her scent wrapped around him, feminine, clean, intoxicating. Through the thinness of her shirt he could feel the warmth radiating off her skin. Her curves, soft, sensual, womanly, pressed into him.

Temptation was furious within him. Pure feeling tried to swamp rational thought. But the soldier in him, highly disciplined, did the clean divide between the emotion he was feeling and what he *needed* to do.

If he continued this, if he accepted the invitation of her lips, the growing urgency of her kiss, if he allowed it to go where it wanted to go, it would be like a wild horse that had broken free, allowed to run. There would be no bringing it back under rein once it had gone too far.

The soldier wanted control; the man wanted to lose control.

The soldier insisted on inserting one more fact. If this carried to its natural conclusion,

Princess Shoshauna would be compromised. The wedding would be off. Her wedding. Again, she wouldn't have made a *choice,* just allowed herself to be carried along by forces she considered out of her control.

It was not what Ronan wanted for her.

He didn't want her to get married to anyone but—

But who?

Him? A soldier. A soldier who didn't believe in marriage? Who *hated* it? This must be a genetic flaw in his family, the ability to convince oneself over a very short period of time, before reality had a chance to kick in, that a marriage could work. He yanked himself away from her.

This was the difference between him and his mother: he didn't have to follow the fantasy all the way through to the end. He already knew the end of every love story.

The soldier won—fact over fiction, practical analysis over emotion, discipline over the wayward leanings of a man's heart.

But he was aware it was a slim victory at best. And he was aware that aggravating word, *love,* had popped up again, banished from his vocabulary since around his thirteenth birthday. It was suddenly presenting itself in his life with annoying frequency.

Ronan made himself hold Shoshauna's gaze, fiery with passion, soft with surrender. He tried to force all emotion from his tone. But the magnitude of his failure to do so—the cold fury of his voice—even took him by surprise. Of course, he really wasn't angry at her, but at himself, at his own vulnerability, his own weakness, his sudden crippling wistfulness.

Hope—a sudden ridiculous wish to regain his own innocence, a desire to be able to believe in things he had long since lost faith in.

"Are you using me to buy your freedom?"

She reeled back from him. If he was not mistaken the tears were back in her eyes, all the proof he needed that insanity had grabbed him momentarily, that moment when he had contemplated her and himself and marriage in the same single thought.

The truth was much more simple. He was a soldier, rough around the edges, hardened, not suitable for the company of a princess or anyone sensitive or fragile.

But there was nothing the least bit fragile about Shoshauna when she planted both her little hands on his chest and shoved him with such amazing strength that it knocked him completely off balance. He stumbled backward, two steps, through her bedroom doorway, and she rushed forward and slammed the door behind him with the force of a hurricane.

As he contemplated the slammed door, he had the politically incorrect thought that it was a mistake that hurricanes weren't still named exclusively after women: volatile, completely unpredictable, even the strongest man could not hope to hold his balance in the fury.

"Just go straight to hell!" she yelled at him through the door. She followed that with a curse that was common among working men and soldiers, a curse so *common* her mother surely would have had heart failure hearing it come from her princess daughter's refined lips.

So he was returning Shoshauna a changed woman. No hair, sunburned, starved *and* she was going to be able to hold her own in a vocabulary contest with a construction crew.

He turned away, muttering to himself, "Well, that didn't go particularly well."

But outside, contemplating a star-studded night, black-velvet sky meeting inky-black ocean, he rethought his conclusions.

Maybe it had gone well. Shoshauna was a woman who needed to discover the depths of her own power, who needed to know how to utilize the hurricane forces within her, so she would not be so easily buffeted by the forces outside of her. In the past it seemed that every shift of wind had made her change direction.

She'd made the decision to get married because her cat died? Only his mother could come up with a fruitier reason than that!

But from the way Shoshauna had shoved him and slammed that door, she was nearly there. Could she hold on to what she was discovering about herself enough to refuse a marriage to a man she did not love? Could she understand she had within her the strength to *choose* the life she wanted for herself?

Despite the peaceful serenity of the night, contemplating such issues made his head hurt. One of the things he appreciated most about his military lifestyle was that it was a cut-and-dried world, regulated, no room for contemplation, few complexities. You did what you were trained to do, you followed orders: no question, no thought, no introspection.

He scrubbed his hand across his lips, but he had a feeling what had been left there was not going to be that easy to erase.

After a long time he looked at his watch. It was past midnight. Just under forty-eight hours to go, and then they were leaving this island, meeting Gray.

What if her life was still in danger?

Well, if it was, if the situation was still not resolved, Gray had to have come up with a protection plan for her that did not involve Ronan.

But was he going to trust anyone else with her protection if she was still in danger? Would he have a choice? If he was ordered back to Excalibur, he was going to have to go, whether she was in danger or not.

He hoped it was a choice he was never going to have to make. Which would he obey? The call of duty or the call of his own heart?

Jake Ronan had never had to ask himself a question like that before, and he didn't like it one little bit that he had asked it now.

The fact that he had asked it meant something had shifted in him, changed. He cared about someone else as much as he cared about duty. Once you had done that, could you ever go back to the way you were before?

That's what he felt over the next twenty-four hours. That he was a man trying desperately to be what he had been before: cool, calm, professional, a man notorious for being able to control emotion in situations gone wild.

He almost succeeded, too.

It wasn't fun, and it wasn't easy, that he was managing to keep the barriers up between them. She was using the kitchen at different times than him. She refused to eat what he left out for her. He found her burnt offerings all over the kitchen, along with mashed fruit. He didn't know if she was trying to torment him by washing her underthings and stringing them on a line by the outdoor shower, but torment him it did, especially since she had managed to turn her bra from pure white to a funny shade of pink.

Of course, he could show her how to do laundry. He *wanted* to, but to what end? Nothing about her life included needing an ability to do laundry without turning her whites to pink.

And nothing about his life needed the complication of inviting her back into it.

No, this might be painful: these silences, the nose tilted upward every time she had to pass him, the hurt she was trying to hide with pride and seething silence, but in the end it was for the best. Even when he found an aloe vera plant and knew how it would soothe her sunburn, bring moisture and coolness and healing to her now badly peeling skin, he would not allow himself to make the offer.

When he saw her sitting at the dining room table by herself, moving chess pieces wistfully, he would not allow himself to give in to the sudden weakness of *wanting* to teach her how to play.

It only led to other wantings: wanting to make her laugh, wanting to see her succeed, wanting to see her tongue stuck between her teeth in concentration, wanting to touch her hair.

Wanting desperately to taste her lips again, just one more time, as if he could memorize how it felt and carry it inside him forever.

But he didn't give in to any of that. He applied every bit of discipline he had ever learned as a soldier to do what was right instead of what he wanted to do.

And he would have made it.

He would have made it right until the end, except that the wind came up.

The surf was up in the bay. And Princess Shoshauna, clad in a T-shirt to cover her burns, was running toward it, laughing with exhilaration and anticipation, the old surfboard they'd uncovered tucked under her arm.

"Hey," he yelled from the steps of the cottage, "you aren't a good enough swimmer for that water."

She glanced back. If he was not mistaken she stuck out her tongue at him. And then she ran even faster, kicking up the sand in her bare feet.

With a sigh of resignation and surrender, Ronan went after her.

CHAPTER SEVEN

SHOSHAUNA FOUND THE waves extraordinarily beautiful, rolling four feet high out in the water where they began their curl, breaking on the beach with a thunderous explosion of white foam and fury.

Her foot actually touched the hard pack of wave-pounded sand, when his hand clamped down on her shoulder with such strength it spun her.

Even though she had spent way too much time imagining his touch, it was not satisfactory in that context! She faced him, glaring. "What?" she demanded.

"You're not a strong enough swimmer for that surf."

"Well, you don't know everything! You said the surf would never even come up in this bay and you were wrong about that!"

"I'm not wrong about this. I'm not letting you go in the water by yourself."

He had that look on his face, fierce; the warrior not to be challenged.

But Shoshauna had been counting days and hours. She knew this time of freedom was nearly over for her. Tomorrow they would be gone from here. And she knew something else. She was responsible for her own life and her own decisions.

She stood her ground, lifted her chin to him.

"I have a lifelong dream of doing this, and I'm doing it."

He looked totally unimpressed with her newfound resolve, indifferent to her discovery of her own power, immune to the sway of her life dreams. He folded his arms over his chest, set his legs, a man getting ready to throw her over his shoulder if he had to.

As delicious as it might be to be carried by him kicking and screaming up to the cottage, this was important to her, and she suddenly had to make him see that.

"It's my lifelong dream, and the waves came. Don't you think you have to regard that as a gift from the gods?"

"No."

"Ronan, all my life people have made my decisions for me. And I've let them. Starting right here and right now, I'm not letting them anymore. Not even you."

Something in him faltered. He looked at the waves and he looked at her. She could see the struggle in his face.

"Ronan, its not that I want to. I *have* to. I have to know what it feels like to ride that kind of power, to leash it. I feel if I can do that, conquer those waves, it's just the beginning for me. If I can do that, I can do anything."

And suddenly she knew she had never spoken truer words. Suddenly she realized she had made a crucial error the other night when she had thought he held the key to the secrets locked away within her.

When they had started this adventure, she remembered saying she didn't know how to find what she was looking for because she didn't know where to look.

But suddenly she knew exactly where to look.

Every answer she had ever needed was there. Right inside herself. And part of that was linked to these waves, to *knowing* what she was capable of, to tapping her sense of adventure instead of denying it. She could not ask Ronan—or anyone else—not her mother or her father or Mahail to accept responsibility for her life. She was in charge. She was taking responsibility for herself. He did not hold the key to her secrets; she did.

She knew that what she was thinking must have shown in her face, because Ronan studied her, then nodded once, and the look on his face was something she would take back with her and cherish as much, maybe more, than the satisfaction of riding the wave.

She had won Ronan's admiration—reluctant, maybe, but still there. He had looked at her, long and hard, and he had been satisfied with what he had seen.

She turned and stepped into the surf, laughed as she leaped over a tumbling wave and it crashed around her, soaking her in foam and seawater.

Then, when she was up to her knees, she placed the board carefully in front of her and tossed herself, belly down, on top of it. It was as slippery as a banister she had once greased with butter, and it scooted out from underneath her as if it was a living thing. A wave pounded over her, awesome in its absolute power, and then she got up and ran after the board.

Drenched, but deliriously happy, she caught the board, shook water from herself, tried again. And then again. It was discouraging. She couldn't even lie on it without getting dumped off. How was she ever going to surf?

Her arms and shoulders began to hurt, and it occurred to her this was going to be a lot harder than she'd been led to believe by watching surfers on TV. But in a way she was glad. She wanted it to be challenging. She wanted to test her spunk and her determination and her spirit of adventure. Life-altering moments were not meant to be easy!

Ronan came and picked her up out of the sand after she was dumped for about the hundredth time, grabbed the board that was being dragged out to sea. She grabbed it back from him.

He sighed. "Let me give you a few tips before you go back out there. The first is this: you don't *conquer* that water. You work with it, you read it, you become a part of it. Give me the board."

It was an act of trust to hand the board to him, because he could just take it and go back to the cottage, but somehow she knew he was now as committed to this as she was. There was nothing tricky about Ronan. He was refreshing in that he was such a what-you-see-is-what-you-get kind of guy.

"You're lucky," he said, "it's a longboard, not a short one, a thruster. But it's old, so it doesn't have a leash on it, which means you have to be very aware where it is at all times. This board is the hardest thing in the water, and believe me, it hurts when it clobbers you."

She nodded. He tossed the board down on the sand.

"Okay, get on it, belly down."

She recognized the gift he was giving her: his experience, and recognized her chances of doing this were better if she listened to him. And that's what he'd said. True power wasn't about conquering, it was about working *with* the elements, reading them.

And that's what Ronan was like: one of the elements, not to be conquered, not to be tamed. To be read and worked with.

When she was down on her belly, he gave her tips about positioning: how to hold her chin, where to have her weight on the board—dead center, not too far back or too far forward.

And so she learned another lesson about power: it was all about balance.

He told her how to spot a wave that was good to ride. "Nothing shaped like a C," he warned her sternly. "Look for waves shaped liked pyramids, small rollers to start with. We'll keep you here in the surf, no deeper than your hips until you get the hang of it."

He said that with absolute confidence, not a doubt in his mind that she would get the hang of it, that she would be riding waves.

"So, practice hopping up a couple of times, here on the sand. Grab the rails."

"It doesn't have rails!"

"Put your hands on the edges," he showed her, positioning her hands. She tried not to find his touch too distracting! "And then push up, bend your back and knees to start, get one leg under you, and pop up as fast as you can. If you do it slow, you'll just tip over once you're in the water."

Under his critical eye, she did it about a dozen times. If he kept this up she was going to be too tired to do it for real!

"Okay," he finally said, satisfied, peeling off his shirt and dropping it in the sand. "Let's hit the water."

They didn't go out very far, the water swirling around his hips, a little higher on her, lapping beneath her breastbone.

"This is the best place to learn, right here." He steadied the board for her while she managed to gracelessly flop on top of it.

"Don't even try to stand up the first couple of times, just ride it, get a sense for how your surfboard sleds."

"Sleds? As in snow?"

"Same word," he said, and she smiled thinking this might be as close as she got to sledding of any kind. Maybe she would have to be satisfied to look after two dreams with one activity!

"Okay, here it comes. Paddle with those arms, not too fast, just to build momentum."

Shoshauna felt the wave lift the board, paddled and then felt the most amazing thing: as if she was the masthead at the head of that wave. The board was moving with its own power now and it shot her forward with incredible and exhilarating speed. The ride lasted maybe a full two seconds, and then she was tossed onto the sand with such force it lifted her shirt and ground sand into her skin.

"Get up," he yelled, "incoming."

Too late, the next wave pounded down on top of her, ground a little more sand into her skin.

He was there in an instant hauling her to her feet.

She was laughing so hard she was choking. "My God, Ronan, is there anything more fun in the entire world than that?"

He looked at her, smiled. "Now, you're *stoked*," he said.

"Stoked?"

"Surfer word for *ready*, so excited about the waves you can barely stand it."

"That's me," she agreed, "stoked." And it was true. She felt as if she had waited her whole life to feel this: excited, alive, tingling with the awareness of possibility.

"Ready to try it standing up?"

"I'm sooo ready," she said.

"You would have made a hell of a soldier," he said with a rueful shake of his head, and she knew she had just been paid the highest of compliments.

"I want to do it myself!"

"Sweetheart, in surfing that's the only way you *can* do it."

Sweetheart. Was it the exhilaration of that offhanded endearment that filled her with a brand-new kind of power, a brand-new confidence?

She went back out, got on the board, carefully positioned herself, stomach down. She turned, watching over her shoulder for just the right wave.

She floated up and over a few rolling waves, and then she saw one coming, the third in a set of three. She scrambled, but despite her practice runs, the board was impossibly slippery beneath her feet. It popped out from under her. The wave swallowed her, curled around her, tossed her and the board effortlessly toward the shore.

She popped up, aware Ronan was right beside her, waiting, watching. But the truth was, despite a mouth full of seawater, she loved this! She loved feeling so part of the water, feeling so challenged. There was only excitement in her as she grabbed the board, swam back out and tried again. And again. And again.

Ronan watched, offered occasional advice,

shouted encouragement, but he'd been right. There was only one way to do this. No one could do it for you. It was just like life. He did not even try to retrieve the board for her, did not try to help her back on it after it got away for about the hundredth time. Was he waiting for her to fail? For exhaustion and frustration to steal the determination from her heart?

But when she looked into the strong lines of his face, that was not what she saw. Not at all. She saw a man who believed she could do it and was willing to hold on to that belief, even while her own faith faded.

It was his confidence in her, the look on his face, that made her turn the board back to shore one last time, watch the waves gathering over her shoulder. It was the look on his face that made Shoshauna feel as if she would die before she quit.

Astonishingly, everything worked. The wave came, and the crest lifted her and the board. She found her feet; they stuck to the board; she crouched at exactly the right moment.

She was riding the sea, being thrust with incredible power toward the shore.

She rode its fabulous power for less than a full second, but she rode it long enough to feel its song beneath her, to feel her oneness with that power, to taste it, to know it, to want it. Her exhaustion disappeared, replaced by exhilaration.

She was really not sure which was more exhilarating, riding the wave or having earned the look of quiet respect in Ronan's face as he came up to her, held up his hand. "Slap my hand," he told her.

She did, and felt his power as surely as she had felt that of the wave.

"That's a high five, surfer lingo for a great ride," he told her.

She achieved two more satisfactory rides before exhaustion made her quit.

He escorted her to shore. She was shivering with exhaustion and exertion and he wrapped her in the shirt he had discarded there in the sand.

"I did it!" she whispered.

"Yes, you did."

She thought of all the things she had done since they had landed on this island and felt a sigh of contentment within her. She was a different person than she had been a few short days ago, far more sure of herself, loving the glimpse she'd had of her own power, of what she was capable of doing once she had set her mind to it.

"I want to see what you can do," she said. She meant surfing, but suddenly her eyes were on his lips, and his were on hers.

"Show me," she asked him, her voice a plea. *Show me where it all can go. Show me all that a person can be.*

He hesitated, looked at her lips, then looked at the waves, the lesser of two temptations. She saw the longing in his eyes, knew he was *stoked.* She caught a glimpse of the boy he must have once been, before he had learned to ride his power, tame it, leash it.

And then he picked up the board and leaped over the crashing waves to the water beyond. He lay down on the board, paddled it out, his strength against the surging ocean nothing less than amazing. He scorned the surf that she had ridden, made his way strongly past the breakers, got up into a sitting position, straddling the board and then waited.

He rode up and over the swells, waiting, gauging the waves, patient. She saw the wave coming that she knew he would choose.

He dropped to his chest, paddled forward, a few hard strokes to get the board moving, glanced back just as the top of the wave picked up the back of his board. She saw the nose of the board lift out of the water, and then, just when she thought maybe he had missed it, in one quick snap, he was up.

He rode the board sideways, one hip toward the nose of the board, the other toward the tail, his feet apart, knees bent, arms out, his position slightly crouched. She could see him altering his position, shifting his weight with his body position to steer the board. He was actually cutting across the face of the wave, down under the curl, his grace easy, confident and breathtaking. He made it look astonishingly easy.

This was where it went, then. When a person exercised their power completely, it became a ballet, not a fight with the forces, but a beautiful, intricate dance with the elements. Ronan rode that wave with such certainty.

Shoshauna had walked all her life with men who called themselves princes, but this was the first time she had seen a man who truly owned the earth, who could be one with it, who was so comfortable with his own power and in his own skin.

There was another element to what he was doing, and she became aware of it as he outran the wave, dropped back to his stomach, moved out to catch another. He was not showing her up, not at all.

Showing *off* for her, showing her his agility and his strength and his grace in this complex dance with the sea.

He may have been mastering the sea, but he was giving in, surrendering, to the chemistry, the sizzle that had been between them from the very moment he had first touched her, dragged her to the ground out of harm's way, a mere week ago, a lifetime ago.

Ronan was doing what men had been doing for woman since time began: he was preening for her, saying, without the complication of words: *I am strong. I am fearless. I am skilled. I am the hunter, and I will hunt for you. I am the warrior, and I will protect you.*

It was a mating ritual, and she could feel her heart rising to the song he was singing to her out there on the waves.

Finally he came in, tossed the board down,

then threw himself down on his stomach and lay panting in the sand beside her.

She wanted to taste his lips again, but knew she was in the danger zone. He questioned her motives, he would never allow himself to be convinced that it was about *them,* not about her looking for convenient ways to escape her destiny.

To even try to convince him might be to jeopardize the small amount of time they had left.

Tomorrow, hours away from now, they would leave here.

As if thinking the same thought, he told her his plan for the day. They would take the boat back across the water, find where the motorcycle was stashed in the shrubbery. Did she know of a fish-and-chips-style pub close to the palace? She told him that almost certainly it was Gabby's, the only British-style pub on the island that she was aware of.

"We'll meet Colonel Peterson there at three," he said.

"And then?"

"If it's safe, you'll go home. If it isn't, you'll most likely go into hiding for a little longer."

"With you?"

"No, Shoshauna," he said quietly. "Not with me."

She would have tonight, then one more ride on that motorcycle, and then, whatever happened next, *this* would be over.

Sadness threatened to overwhelm her, and she realized she did not want to ruin one moment of this time she had left contemplating what was coming. She suspected there was going to be plenty of time for sadness.

Now was the time for joy. For connection. He knew they were saying goodbye, it had relaxed his guard.

Shoshauna looked at the broadness of Ronan's shoulders as he lay in the sand beside her, how his back narrowed to the slenderness of his waist, she looked at how the wet shorts clung to the hard-muscled lines of his legs and his buttocks.

She became aware he was watching her watching him, out of the corner of his eye, letting it happen, maybe even enjoying it.

She reached out and rested her hand on the dip of his spine between his shoulders. For a minute his muscles stiffened under her touch, and she wondered if he would deprive her of this moment, get up, head to the cottage, put distance between them. She wondered if she had overplayed.

But then he relaxed, closed his eyes, let her touch him, and she thought, *See? I knew I would be a good chess player.* Still, she dared not do more than that, for fear he would move away, but she knew he was as aware as she was that their time together was very nearly over. That was the only reason he was allowing this. And so she tried to memorize the beauty of his salt- and sand-encrusted skin beneath her fingertips, the wondrous composition of his muscle and skin. She felt as if she could feel the life force flowing, vibrating, throbbing through him with its own energy, strong, pure, good.

Night began to fall, and with it the trade winds picked up and the wind chilled. She could feel the goose bumps rising on his flesh and on her own. The waves crashed on the shore, throwing fine spray droplets of water up toward them.

Still, neither of them made a move to leave this moment behind.

"Do you think we could have a bonfire to-night," she asked, "right here on the beach?"

Silence. Struggle. It seemed as if he would never answer. She was aware she was holding her breath.

"Yeah," he said, finally, gruffly. "I think we could."

She breathed again.

Ronan slid a glance at Shoshauna. She had changed into a striped shirt and some crazy pair of canvas slacks she had found in the cottage, lace-up front with frayed bottoms that made her look like an adorable stowaway on a pirate's ship.

Despite the outfit, she was changed since the surfing episode, carrying herself differently. A new confidence, a new certainty in herself. He was glad he'd let down his guard enough to be part of giving her that gift, the gift of realizing who she would be once she went back to her old world.

Surely, he thought looking at her, at the tilt of her chin, the strength in her eyes, the fluid way she moved, a woman certain of herself, she would carry that within her, she would never marry a man for convenience, or because it would please others. He remembered her hand resting on his back. Surely, in that small gesture, he had felt who she was, and who she would be.

Tonight, their last night together, he would keep his guard down, just a bit, just enough.

Enough to what? he asked himself.

To have parts of her to hold on to when he let her go, when he did not have her anymore, when he faced the fact he would probably never look at her face again.

Then he would have this night: the two of them, a bonfire, her laughter, the light flickering on her skin, the sparkle in her eyes putting the stars to shame.

In the gathering darkness they hauled firewood to the beach. As the stars came out, they roasted fish on sticks, remembered her antics in the water, laughed.

Tomorrow it would be over. For tonight he was not going to be a soldier. He was going to be a man.

And so they talked deep into the night. When it got colder, he went and got a blanket and wrapped it around her shoulders, and then when it got colder still and she held up a corner, he went and sat beneath the blanket with her, shoulder to shoulder, watching the stars, listening to the waves and her voice, stealing glimpses of her face, made even more gorgeous by the reflection of the flame that flickered across it.

At first the talk was light. He modified a few jokes and made her laugh. She told him about tormenting her nannies and school-teachers.

But somehow as the night deepened, so did the talk. And he was hearing abut a childhood that had been privileged and pampered, but also very lonely.

She told him about the kitten she had found on a rare trip to the public market, and how she had stuck it under her dress and taken it home. She smiled as she told the story about a little kitten taking away the loneliness, how she had talked to it, slept with it, made it her best friend.

The cat had died.

"Silly, maybe to be so devastated over a cat," she said sadly, "but I can't tell you how I missed him, and how the rooms of my apartment seemed so empty once he was gone. I missed all his adorable poses, and his incredible self-centeredness."

"What was his name?"

"Don't laugh."

"Okay."

"It was Retnuh. In our language it means Beloved."

He didn't laugh. In fact, he didn't find it funny at all. He found it sad and lonely and it confirmed things about her life that she had wanted to tell him all along but that he had already guessed anyway.

"Prince Mahail's proposal came very shortly after my Beloved died. Ronan, it felt so much easier to get swept along in all the excitement than to feel what I was feeling. Bereft. Lonely. Pathetic. A woman whose deepest love had been for a cat."

But he didn't see it as pathetic. He saw it as something else: a woman with a fierce capacity to love, giving her whole heart when she decided to love, giving it her everything. Would the man who finally received that understand what a gift it was, what a treasure?

"Will you tell me something about you now?"

It was one of those trick questions women were so good at. She had shared something *deep*, meaningful. She wasn't going to be satisfied if he talked about his favorite soccer team.

"I wouldn't know where to begin," he said, hedging.

"What kind of little boy were you?" she asked him.

Ah, a logical place to begin. "A very bad one," he said.

"Bad or mischievous?"

"Bad. I was the kid putting the potatoes in the tailpipes of cars, breaking the neighbors' windows, getting expelled from school for fighting."

"But why?"

But why? The question no one had asked. "My Dad died when I was six. Not using that as an excuse, just some boys need a father's hand in their lives. My mother seemed to know she was in way over her head with me. I think wanting to get me under control was probably motivation for most of her marriages."

"*Marriages?* How many?" Shoshauna whispered, wide-eyed. This would be scandalous in her country where divorce was nearly unheard of. It had been scandalous enough in his own.

"Counting the one coming up? Seven?"

"You can't be responsible for that one!"

Still, he always felt vaguely responsible, a futile sense of not being able to protect his mother. When he was younger it was a sense of not being enough.

"What was that like for you growing up? Were any of her husbands like a father to you?" Shoshauna asked.

And for some reason he told her what he had never told anyone. About the misery and the feelings of rejection and the rebellion against each new man. He told her about how that little tiny secret spark of hope that someday he would have a father again had been steadily eroded into cynicism.

He didn't know why he told her, only that when he did, he didn't feel weaker. He felt lighter.

And more content than he had felt in many years.

"What was your mother's marriage to your father like?" she asked softly.

He was silent, remembering. Finally he sighed, and he could hear something that was wistful in him in that sigh. He had thought it was long dead, but now he found it was just sleeping.

"Like I said, I was only six when he died,

so I don't know if these memories are true, or if they are as I wish it had been."

"Tell me what you think you remember."

"Happiness." He was surprised by how choked he sounded. "Laughter. I remember, one memory more vivid than any other, of my dad chasing my mom around the house, her running from him shrieking with laughter, her face alight with life and joy. And when he caught her, I remember him holding her, covering her with kisses, me trying to squeeze in between them, to be a part of it. And then he lifted me up, and they squeezed me between them so hard I almost couldn't breathe for the joy of it."

For a long time she was silent, and when she looked at him, he saw what the day had given her in her face: a new maturity, a new ability to be herself in the world.

And he heard it in her voice, in the wisdom of what she said.

She said, "Once your mother had that, what she had with your father, I would think she could not even imagine trying to live without it. By marrying all those men, she was only trying to be alive again. Probably for you, as much as for herself. It wasn't that she wanted those men to give you something you didn't have, it was that she wanted to give you what she had been before, she saw you grieving for her as much as for him."

It was strange, but when he heard those words, he felt as if he had searched for them, been on a quest that led him exactly to this place.

A place where, finally, he could forgive his mother.

Ever since he'd left home, it was as if he had tried desperately to put a lid on the longing his earliest memories had created. He had tried to fill all the spaces within himself: with discipline, with relentless strength, with purpose, with the adrenaline rush of doing dangerous things.

But now he saw that, just like Shoshauna, he had been brought to this place to find what was really within himself.

He was a man who wanted to be loved.

And deserved to be loved.

A man who had come to know you could fill your whole world, but if it was missing the secret ingredient it was empty.

With the fire warm against their faces and the blanket wrapped around them, they slept under the winking stars and to the music of the crashing waves. He had not felt so peaceful, or so whole, for a long, long time.

But he awoke with a fighting man's instinct just before dawn.

For a moment he was disoriented, her hair, soft as eiderdown, softer than he could have ever imagined it, tickling the bottom of his chin, her head resting on his chest, her breath blowing in warm puffs against his skin.

The feeling lasted less than half a second.

He could hear the steady, but still far off, *wop-wop-wop* of a helicopter engine, beneath that the steady but still-distant whine of powerboats.

He sat up, saw the boats coming, halfway between the island and the mainland, three of them forming a vee in the water, the helicopter zooming ahead of them to do reconnaissance.

The fire, he thought, amazed at his own stupidity. He'd been able to see the lights of the mainland from here, how could he have taken a chance by lighting that fire?

Because he'd been blinded, that's how. He'd forgotten the number-one rule of protection, no not forgotten it, been lulled into believing, that just this once it would be okay to set it aside. But he'd been wrong. He'd broken the rule he knew to be sacred in his business, and now he was about to pay the price.

He knew that emotional involvement with the principal jeopardized their well-being, their safety. And he had done it anyway, putting his needs ahead of what he knew was right.

He'd acted as if they were on a damn holiday from the moment they'd landed on this island. Instead of snorkeling and surfing, he should have spent his time creating a defensible position: hiding places, booby traps, a fallback plan.

He felt the sting of his greatest failure, but there was no time now for self-castigation. There would probably be plenty of time for that later.

He eyed their own boat, the tide out, so far up on the sand he didn't have a chance of getting it to the water before the other boats were on them, and he didn't like the idea of being out in the open, sitting ducks. He could hear the engines of those other boats, anyway. They were far more powerful than the boat on the beach.

"Wake up," he shouted at her, leaping to his feet, his hand rough on her slender shoulder.

There was no time to appreciate her sleep-ruffed hair, her eyes fluttering open, the way a line from his own chest was imprinted on her cheek. She was blinking at him with sleepy trust that he knew himself to be completely unworthy of.

He yanked her to her feet. She caught his urgency instantly, allowed herself to be pushed at high speed toward the cottage. He stopped there only briefly to pick up the Glock, two clips of ammo, and then he led the way through the jungle, to where he had chopped down the tree earlier.

He tucked her under the waxy leaves of a gigantic elephant foot shrub. "Don't you move until I tell you you can," he said.

"You're not leaving me here!"

He instantly saw that her concern was not for herself but for him. This was the price for letting his barriers down, for not maintaining his distance and his authority. She thought listening to him was an option. She did not want to understand it was his job to put himself between her and danger.

She did not want to accept reality.

And his weakness was that for a few hours yesterday he had not accepted it either.

"Princess, do not make me say this again," he said sharply. "You do not move until you hear from me, personally, that it's okay to do so."

Three boats and a helicopter. He had to assume the worst in terms of who it was and what their intent was. That was his job, to react to worst-case scenarios. There was a good chance she might not be hearing from him, personally, ever again. He might be able to outthink those kind of numbers, but their only chance was if she cooperated, stayed out of the way.

"*My* life depends on your obedience," he told her, and saw, finally, her capitulation.

He raced back to the tree line, watched the boats coming closer and closer, cutting through the waters of the bay. His mind did the clean divide, began clicking through options of how to keep her safe with very limited resources. Not enough rounds to hold off the army that was approaching.

The boats drew closer, and suddenly he stood down. His adrenaline stopped pumping. He recognized Colonel Gray Peterson at the helm of the first boat, and he stepped from the trees.

Ronan moved slowly, feeling his sense of failure acutely. This was ending well, but not because of his competence. Because of luck. Because of that thing she had always seemed to trust and he had scorned.

Gray came across the sand toward him.

"Where's the princess?" he asked.

"Secure."

Of course she picked that moment to break from the trees and scamper down the beach. She must have left her hiding place within seconds of Ronan securing her promise she would stay there.

"Grandpa!" She threw herself into the arms of a distinguished-looking elderly man.

Ronan contemplated her disobedience—the complete disintegration of his authority over her—with self-disgust.

Gray looked at her, his eyebrows arched upward. "Good grief, man, tell me that's not the princess."

"I'm afraid it is."

But Gray's dismay was not because she had broken cover without being given the go-ahead.

"What on earth happened to her hair?"

The truth was Ronan could only vaguely remember what she had looked like before.

"She's safe. Who cares about her hair?"

Gray's look said it all. People cared about her hair. Ronan was glad she had cut it if it made her less of a commodity.

"She is safe, isn't she?" Ronan asked. "That's why you're here? That's why you didn't wait for me to come in?"

"We made an arrest three days ago."

"Who?" He needed to know that. If it was some organized group with terror cells all over the place, she would never be safe. And what would he do then?

Peterson lowered his voice. "You gave us the lead. Princess Shoshauna's cousin, Mirassa. She was an old flame of Prince Mahail's. You've heard that expression 'Hell hath no fury like a woman scorned,' but in this case it was more like high school high jinx gone very wrong."

Ronan watched Shoshauna, felt her joy at being with her grandfather and felt satisfied that her instincts had been so correct. If she had that—her instincts—and now the ability to capture the power of the wave, she was going to be all right.

"You went deep," Gray said, "if I could have found you I would have pulled you out sooner."

Oh, yeah, he'd gone deep. Deep into territory he had no right going into, so deep he felt lost even now, as if he might never make his way out.

"But when one of the villagers saw the fire last night and reported it to her grandfather he knew right away she'd be here." Gray glanced down the beach at her, frowning. "She doesn't look like the same person, Ronan."

Ronan was silent. She was the same person. But now she had a better idea of who that was, now, he hoped she would not be afraid to let it show, to let it shine.

He was aware of Gray's sudden scrutiny, a low whistle. "Anything happen that I should know about?"

So, the changes were in him, too, in his face.

"No, sir." Nothing anybody should know about. He would have to live with the fact his mistakes could have cost her her life. Because they hadn't, no one else had to know. Ronan watched the other two boats unload. Military men, palace officials, bodyguards.

"Where's Prince Mahail?' he asked grimly.

"Why would he be here?"

"If I was going to marry her and she'd disappeared, I'd sure as hell be here." But only her grandfather had come. Not her mother. Not her father. Not her fiancé. And suddenly he understood exactly why she had loved a cat so much, the loneliness, the emptiness that had driven her to say yes instead no.

But she knew herself better now. She knew what she was capable of. As far as gifts went, he thought it was a pretty good one to give her.

Gray was looking at him strangely now, then he shook it off, saying officiously, "Look, I've got to get you out of here. Your commanding officer is breathing down my neck. Your Excalibur team is on standby waiting to be deployed. I've been told, in no uncertain terms, you'd better be back when they pull the plug. I'm going to signal the helicopter to drop their ladder."

Ronan was a soldier; he trained for the unexpected; he expected the unexpected. But somehow it caught him completely off guard that he was not going to be able to say good-bye.

The helicopter was coming in low now in response to Gray's hand signals, sand rising around it. The ladder dropped.

Don't think, Ronan told himself and grabbed the swaying rope ladder, caught it hard, pulled himself up to the first rung.

With each step up the ladder, he was aware of moving back toward his own life, away from what had happened here.

Moments later, hands were reaching out to haul him on board.

He made the mistake of looking down. Shoshauna was running with desperate speed. She looked as if she was going to attempt to grab that ladder, too, as if she was going to come with him if she could.

But the ladder was being hauled in, out of the way of her reaching hands. Had he really been holding his breath, *hoping* she would make it, hoping by some miracle she could come into his world. Was he really not ready to let go? But this was reality now, the chasms between them uncrossable, forces beyond either of their control pulling them apart.

She went very still, a small person on a beach, becoming smaller by the second. And then, standing in the center of a cyclone of dust and sand, she put her hand to her lips and sent a kiss after him. He heard the man who had hauled him in take in a swift, startled gasp at the princess's obvious and totally inappropriate show of affection for a common man, a soldier no different from him.

But he barely registered that gasp or the startled eyes of the crew turning to him.

Jake Ronan, the most pragmatic of men, thought he felt her kiss fly across the growing chasm between him and touch his cheek, a whisper of an angel's wings across the coarseness of his whiskers, as soft as a promise.

CHAPTER EIGHT

SHOSHAUNA LOOKED AROUND her bedroom. It was a beautiful room: decorated in turquoises and greens and shades of cream and ivory. Like all the rooms in her palatial home, her quarters contained the finest silks, the deepest rugs, the most valuable art. But with no cat providing lively warmth, her space seemed empty and unappealing, a showroom with no soul.

She was surrounded by toys and conveniences: a wonderful sound system; a huge TV that slid behind a screen at the push of a button; a state-of-the-art laptop with Internet access; a bathroom with spa features. But today, despite all that luxury, all those things she could occupy herself with, her room felt like a prison.

She longed for the simplicity of the island, and she felt as if she had been *robbed* of her last few hours with Ronan. She had thought they would at least have one more motorcycle ride together. No, she had even been robbed of her chance to say goodbye, and to ask the question that burned in her like fire.

What next?

The answer to that question lay somewhere in the six days of freedom she had experienced. She could not go back to the way her life had been before, to the way she had been before.

Where was Ronan? She still felt shocked at the abruptness of his departure. After that final night they had shared, she had wanted to say goodbye. No, *needed* to say goodbye.

Goodbye? That isn't what she wanted to say! *Hello. I can't wait to know you better. I love the way I feel when I'm with you. You show me all that is best about myself.*

There was a knock on her door, and she leaped off her bed and answered it, but it was one of the maids and a hairdresser.

"We've come to fix your hair," the maid said cheerfully, "before you meet with Prince Mahail. I understand he's coming this afternoon."

Shoshauna did not stand back from the

door to invite them in. She said quietly but firmly, "I happen to like my hair the way it is, and if Prince Mahail would like to see me he will have to make an appointment to see if it's convenient *for me*."

And then she shut the door, her maid's mouth working soundlessly, a fish gasping out of water. For the first time since she had come back to this room, Shoshauna felt free, and she understood the truth: you could live in a castle and be a prisoner, you could live in a prison and be free. It was all what was inside of you.

A half hour later there was another knock on her door, the same maid, accompanied by a small boy, a street ragamuffin.

"He said," the maid reported snippily, "he has something that he is only allowed to give to you. Colonel Peterson said it would be all right."

The boy shyly held out the basket he was carrying and a book.

Shoshauna took the book and smiled at him. She glanced at the book. *Chess Made Simple*. Her heart hammering, she took the basket, heard the muted little whimper even before she rolled back the square of cloth that covered it.

An orange kitten stared at her with round green eyes.

She felt tears film her eyes, knew Ronan was gone, but that he had sent her a message.

Did he know what it said to her? Not "Learn to play chess," not "Here's a kitten to take the edge off loneliness."

To her his message said he had seen the infinite potential within her.

To her his message said, "Beloved." It said that he had heard her and seen her as no one else in her life ever had.

But then she realized this gift was his farewell gift to her. It said he would not be delivering any messages himself. Had he let his guard down so completely on that final day together because he thought he would never see her again?

Never see him *again?* The thought was a worse prison than this room—a life sentence.

She wanted to just slam her bedroom door and cry, but that was not the legacy of her week with Ronan. She had learned to be strong. She certainly had no intention of being a victim of her own life! No, she planned from this

day forward to be the master of her destiny!
To take charge, to go after what she wanted.

And to refuse what she didn't want.

"Tell Prince Mahail I will see him this afternoon after all," she said thoughtfully.

She realized she had to put closure on one
part of her life before she began another. She
did not consult her father or her mother about
what she had to say to Mahail.

He was waiting for her in a private drawing
room, his back to her, looking out a window.
When she entered the room, she paused for
a moment and studied him. He was a slight
man, but handsome and well dressed.

She saw the boy who had said to her, years
ago, as he was learning to ride a pony at his
family's compound, "Girls aren't allowed."

He turned and smiled in greeting, but the
smile faltered when he saw her hair. She deliberately wore short sleeves so he could see
the chunks of skin peeling off her arms, too.

He regained himself quickly, came to her
and bowed, took both her hands.

"You are somewhat worse the wear for your
adventure, I see," he said, his voice sorrow-
ful, as if she had survived a tsunami.

"Not at all," she said, "I've never *felt* better."

Of course he didn't get that at all—that how she felt was so much more important than how she looked.

"I understand you have been unaccompanied in the presence of a man," he said. "Others might see that as a smirch on your character, but of course, I do not. I understand the man's character is unimpeachable."

She knew she should be insulted that the *man's* character was unimpeachable, but in fact it *had* been Ronan who had exercised self-control, not her. Still!

"How big of you," she said. "Of course that man saved me from a situation largely of your making, but why think of that?"

"My making?" the prince stammered.

"You were cruel and thoughtless to Mirassa. She didn't deserve that, and she retaliated. I'm not excusing what she did, but I am saying I understand it."

The prince was beginning to look annoyed, not used to anyone speaking their mind around him, especially a woman. What kind of prison would that be? Not being able to be honest with the man you shared the most intimate things in the world with?

"And that man, whom *others* might see as

having put a smirch on my character, was absolutely devoted to protecting me. He was willing to put my well-being ahead of his own." *To refuse everything I offered him, if he felt it wasn't in my best interests.*

"How noble," the prince said, but he was watching her cautiously. She wasn't supposed to speak her mind, after all, just toss her hair and blink prettily.

"Yes," she agreed, "noble." Ronan, her prince, so much more so than this man who stood in front of her in his silk and jewels, the aroma of his expensive cologne filling the room.

What would he say if she said she would rather smell Ronan's sweat? She smiled at the thought, and Mahail mistook the smile for a change in mood, for coy invitation.

"Are you well enough, then, to reschedule the day of our marriage?" he asked formally.

So, despite the hair, the skin, her new outspokenness, he was not going to call it off, and suddenly she was glad, because that made it her choice, rather than his—that made it her power that had to be utilized.

She needed to *choose*.

"I've decided not to marry," she said firmly,.

with no fear, no doubt, no hesitation. A bird within her took wing.

"Excuse me?" Prince Mahail was genuinely astonished.

"I don't want to get married. I have so many things I want to achieve first. When I marry I want it to be for love, not for convenience. I'm sorry."

He glared at her, put out. "Have you consulted your father about this?"

Of all the maddening things he could have said, that about topped her list!

"It's my choice," she said dangerously, "not his."

Prince Mahail looked at her, confused, irritated, annoyed. "Perhaps it is for the best," he decided. "I think I might like your cousin, Mirassa, better than you after all."

"You would," Shoshauna muttered as he marched from the room.

And yet the next day, when she met with her father, she felt terrible trepidation, aware her legs were shaking under her long skirt.

Meetings with him always had a stilted quality, formal, as if his children were more his subjects than his blood.

"I understand," he said, without preamble,

"that you have told Prince Mahail there will
be no wedding."

"Yes, Father."

"Without consulting me?" he asked with a
raised eyebrow.

Shoshauna took a deep breath and told him
who she was. She did not tell him she was the
girl he wanted her to be, meek, docile, pliable,
but she told him of longing for education and
adventure…and love.

"And so you see," she finished bravely, "I
cannot marry Mahail. I am prepared to go to
the dungeon first."

Her father's lips twitched, and then he
laughed. "Come here," he said.

As she stepped toward him, he stood up
and embraced her. "I want for you what every
father wants for his daughter—your happiness. A father thinks he knows best, but you
have always been a strong-spirited girl, able,
I think, to find your own way. Do you want
to go to school?"

"Yes, Father!"

"Then it will be arranged, with my blessing."

As she turned to go, he called her back.

"Daughter," he said, laughing, "we don't

have a dungeon. If we did I suspect your poor mother would have locked you away in it a long time ago. I will explain this, er, latest development to her."

"Thank you."

Funny, she thought walking away, her whole life she had sought her father's love and approval. And she had gotten it, finally, not when she had tried to please him, but when she had been brave enough to please herself, brave enough to be herself.

This was news she had to share with Ronan. She asked Colonel Peterson where he was.

He looked at her carefully. "He's been deployed," he said, "even if I knew where he was, I wouldn't be able to tell you."

And then she realized that was the truth Ronan had tried to tell her about his life.

And she recognized another truth: if you were going to be with a man like that, you had to have a life—satisfying and fulfilling—completely separate from his. If Ronan was going to be a part of her life, she had to come to him absolutely whole, certainly able to function when his work called him to be away.

She renewed her application for school and

was accepted. In two months she would be living one more dream. She would be going to study in Great Britain.

And until then?

She was going to learn to surf! There was no room in a world like Ronan's for a woman who was needy or clingy. She needed to go to him a woman confident in her ability to make her own life.

And then she would be a woman who could make a life with him.

An alarm was going off, and men were pouring through the doors of an abandoned warehouse, men in black, their faces covered, machine guns at the ready. Ronan was with Shoshauna, his body between her and the onslaught, but he felt things no soldier ever wanted to feel—outnumbered, hopeless, helpless. He couldn't protect her. He was only one man...

Ronan came awake, drenched in sweat, grateful it wasn't real, perturbed that after six months he was still having that dream, was unable to shake his sense of failure.

Slowly he became aware that the alarm from his dream was really his phone ring-ing. He'd picked up the phone, along with a whole pile of other things he needed, when he'd moved off base a few months ago. Next time he bought a phone, he'd know to test the damned ringer first. This one announced callers with the urgency of an alarm system announcing a break-in at the Louvre.

He got up on one elbow and looked at the caller ID window.

"Hi, Mom," he said.

"Are you sleeping? It's the middle of the day."

"We're just back from a deployment. I'm a little turned around."

Six months ago he wouldn't have imagined voluntarily giving his mother that information, but then, six months ago she would have been asking all kinds of questions about what he'd been up to, trying to get him to quit his job, do something safer.

Interestingly, Ronan found he wasn't enjoying the emergency call-outs the way he once had. He recognized that adrenaline had become his fix, his drug, it had filled something in him.

It didn't work anymore. Not since B'Ranasha.

He'd felt something else then, softer, kinder, ultimately more real.

Adrenaline had been a substitute, a temporary solution to a permanent problem. Loneliness. Yearning.

He'd been asked if he would consider taking an instructor's position with Excalibur. Maybe he was just getting older, but the idea appealed.

Now his mother didn't even ask a single detail about the deployment, which was good. Even though she now had her own life and it had made her so much more accepting of his, Ronan thought it might set their growing trust in each other back a bit if he told her he'd just been behind the lines in a country where a military coup was in full swing rescuing the deposed prime minister.

Or, he thought, listening to the happiness in her voice, maybe not.

The big news that she had been trying to reach him about when he'd taken the wedding security position on B'Ranasha, amazingly, had nothing to do with another wedding, or at least not for her. No, she'd had an idea.

She'd wanted to know if he would invest in her new company.

But of course, that wasn't really what she had been asking. Sometime, probably in that week with Shoshauna, Ronan had developed the sensitivity to know this.

She was *really* asking for an investment in her. She was asking him, fearfully, painfully, *courageously,* to believe in her. One last time, despite it all, *please.*

And isn't that what love did? Believed? Held the faith even in the face of overwhelming evidence that to believe was naive?

The truth was he had all kinds of money. He'd had a regular paycheck since leaving high school. Renting this apartment was really the first time he'd spent any significant amount of it. His lifestyle had left him with little time and less inclination to spend his money.

Why not gamble it? His mother wanted to start a wedding-planning service and a specialized bridal boutique. Who, after all, was more of an expert on weddings than his mother? There was no *sideways* feeling in his stomach—not that he was at all certain it worked anymore—so he'd invested. When she'd told him she'd decided on a name for their new company, he'd expected the worst.

"'Princess,'" she said, "the *princess* part in teeny letters. That's important. And then in big letters 'Bliss.'"

Into his telling silence she had said, "You hate it."

That was putting it mildly. "I guess I just don't understand it."

"No, you wouldn't, but Ronan, trust me, every woman dreams of being a princess, if only for a day. Especially on *that* day."

And then Ronan had been pleasantly surprised and then downright astounded at his mother's overwhelming success. Within a few months of opening, Princess Bliss had been named by *Aussie Business* as one of the top-ten new businesses in the country. His mother had been approached about franchising. She was arranging weddings around the globe.

"Kay Harden just called," his mother told him breathlessly. "She and Henry Hopkins are getting married again."

"Uh-huh," Ronan said.

"Do you even know who they are, Jacob?"

"No, ma'am."

"Don't call me that! Jacob, you're hopeless. Movie stars. They're both movie stars."

He didn't care about that, he'd protected

enough important people to know the truth. One important person in particular had let him know the truth.

All people, inside, were the very same.

Even soldiers.

"We're going to have a million-dollar year!" his mother said.

Life was full of cruel ironies: Jake Ronan the man who hated weddings more than any other was going to get rich from them. He'd told his mother he would be happy just to have his initial investment back, but she was having none of it. He was a full, if silent, partner in Princess Bliss, if he liked it or not. And when he saw how happy his mother was, for the first time in his memory since his father had died, he liked it just fine.

"Mom," he said. "I'm proud of you. I really am. Please, don't cry."

But she cried, and talked about her business, and he just listened, glancing around his small apartment while she talked. This was another change he'd made since coming home from B'Ranasha.

After a month back at work he had decided to give up barrack life and get his own place. The brotherhood of his comrades was no longer as comfortable as it once had been. After he'd gotten back from B'Ranasha he had felt an overwhelming desire to be alone, to create his own space, a life separate from his career.

If the apartment was any indication, he hadn't really succeeded. Try as he might to make it homey, it just never was.

Try as he might to never think about *her* or that week on the island, he never quite could. He was changed. He was lonely. He hurt.

The apartment was just an indication of something else, wanting *more,* wanting to have more to life than his work.

And all that money piling up in his bank account, thanks to his partnership in Bliss, was an indication that something *more* wasn't about money, either.

He'd contacted Gray Peterson once, a couple of days after leaving B'Ranasha. He'd been in a country so small it didn't appear on the map, in the middle of a civil war. Trying to sound casual, which was ridiculous given the lengths he'd gone to, to get his hands on a phone, and hard to do with gunfire exploding in the background, he'd asked if she was all right.

And found out the only thing he needed

to know: the marriage of Prince Mahail and Princess Shoshauna had been called off. Ronan had wanted to press for details, called off for what reason, by *whom,* but he'd already known that the phone call was inappropriate, that a soldier asking after a princess was not acceptable in any world that he moved in.

Ronan heard a knock on his door, got up and answered it. "Mom, gotta go. Someone's at the door."

Was it Halloween? A child dressed as a motorcycle rider stood on his outside step, all black leather, a helmet, sunglasses.

And then the sunglasses came off, and he recognized eyes as turquoise as the sunlit bay of his boyhood. His mouth fell open.

And then she undid the motorcycle helmet strap, and struggled to get the snug-fitting helmet from her head.

He had to stuff his hands in his pockets to keep from helping her. Finally she had it off.

He studied her hair. Possibly, her hair looked even worse than it had on the island, grown out considerably but flattened by the helmet.

"What are you doing here?" he asked gruffly,

as if his heart was not nearly pounding out of his chest, as if he did not want to lift her into his arms and swing her around until she was shrieking with laughter. As if he had not known, the moment he had recognized her, that she was the something *more* that he yearned for, that filled him with restless energy and a sense of hollow emptiness that nothing seemed to fill.

This was his greatest fear: that with every moment he'd dedicated to helping her find her own power, he had lost some of his own.

"What am I doing here?" she said, with a dangerous flick of her hair. "Try this— 'Shoshauna, what a delightful surprise. I'm so glad to see you.'"

He saw instantly she had come into her own in ways he could not even imagine. She exuded the confidence of a woman sure of herself, sure of her intelligence, her attractiveness, her power.

"I'm going to university here now."

That explained it. Those smart-alec university guys were probably all over her. He tried not to let the flicker of pure jealousy he felt show. In fact, he deliberately kept his voice remote. "Oh? Good for you."

She glared at him, looked as if she wanted to stamp her foot or slap him. But then her eyes, smoky with heat, rested on his lips, and he knew she didn't want to stamp her foot or slap him.

"I didn't get married," she announced in a soft, husky purr.

"Yeah, I heard." No sense telling her he had celebrated as best he could, with a warm soda in one hand and his rifle in the other, watching the sand blow over a hostile land, *wishing* he had someone, something more to go home to. Feeling guilty for being distracted, wondering if he was just like his mother. Did all relationships equal a surrender of power? Wasn't that his fear of love?

"But I have dated all kinds of boys."

"Really." It was a statement, not a question. He tried not to feel irritated, his sense of having given her way too much power over him confirmed! Seeing her after all this time, all he wanted to do was taste her lips, and he had to hear she was dating guys? *Boys*. Not men. Why did he feel faintly relieved by that distinction?

"I thought I should. You know, go out with a few of them."

"And you stopped by to tell me that?" He folded his arms more firmly over his chest, but something twinkled in her eyes, and he had a feeling his defensive posture was not fooling her one little bit. She knew she had stormed his bastions, taken down his defenses long ago.

"Mmm-hmm. And to tell you that they were all very boring."

"Sorry."

"And childish."

"Males are slow-maturing creatures," he said. Had she kissed any of them, those boys she had dated? Of course she had. That was the way things worked these days. He remembered all too well the sweetness of her kiss, felt something both possessive and protective when he thought of another man—especially a childish one—tasting her.

"I didn't kiss anyone, though," she said, and the twinkle in her eyes deepened. Why was it she seemed to find him so transparent? She had always insisted on seeing who he really was, not what he wanted her to see.

He wanted to tell her he didn't care, but he had the feeling she'd see right through that, too, so he kept his mouth shut.

"I learned to surf last summer. And I can ride a motorcycle now. By myself."

"So I can see."

"Ronan," she said softly, "are you happy to see me?"

He closed his eyes, marshaled himself, opened them again. "Why are you here, Shoshauna?"

Not princess, a lapse in protocol that she noticed, too. She beamed at him.

"I want to play you a game of chess."

He didn't move from the doorway. A game of chess. He tried not to look at her lips. A game of chess was about the furthest thing from his poor, beleaguered male mind. "Why?" he croaked.

"If I win," she said softly, "you have to take me on a date."

He could have gotten her killed back there on that island. She apparently didn't know or didn't care, but he was not sure he'd ever be able to forgive himself or trust himself either.

"I can't take you on a date," he said.

"Why not? You aren't in charge of protecting me now."

If he was, she sure as hell wouldn't be riding a motorcycle around by herself. But he only said, "Good thing, since I did such a crack-up job of it the first time."

"What does that mean?"

"Don't you ever think what could have happened if those boats that arrived that day hadn't been the colonel and your grandfather? Don't you ever think of what might have happened if it hadn't been your cousin, if it had been a well-organized terror cell instead?"

There it was out, and he was glad it was out. He felt as if he had been waiting months to make this confession. Why was it always so damned easy to show her who he really was? Flawed, vulnerable, an ordinary man under his warrior armor.

"No," she said, regarding him thoughtfully, *seeing* him, "I don't. Do you?"

"I think of the possibilities all the time. I didn't do my job, Shoshauna, I just got lucky."

"The boys at school use that term sometimes," she said, her voice sultry.

"Would you be serious? I'm trying to tell you something. I can't be trusted with you. I've never been able to protect the people I love the most." The look wouldn't leave her face, as if she thought he was adorable, and so he rushed on, needing to convince her, very sorry the word *love* had slipped out, somehow. "I have this thing, this *sideways* feeling, that tells me what to do, an instinct, that warns of danger."

"What's it doing right now?" she asked.

"That's just it. It doesn't work around you!"

She touched his arm, looked up at him, her eyes so full of acceptance of him that something in him stilled. Completely.

"You know why it doesn't work around me, Ronan? Because nothing is wrong. Nothing was wrong on the island. You were exactly where you needed to be, doing exactly what you needed to do. And so was I."

"I forgot what I was there to do and, Shoshauna, that bugs the hell out of me. I didn't do a good job of protecting you. I didn't do my job, period."

"I seem to still be here, alive and kicking."

"Not because of anything I did," he said stubbornly.

She regarded him with infinite patience. "Ronan, there are some things that are bigger than even you. Some things you just have to surrender to."

"That's the part you don't get! *Surrender* is not in any soldier's vocabulary!"

She sighed as if he was being impossible and childish just like those boys she had dated. "Thank you for the kitten, by the way. I was able to bring him with me. He's a monster. I called him Hope."

He wasn't really done discussing his failures with her, but he said reluctantly, "That sounds like a girl's name." The name said it all, named the thing within him that he had not been able to outrun, kill, alter.

He *hoped*. He hoped for the life he saw promised in her eyes: a life of connection, companionship, laughter, *love*.

"You know what I think, Ronan?"

"You're going to tell me if I want to know or not," he said.

"Just like I want someone to see me for who I am, someone I don't have to put on the princess costume for, you want someone to see you without your armor. You want someone to know there is a place where you are not all strength and sternness. You want someone to see you are not all warrior."

"No, I don't!"

"Now," she said, casually, as if she had not ripped off his mask and left him feeling trembling and vulnerable and on the verge of surrendering to the mightiest thing of all, "let's play chess. I told you the terms—if I win you have to take me on a date."

"And if I win?" he asked.

She smiled at him, and he saw just how completely she had come into herself, how confident she was.

"Ronan," she said softly, her smile melting him, "why on earth would you want to win?"

CHAPTER NINE

"I CAN'T BELIEVE you'd ever accept anything but my very best effort," he said, though the truth was he already knew he was lost.

She contemplated him. "That's true. So if you win?"

"I haven't even agreed to play yet!"

"Well, we've stood at this point before, haven't we, Ronan? Where you have to decide whether or not to let me in."

They had stood at this point before. On the island he'd refused to play chess with her, and he'd made her cry. But then he had only been doing his job, and in the end that barrier had not been enough to keep him from caring about her.

Without that barrier where would it go?

A single word entered his mind. And oddly enough, it was not surrender. *Bliss.*

He stood back from his door, an admission

in his heart. He was powerless against her; he had been from the very beginning. Princess Shoshauna of B'Ranasha walked into his humble apartment, took off the black jacket and tossed it on his couch as if she belonged here.

The form-fitting white silk shirt and black leather pants were at least as sexy as that bikini she had nearly driven him crazy in, and his feeling of powerlessness increased.

She looked around his place with interest. He shoved a pair of socks under the couch with his foot. She looked at him.

"I want to live in a cute little place just like this, one day."

His mother had claimed that every girl wanted to be a princess, but somehow, someway he had lucked into something very different. A girl who had already been a princess and who wanted to be ordinary.

He got his chess set out of a cabinet, set it up at the small kitchen table.

"Why didn't you call me?" she asked, sitting down, taking a black and a white chess piece and holding them out to him, closed fist.

He chose. Black, then. Let her lead the way.

He snorted. "Call you? You're a princess.

You're not exactly listed in the local directory."

"You knew how to get ahold of me, though, if you'd wanted to."

"Yes."

"So you didn't want to?"

He was silent, contemplating her first move, her opening gambit. He made a defensive move.

"I couldn't. I still dream about what could have happened on that island. I failed you. There I was snorkeling and surfing, when really I should have been setting up defenses."

"I'd been protected all my life. You didn't fail me. You gave me what I needed far more than safety. A wake-up call. A call to live. To be myself. You gave me a gift, Ronan. Even when you didn't call it that, it was a gift."

He waited.

"I needed to choose and I have. I've chosen."

"To play chess with a soldier?"

"No, Ronan," she said gently. "It was never about the chess."

"So I see." He was surrendering to her, just as he had on the island, even though he didn't want to, even though he knew better. *Bliss.*

It unfolded in him like a sail that had finally caught the wind, it filled him, it carried him forward into a brand-new land.

She beat him soundly at chess, though he might have been slightly distracted by the scent of her, by the pure heaven of having her in the same room again, by the sound of her voice, the light in her eyes, the way she ran her hand through the disaster that was her hair.

"Do you know why I dated those other boys?" she asked.

He shook his head.

"So that you wouldn't have one single excuse to say no to me. So that you couldn't say, 'You only think you love me. You don't know anyone else.'"

"Love?" he said.

She sighed. "Ronan, I made it perfectly clear it wasn't about the chess game."

That was true, she had.

"So," he said, "what do you want to do for that date?"

What would a princess want to do? The opera? Live theater? Was he going to have to get a new wardrobe?

"Oh," she said, "I want to go to a pub for

fish and chips and then to a movie after. Just like an ordinary girl."

His mother had been so wrong. Not every girl wanted to be a princess, not at all. Still, when he looked at her and smiled, he knew there was no hope she would ever be an ordinary girl, either.

And suddenly it came to him, a truth that was at the very core of humanity. A truth that was humbling and reassuring at the very same time.

Love was more powerful than he was.

He got up from his chair, came around to hers and tugged her out of it. Shoshauna came into his arms as if she was coming home.

"I guess," he whispered against her hair, "it's time for you to start calling me Jake."

He picked her up for their first official date three nights later. He felt like a teenager getting ready. He wore jeans and a T-shirt, trying for just the right note of casual.

As he approached her address, he was aware that for a man who had done the most dangerous things in the world with absolute icy calm, his heart was beating faster, and his palms were sweat-slicked.

She lived on campus in what looked to be a very ordinary house until he went to the front door, rang the bell and was let in.

There were girls everywhere, short girls, tall girls, skinny girls, heavy girls. There were girls dressed to go to nightclubs and girls in their pajamas. There were girls with their hair in rollers and girls hidden behind frightening facial masks of green creams and white creams. And it seemed when he stood in that front foyer, every single one of them stopped and looked at him. Really looked.

"Sexy beast," one of them called out. "Who are you here for?"

The last time he had blushed was when Shoshauna had kissed him on the cheek and called him Charming in that little market in B'Ranasha. She was determined to put him in predicaments that stretched him! At least now he knew a little blush wouldn't kill him.

"I'm here for Shoshauna." There were groans and calls of "lucky girl," and he found himself blushing harder.

But when he saw her, coming down the steps, two at a time, flying toward him, all thought of himself, of his wild discomfort at finding himself, a man so used to a man's world, so surrounded by women, was gone.

There was a look on her face when she saw him that he knew he would never forget, not if he lived to be 102.

It was unguarded and filled with tenderness.

A memory niggled at him, of a moment a long, long time ago. His father coming up the steps from work, in combat uniform, his mother running to meet him, a look just like the one on Shoshauna's face now in her eyes. And he remembered how his father had looked at her. Despite the uniform, in that moment his father had not been a warrior. No, just a man, filled with wonder, gentled by love, amazed.

In the next few weeks, even though Ronan had to run the gauntlet of her housemates every time he saw her, he spent every moment he could with her. Every second they could wangle away from hectic schedules, they were together. Simple moments—a walk, holding hands, eating pizza, playing darts at the pub—simple moments became infused with a light from heaven.

Ronan was aware that, left to his own devices, he would have performed his duties perfectly on B'Ranasha. He would have been a perfect professional, he would never have allowed himself to become personally involved with the principal.

And he would have missed this: the tenderness, the sweetness of falling head over heels in love. But somehow, some way, a kind universe had taken pity on him, given him what he needed the most, even though he had been completely unaware of that need. Even though he had strenuously denied that need and tried to fight against it.

Falling in love with Shoshauna was like waking from a deep hypnotic state. When he woke in the morning, his first thought was of her. He felt as if he was living to make her laugh, to feel the touch of her hand, to become aware of her eyes resting on his face, something in them so unguarded and so breathtakingly, exquisitely beautiful.

For some reason he, a rough soldier, had come to be loved by a woman like this one. He planned to be worthy of it.

Shoshauna looked around, let the trade winds lift her hair. There was a flower-laced pagoda set up on the beach, the royal palace of B'Ranasha white and beautiful in the background. They had tried to keep things small, but even so the hundred chairs facing the wedding pagoda were filled. The music of a single flute intertwined with the music of the waves that lapped gently on the sand.

Jake's mother, Bev, had managed to get over her disappointment that, despite the fact it was a royal wedding, her first, they wanted nothing elaborate. Now Shoshauna saw why her mother-in-law's business was so successful: she had read their hearts and given them exactly what they wanted—simplicity—the beauty provided by the ocean, the white-capped waves in the blue bay the perfect backdrop to the day.

Shoshauna wore a simple white sheath, her feet were bare, she had a single flower in her hair.

She watched from the tree line as Jake made his way across the sand and felt the tears rise in her eyes. *Beloved.*

He was flanked by Gray Peterson, just as he had been the first time she had seen him, but this time Jake looked calm and relaxed, a man at ease despite the formality of the black suit he was wearing, the people watching him, the fact it was his wedding day.

It had been almost a year since she had first laid eyes on him, six months since she had won her first date with him in that chess match.

Since then there had been so much laughter as they discovered a brand-new world together—a world seen through the viewfinder of love.

They had ridden motorcycles, gone to movies, walked hand in hand down rain-filled streets, played chess and done nothing at all. Everything was equally as astounding when she did it with him.

He was so full of surprises. Who would have ever guessed he had such a romantic nature hidden under that stern exterior? The kitten as a gift should have been her first clue! He was constantly surprising her with heartfelt or funny little gifts: a tiara he'd gotten at a toy store; a laser pointer that drove the kitten, Hope, to distraction; a book of poems; a pink bikini that she would use now, for the first time, on her honeymoon.

And the stern exterior was just that. An exterior. She'd always thought he was good-looking, but now the hard lines on his face were relaxed around her, and the stern mask was gone from his eyes. The remoteness was gone from him and so was his need to exercise absolute control over everything. Jake Ronan seemed to have enjoyed every second of letting go of control, seeing where life— and love—would take them, if they gave it a chance.

It had taken them to this day and this moment. He stood at the pagoda, his eyes searched the tree line until they found her.

And he smiled.

In his smile she saw such welcome and such wonder—and such sensual promise— that her own heart beat faster.

Of course, there was one thing they had not done, one area where he had maintained every ounce of his formidable discipline. Jake Ronan had proven to be very old-fashioned when it came to the question of her virtue.

Oh, he had kissed her until she had nearly died from wanting him, he had touched her in ways that had threatened to set her heart on fire, but always at the last moment he had pulled away. He had told her his honor was on the line, and she had learned you did not question a warrior's honor!

But tonight she would lie in his arms, and they would discover the breathtaking heights of intimacy. After the reception, they would take her grandfather's boat, and they would go to *their* island, Naidina Karobin, *my heart is home*. The island would be once again inhabited only by them.

Last night, even though he wasn't supposed to see her until today, Jake had managed to charm his way past all her girlfriends and her cousins and aunts.

"I brought you a wedding present."

"You're not supposed to be here," she told him, but not with a great deal of conviction. She loved seeing him.

"I know. I couldn't stay away. Knowing you were here, just a few minutes away from me, I couldn't not be with you. Shoshauna, that's what you do to me. Here I am, just about the most disciplined guy in the world, and I'm helpless around you. Worse," he moved closer to her, touched her cheek with the familiar hardness of his hands, "I like being helpless. You make me want to be with you all the time. You make everything that is not you seem dull and boring and like a total waste of time.

"You make me feel as if all those defenses I had, had kept me prisoner in a world where I was very strong but very, very alone. You rescued me."

Her eyes filled with tears. "Ronan, you could not have given me a more beautiful gift than those words."

He smiled, a little bit sheepishly. "There's still enough soldier in me that I don't see words as any kind of gift." He opened the door and brought in what he had left in the hallway.

She burst out laughing. That's what he did to her, and for her—took her from tears to laughter and back again in the blink of an eye.

A brand-new surfboard, and she had been delighted, but at the same time she rather hoped, much as she was *stoked* about surfing, that the waves would never come up. She rather hoped they would never get out of bed! Not for the whole two weeks. That she could touch him until she had her fill of the feel of his skin under her fingertips, until she had her fill of the taste of his lips, and she already knew she was never going to get her fill of that!

Shoshauna was still blushing from the audacity of her own thoughts when her mother and her father came up beside her, not a king and a queen today but proud parents. Each of them kissed her on the cheek and then took their seats.

Her father in particular was very taken with Jake. Her mother had been more slow to come around, but no one who truly got to know Jake could do anything but love him.

Her mother had also been appalled by the simplicity of the wedding plans, but she and Bev had managed to console each other and had become quite good friends as they planned the wedding of their children.

Her grandfather came to her side, linked his arm through hers, smiled at her, though his eyes were wet with tears of joy.

And then Shoshauna was moving across the sand toward her beloved, toward Jake Ronan, and she could see the whole future in his eyes. Her grandfather let her go, and she walked the last few steps to him on her own, a woman who had chosen exactly the life she wanted for herself.

* * *

Jake watched Shoshauna move toward him across the fineness of the pure white sand.

She had chosen the simplest of dresses, her feet were bare, but when you were as beautiful as she was, even his mother had agreed that simplicity was the best way to let her true beauty shine through.

His mother and his wife-to-be, here together.

And in him the most wonderful surrender. He would protect them with his life, if he ever had to, and they both knew that.

Someday he would have children with Shoshauna, and he could feel the fierce protectiveness within himself extend to them, but something new was there, too.

A trust, that he would do whatever he could do, but when his strength ran dry, then there would be *something* else there to step in, *something* that seemed to have a better plan for him than anything he could have ever planned for himself, if the woman walking over the sand toward him was any indication.

He knew that *something* went by a great many names. Some called it the Universe, the life force, God.

He had come to call it Love, and to recognize it had been running the show long before he'd come along, and would be running it long after.

There came a point when a man had to realize that there were things he did not control, and that he would only exhaust himself, drain away his strength and his soul, if he continued to think the whole world would fall apart if he was not running it.

Ronan had come to believe that he could trust the protection and care of a force larger than himself.

It was the same force that brought a certain man and a certain woman together, against impossible odds, across cultural and social differences, the force that made one heart recognize another.

And it was that force that would protect them and see their children into the world.

Once upon a time Jake Ronan had thought if he ever had to stand where he was standing today, he would probably faint.

And yet the truth was, he had never felt so calm, so strong, so *right*. And the strangest thing of all was that, even as Ronan admitted he was powerless in the face of this thing called love, with each day of his surrender he felt more powerful, more alive and more relaxed, more grateful, more everything.

This was the something *more* he had longed for all his life: to be a part of the magnificent mystery that flowed around him and in him as surely as it flowed through the waves on the sea. He longed to ride that incredible energy with the ease and joy with which he could ride the most powerful of waves. Not to conquer but to feel connected.

He watched Shoshauna move toward him, and he almost laughed out loud.

For one thing he had come to know that this thing he chose to call Love had the most delicious sense of humor.

And for the longest time he had thought it was his job to rescue the princess.

But now he saw that wasn't it at all.

That she had come to rescue him. And that allowing himself to be rescued had not made him a weaker man but a better one.

She reached him, looked him in the face, his equal, the woman who would be the mother of his children, his companion, his friend, his lover through all the days of his life.

"Beloved," she said, her voice hushed with

reverence of what they stood in the presence of, that Force greater than all things. "Ret-nuh."

And he said to her, his eyes never leaving her face, in her own language, a greeting and a vow, "My heart is home."

* * * * *

COMING NEXT MONTH from Harlequin® Romance
AVAILABLE JUNE 4, 2013

#4379 THE MAKING OF A PRINCESS
Teresa Carpenter

Amanda Carn could be Pasadonia's long-lost princess. Xavier LeDuc is bound by duty to protect her—and where could be safer than in his own arms?

#4380 MARRIAGE FOR HER BABY
The Single Mom Diaries
Raye Morgan

Sara Darling marries Jake Martin to keep custody of her niece. But this damaged soldier might just need their ready-made family as much as she does....

#4381 THE MAN BEHIND THE PINSTRIPES
Melissa McClone

Becca Taylor finally has a chance to start over—until CEO Caleb Fairchild marches into her life. Is she the one woman who can crack the iron walls around his heart?

#4382 FALLING FOR THE REBEL FALCON
The Falcon Dynasty
Lucy Gordon

Journalist Perdita Hanson jumps at the chance to be famous Leonid Falcon's date. But when he discovers who she is, can their budding romance ever recover?

You can find more information on upcoming Harlequin® titles, free excerpts and more at www.Harlequin.com.

*Have you ever dreamed of discovering that you're really
a princess? That's exactly what happens to Amanda Carn
in THE MAKING OF A PRINCESS by Teresa Carpenter!*

"I MUST SAY good night." With obvious reluctance, Xavier
saw her safely seated. And then he stepped back and raised
his hand in farewell.

Amanda pressed her hand to the window and made herself drive away. Oh, boy. She was so lost. Absolutely gone.
He made her feel alive, feminine, desirable.

She knew she was setting herself up for heartbreak. He'd
be leaving in a few weeks and her life was here. There was
no future to this relationship.

But better heartache than regret. She was tired of being
afraid to trust. Tired of letting fear rule her. She felt safe
with Xavier. And she longed to explore the chemistry that
sizzled between them.

Xavier strolled back to the museum, his gaze locked on
the vehicle carrying Amanda Carn into the night. When the
car turned from his sight, he fixed his gaze forward and
tried to calculate exactly how big a mistake he'd just made.

For the first time, man and soldier were at odds as desire warred with duty. He liked this woman, he wanted her
physically, but if she was of the royal family, his duty was
to protect her against all threats, including himself. With
the addictive taste of her still on his lips, he recognized the
challenge that represented.

Inside, he did a final walk-through of the entire museum, as was his habit, ending with the exhibit rooms.

He knew his duty, lived and breathed it day in and day out. Duty was what kept the soldier from kissing her when she so obviously wanted a kiss as much as he wanted to get his mouth on her. The shadow of hurt as she moved away drew the man in him forward as he sought to erase her pain.

And his.

Now may be the only time he had with her, this time of uncertainty while the DNA test was pending. Once her identity was confirmed, she'd be forever out of his reach....

If she's proved to be royalty, then Xavier will have to keep his distance, but he's been bound by royal command to protect Amanda until the truth is discovered. Keeping Amanda safe is his new mission—and where could be safer than in his own arms?

Available in June 2013 from Harlequin® Romance wherever books are sold.

HARLEQUIN

Romance

His pinstripe suit is normally his armor....

Becca Taylor has worked hard to overcome her troubled past. But when Caleb Fairchild marches into her life, the instant attraction between them is the last thing she needs!

CEO Caleb has learned the hard way not to suffer fools and to be careful of whom to trust. Why should Becca, gorgeous as she is, be any different? But he can't help but be drawn to her, to want to get close to her. So when her secrets are blown into the open, betrayal seems inevitable. Unless the truth can start to crack the iron walls he's built around his heart...

The Man Behind the Pinstripes
by Melissa McClone

Available June 2013, wherever books are sold!